Mirror Murder

Doreen smiled. She crouched down by Dr. Walters and looked intently at his blood-stained face.

"You shouldn't have done it, Doc," she whispered hoarsely. "You ruined me playing God. Why me anyway? Why did you choose me and not Debbie? Do you hurt, Dr. McClusky? I hurt. I always hurt. All my life, Doctor. All of my miserable, fucking life!"

She listened to the gurgling sounds coming from his throat. "Can you hear me, Doc? Do you understand that you have to pay? Everyone pays for damages, Doc, even you. I'm paying and I don't even know why. Do you hear me, Dr. McClusky?" There was no answer, only that raspy, choking sound. She rolled Dr. Walters over onto his stomach.

"Are you crying, Doc?" Doreen put her ear close to his mouth and listened. She momentarily felt sad. She didn't want him to cry. She hated when someone cried, especially if she had been the reason for their pain. But that was ridiculous! She had not given the good doctor a reason to cry! It was him that had caused HER to cry! She rolled him over again. And again. And again.

Mirror Murder

by

Marjaree Mayne

Dreams do come
true. Hope you
enjoy my dream!
Thank you.
Marjaree Mayne
6-4-98

Commonwealth
Publications

A Commonwealth Publications Paperback
MIRROR MURDER

This edition published 1997
by Commonwealth Publications
9764 - 45th Avenue,
Edmonton, AB, CANADA T6E 5C5
All rights reserved
Copyright © 1996 by Marjaree Mayne

ISBN: 1-55197-911-X

Printed in Canada

Acknowledgments

I would like to publicly thank:

Detective James Schweers of the Flagler County Sheriff's Department, Florida, and Robert J. McConaghie, M.D., F.A.C.P., medical examiner for District 23 (Flagler, Putnam and St. Johns Counties), Florida (now deceased), for all their time spent with me on the technical data and advice; my sons, Richard, Gary, Robert and William Panek, and my parents, Roy (now deceased) and Margaret Lenois, Joseph and Josephine Santore, for their mental and financial support; my friends Kerry Klinker, Robert Zuber for believing that this novel could be written; and especially my youngest son, Will, who was willing to do without, and who never complained throughout the time it took to write this book, but instead cheered me on and pushed me when I needed it.

THANK YOU ALL!

Dedication

This book is dedicated to my four wonderful sons, Richard, Gary, Robert and William, and to my terrific parents, Roy (now deceased) and Margaret Lenois, for their total confidence and support, and especially to Will, who stood by me through it all.

Prologue

It was Saturday, November 18, 1972, and a beautiful, clear, brisk autumn day. Mother Nature had spared nothing to create the colorful landscape with its brown, gold and orange decor. There was just enough chill in the air to require heavy sweaters and wool slacks. Judy Price stared at the colorful New Jersey mountains in the distance from her hospital room window and sighed long and deep. This was supposed to have been her wedding day. Instead, she was here in Shadowbrook Hospital and the long, tier on tier, chantilly white lace gown hung limply in her bedroom closet at her parents' home in Plainfield.

"I'm sorry, Judy. I'm just not ready for all this," Gary said. "I mean, you know, I wanted to marry you, sure, but a baby already? I was scared about the whole marriage set-up, especially with me being still in college and all, but how can I possibly handle it with a baby to worry about, too? I'm just not ready for that."

No, he wasn't ready for it, but he had done it, damn him! Why were men such self-centered cowards? Thinking only of THEIR pleasures, THEIR plans, THEIR futures? What about her pleasures, her plans, her future? She was only eighteen years old. What was going to happen to her now that all of HER plans had been shot to hell?

"I know you're upset, Judy, and I guess I don't blame you for hating me. I just don't know what else to say." What else was there to say? Thanks for not marrying me? Thanks for knocking me up? Thanks for fucking up the rest of my life? Judy's thoughts were interrupted when Nurse Stevenson came in carrying a lunch tray. She set it down on the bedside table, and started to open the clear plastic package that surrounded a small white paper napkin, stainless steel eating utensils, and small packets of salt and pepper.

"Don't bother," Judy said roughly. "I'm not hungry!"

"You have to eat something, Judy," the nurse answered, continuing to prepare the tray. "You need to build up your strength again. Don't you want to get out of here? You'll need your stamina intact if you're going to raise those darling babies of yours." Her round plump face flashed Judy a smile, showing straight small teeth. Judy didn't answer, but her large blue eyes filled with tears, and her small pointed chin quivered. She bit her lower lip to help stifle the sob that was trapped in her throat.

"Today would have been my wedding day," Judy said quietly. The tears brimmed over and ran down her pale cheeks. She covered her face with her delicate hands as the sob surfaced and she could no longer hide her pain. Turning her face into the pillow, she cried, her body racked with tremors. Nurse Stevenson gently smoothed Judy's dark brown hair away from her face.

When Judy continued to cry, Nurse Stevenson gathered Judy in her meaty arms, and gently rocked her back and forth like a baby. *Just a child herself,* the nurse thought. *So young to be making so many hard decisions; so young to be the mother of Siamese twin girls, born four days ago by Cesarean section; so young to raise these babies alone. Such an awful way to start a future.* She laid Judy down softly on her pillow, fixed her covers, and left the room. She was back in a flash with a hypodermic filled with prescribed Darvon and gave her the shot. Within a few minutes Judy began to quiet down, and within a half hour was sleeping peacefully.

While Judy slept, her new twin daughters were upstairs being surgically separated. Beautiful babies, each with a crop of fine black hair, they had been born joined at their sides from under the armpit down to the top of the thigh.

"What do you think, John?"

"There's no other way," Dr. John McClusky answered. "We can successfully do it, but only one will come out perfect, except for a small scar on her left side. Unfortunately, the other girl will have an awful scar. She'll be perfect health wise, but there's no way to escape the mark she'll have. When she's older, cosmetic surgery will definitely be needed."

"You know, Doctor, there's something different about these twins," Nurse Anne Dobney said as she moved the surgical tray closer to the operating table where the two babies lay sleeping under the anesthesia.

"Different? Different how?"

"Well, some of the nurses and I have noticed some unusual things, like when one baby cries the other one cries, too."

"Anne, that's natural. One baby's crying will wake or disturb another baby, whether they're twins or not. What's so different about that?"

"What's so different about that? How about if you soothe the one that started crying and you quiet her down, and lo and behold! The other one automatically stops crying without being touched or soothed! Huh? You don't find that strange?"

"No. As a matter of fact, I don't. It only seems natural that twins, especially Siamese twins, would react to each other. Sponge."

"Well, we all think it's strange," she said handing him the sponge. "Call it women's intuition, if you want, but there is definitely something strange about those babies. I guess only time will tell."

Chapter 1

In her spacious one bedroom apartment in Edison, New Jersey, twenty-four year old Doreen Price stood staring at her slim naked body in the full length mirror on the back of her bathroom door. Her gaze started at her feet, scanned her long legs, and came to rest on her right hip, where the scar began. Her gaze always stopped at the hip and stayed fixed there for a while before continuing up her right side to where the scar ended just below her armpit. She never seemed to notice her hard, flat stomach, her small, tight waist, or her small, firm breasts. Nor did she notice the frown that creased her forehead, or the glazed look that clouded her large dark blue eyes. Her eyes just always seemed to be drawn to that ragged, discolored cross-stitch that was a constant reminder that she was one-half of a Siamese twin set.

She slowly turned to the right, so that the scar was no longer visible in her reflection in the mirror. Her body now looked totally normal. In fact, it was a beautiful body. She raised her arms up over her head, and stood on her tiptoes as she stretched her body to her full five foot six inch height. *Gorgeous*, she thought to herself. She let her heels again touch the floor, keeping her arms up in the air, and slowly turned back to the left until just her right side showed in the mirror. Her eyes were frozen on the scar that disfigured her beautiful body, and she clenched her teeth as the bitterness swept over her again.

"D is for Dory, Dirty, dirty, Dory,
S is for scar, and that is the story."

They had sung it, over and over, as they skipped rope. Debbie had stood quietly on the side watching. Watching while Dory had cried and then run home alone, small hands covering her ears to block out the chant. Her mother had tried to soothe her, telling her that children were just cruel and that they had not meant it. But Dory had known better. She was ugly and she knew it. Her mother knew it! Everybody knew it! Debbie was perfect, and everybody knew that, too. Debbie was popular. Nobody sang those songs to Debbie!

Doreen looked at her face and realized that tears were streaming down her cheeks. Her head ached, and her vision was getting blurry. She knew that she had to lie down. She felt for the doorknob and opened the door, groping along the bedroom wall trying to find the large bed which dominated her room. The pounding in her temples had spread to behind her eyes, causing them to burn like fire.

"D is for Dory, Dirty, dirty, Dory..." Oh, Momma, make them stop! Please make them stop!

* * * *

The hot Florida sunshine streamed through the window of the cozy country kitchen where Deborah Price Sterling stood preparing breakfast for her husband, Joe. Her head had started to ache, and it was getting difficult to breathe. Her ears seemed to echo every little sound. She shook her head, trying to clear it.

What was happening to her lately? She had had these spells before, but now they seemed to be getting worse each time. Joe had insisted that she see Dr. Brenner, and he had done what he could. He had put her in the hospital, run every neurological test he could find, including a brain scan, but could find no reason for these "spells". Her headaches, the shortness of breath, the dizziness, and most of all the loss of memory were all scaring her to death.

The memory lapses were for short periods of time, an hour or two here and there, but it was frustrating to lose time out of your life and not know where it had gone or what you had done. Waves of nausea swept over her and she clutched the edge of the sink, taking a deep breath. She felt flushed and warm. Deborah turned on the faucet and splashed cold water on her face, neck and wrists.

"Debbie? Are you feeling okay?" Joe asked coming into the kitchen. His blond curly hair was still damp from the hot shower he had taken a few minutes before, but his square jaw was set and his brown eyes showed his concern. "Is it another attack?"

"Yes, I guess so. Oh, Joe, what's the matter with me? Why is this happening?" Joe put his arm around her expanded waist and guided her to one of the solid maple kitchen chairs. He noticed that beads of sweat had broken out across her forehead, on her small upturned nose, and above her top lip. Her blue eyes were glassy and heavy-lidded.

"You just didn't want to make breakfast this morning," he chided her. "That's all right, I got the hint. They taught us how in 'Breakfast Making-

101' at the police academy." He brought her a mug of steaming coffee and set it on the brown straw place mat on the table. She looked up at him and smiled weakly.

"Do you think it's psychosomatic?"

"It's possible, I guess. I'm no psychiatrist, Debbie, but maybe we should get you one. I mean, maybe you're under stress, or worried about something. Has anything been bothering you lately? Any problems at work?"

"Not that I am aware of. My job at the hospital is fine. We're fine. I have absolutely no idea."

"Maybe you're just upset that..."

"That what?"

"Well, you are six months pregnant now. Maybe it's due to that. I know you're happy about it, but it might be a worry to you, whether you're aware of it or not. Maybe that's on your mind, consciously or unconsciously."

He watched her blow on her coffee before she sipped it. He loved her full sensuous lips, her moist, sweet tasting tongue, her straight, perfect teeth. He felt his groin start to pulsate. God, how he loved her. A baby would make their life complete. She'd be all right. Just as soon as she had her baby, she'd be fine. He just knew it.

* * * *

Doreen had decided to walk to work. It was less than a mile, and a beautiful October morning. She loved New Jersey in the fall with all its different colors. The breeze was cool against her skin and she inhaled the fresh air, letting it fill her lungs. Her crisp white uniform rustled as she walked, but she was unaware of the sound. She carried her white cap in a clear plastic bag and it swung slightly as she walked.

Doreen loved being a registered nurse at Metropolitan Hospital. If she wasn't loved, at least she felt needed. She took good care of the patients entrusted to her. Unlike many of the other nurses, she was compassionate, caring and understanding of their problems. When her patients hurt, she could almost feel their pain. She was most understanding with her surgical patients. She pitied them their scar, no matter where they had it. And she was most loving with her surgical patients who were children. She worried whether or not their scar might show, and then worried if other kids might make fun of them.

"D is for Dory, Dirty, dirty Dory..." She stopped and swung around quickly, looking for them. Three little girls were skipping rope across the street in front of a neatly landscaped, two-story colonial white house.

"B my name is Bonnie, and"

"Stop it!" Doreen yelled at them, hands clenched at her sides, arms straight as pokers. "Stop it right now! That's not very nice! You're mean and I hate you!" She turned on her heel and continued to walk quickly to work. The three girls stood staring, watching her walk away.

"Is she weird or what?" the smallest girl said to her friends, using her thumb over her shoulder to indicate the direction that Doreen had taken.

"I wonder why she said we were mean," said the girl with red curls surrounding her freckled face.

"Let's go or we'll be late for school."

* * * *

Deborah looked over her lab list for the day. She had twelve CBC tests to do, and then she would do the nine EKGs. Lucy Daniels was the regular lab technician whose job it was to do the electrocardiograms, but she had called in sick today with a virus, so Deborah had to fill in for her. Deborah didn't mind.

Beachside Memorial Hospital was just a small one floor hospital in a small fishing town named Flagler Beach, so there usually wasn't too much to do in a day, and she would rather keep busy. When Doreen had decided to become a nurse, Deborah had decided on a lab technician career. She liked the idea of working in a hospital, but she knew she could never handle being a nurse.

Deborah hated to see really sick people, and it devastated her to hear that someone she knew had died. It left her with a feeling of helplessness and failure. As a lab tech she had only minimal contact with the patients, and her contact with them was mostly just routine testing for admission to the hospital. Whenever she had to do tests on a terminally ill patient, she would be all business, getting her testing done and then moving on to the next room. She tried not to look at the very sick, as if whatever they had she would catch if she didn't stay clear of them.

Deborah's mind flashed to Joe. Sunday was their third anniversary and she bought him a black onyx tie tack with a diamond in the center, and matching cuff links for his very dressy shirts with the French cuffs. She had a quiet candlelit dinner planned for the two of them, complete with stuffed lobsters, and she was really looking forward to the week-end. Tonight she had to stop by Goldstein Jewelers after work and pick up his present.

She loved being married to Joe. He was so handsome with his soft blond hair, warm sexy brown eyes, and strong square jaw. He was six feet two inches tall, with broad shoulders and a muscular body. She was so proud of him, especially when they were out together. She liked the way other women looked at her husband. She liked the look of envy on their faces when they looked at her. Oh, yes, she never doubted her love for Joe and she had never regretted her decision to marry him and move to Florida. Her life was just as she wanted it-- quiet, loving and peaceful.

* * * *

Metropolitan Hospital in Edison was a modern eight story facility which rose up against the sky, clearly visible from within a mile of its parking lot.

"Doreen, would you accompany me on my rounds, please," Dr. Walters said, more a command than a question.

"Of course, Doctor," she said, putting down the patient's chart that she had been writing comments in.

"How's Mrs. Redderman?"

"She's still requesting pain med every four hours on the nose. I think she's timing her shots. We've been stalling fifteen minutes to a half hour to prolong it before we dope her up again, but she's starting to get wise, and is now asking for her shot a half hour before it's due."

"How long has she been in now?"

"Almost ten days. Also, I found chocolate bar wrappers in the waste basket. If she's in as much pain as she claims to be, she would not touch candy knowing that chocolate makes her ulcer act up."

"The more I get to know people, the more I need to jog. I'll have to change her medication. Maybe give her some sugar to see if she still times it. If it continues to be every four hours, we'll know for sure, won't we?"

"You jog, Doctor?" Doreen asked him innocently, looking up at him as they walked down the corridor. *You run like a duck,* she thought. *If only you knew how stupid you look, Doctor! To see yourself as others see you, jogging around the park every night, running around the lake without a care in the world. See Doctor run. Run, Doctor, run!*

"Yes, it's one of my favorite things to do. It gives me a chance to think and feel good about things." *And keeps me in shape for those cute nurses that keep entering our hospital doors,* he thought to himself. "Good morning, Mrs. Redderman. How do you feel today?" he asked, walking into Room 226.

Doreen stood to the side of Mrs. Redderman's bed watching Dr. Walters press slightly on Mrs. Redderman's soft, plump stomach. She studied his tanned round face, his hard muscled body, the way he moved his eyes when he talked. She memorized every movement, every mannerism, every trait. Just like yesterday, last week, last month. He was so easy to learn, a real creature of habit.

"I understand you're still having pain," he remarked, listening to Mrs. Redderman's stomach noises with his stethoscope.

Doreen turned her attention to Mrs. Redderman's face. Most patients adored their doctors, and Mrs. Redderman was no exception. Shame, Doreen thought, how these naive people put all their faith, trust and admiration into a mere man called doctor. How stupid people could be. Doctors were men, not gods, but everyone treated them like they were. EVERYONE! Doctors always got the royal treatment every place they went: the

best table at the finest restaurants without a reservation; the best cuts of meats at the butcher's at
a reduced price; the highest fees, even when they
botched up surgery and ruined someone's life! *Oh,
yes! The surgery was a success, even though the
patient died, and the bill was expected to be paid
by the end of the week because the new Rolls was
due in. Thank you for coming in.*

"Is there a problem, Nurse?" Dr. Walters asked,
cutting into her thoughts. Doreen felt herself blush.

"No, Doctor, not at all," she answered quickly.
"I'm just tired."

"Then maybe you should get some more sleep
at night, instead of whatever it is you now do to
make yourself tired," he said, giving Doreen a wink,
lowering his voice into a conspiratorial whisper,
his voice husky, eyes shining as if he shared some
deep dark secret that only he and Doreen knew.
Doreen blushed again. Dr. Walters smiled a wide
smile, turned and walked out of the room, leaving
Doreen to regain her composure, and then hurry
behind him, head down.

* * * *

It had been a long tedious day for Deborah,
the highlight of which was lunch time in the
hospital courtyard. The peace and tranquillity; the
cool breeze blowing down from the North,
reminding the South that it was autumn; the sweet
sounds of robins and bluebirds again singing in
the trees now that they had migrated to the warmer
climate of Florida for the winter. Deborah had just
sat there quietly, nibbling a bologna sandwich
which she had brought from home, and soaking
up the sights and sounds around her, feeling the
anxiety that had plagued her all morning slipping

away. The smell of the fresh cut grass, the clarity of the bright blue sky, the chill of the wind, all wonderful gifts from the angels.

In her mind's eye, she saw her sister, Doreen, back when they were only eight years old, sitting there under the massive old oak tree with its leaves of brown and gold rustling in the breeze. Dory's legs were curled up under her blue plaid shirt, her little hands folded in her lap, her long dark hair blowing around her sad small face, giving it a halo effect. She sat quietly and watched the other kids playing in the school yard. She always sat there during lunch recess, always quiet and always alone.

Debbie would stand to one side and watch her sister sit there under that oak tree, day in and day out. She had tried a few times to sit with Dory, but Dory would only get upset and run away. Dory didn't want Debbie near her when they were at school because wherever Debbie was, the other children flocked around her. Dory did not want the other children's attention. To have their attention meant being the subject of their ridicule, and then the chant might start.

That chant! Debbie could hear the chant, over and over; she could see her sister crying, running blindly into the wooded area behind the school; she could feel the tightness in her chest and the pain across her forehead that she always got when Dory was upset. Poor Dory. That awful scar. Why hadn't it been her, not Dory. Deborah was sure that she could have tolerated the mark better than Dory. She had hated for Dory to be upset because she also got upset, and then she would have one of her attacks. Maybe that was what was causing her attacks now. Maybe she was subconsciously worrying about Dory. But that was ridiculous. They were adults now. No one would sing that chant to

Dory anymore.

Deborah spent the rest of the day thinking about Doreen, wondering how she was doing. She would definitely have to give her a telephone call soon. Deborah stopped at the butcher shop after work, purchased two thick Delmonico steaks, and then stopped by the florist for some fresh cut flowers for the table. She had to hurry dinner or else be late for her late night bowling league. She was anchor woman on her hospital team, The Bloodsuckers, and her colleagues would never let her live it down if they had to default a game because she wasn't there.

Deborah quickly rinsed the dinner dishes, put them in the dishwasher and grabbed her blue-marbled bowling ball. Joe came out of the bathroom, a large fluffy green towel wrapped around his waist, his almost hairless chest, golden brown from the Florida sun, glistening with drops of water.

"Want to see the surprise I have for you under my towel?" Joe asked with a smirk, holding the ends of the towel in anticipation, his eyebrows raised, his big brown eyes wide open and shining.

"Just hold your surprise till I get home," Deborah laughed. "I'll be home around midnight."

"Cute. Real cute," he said, looking genuinely disappointed.

Deborah ran over and kissed his full mouth. She patted his small, hard backside, picked up her keys and hurried to her car.

* * * *

Doreen had had an even worse day. After the humiliation that she had suffered with Dr. Walters, Doreen had encountered several emergencies.

First, Mr. Diriksen had had a cardiac arrest, and then, while that Code Blue was going on, they had brought in Danny Lenoire with a broken back from an automobile accident that he had just been involved in. And as if that hadn't been enough, old Mrs. Dominico had decided to choose that very moment to die, and being visitor's hours, her family had been there in the room. Her daughter had come running out of the room screaming for a nurse, while the rest of the family cried and wailed.

"Damn emotional, fanatical Italians!" Doreen had murmured to herself as she sent one of the other nurses to Mrs. Dominico's room to settle everyone down. Oh, yes, it had been one of those days you'd sooner forget. But now Doreen felt great. It was a clear, brisk night. The stars looked close enough to pick. Doreen liked that idea, and visualized herself picking a bunch of the little twinkling stars and sprinkling them all over her hair so that she would appear to be in a dazzle of sheer light rays.

The light would make her perfect...her body would be perfect. She walked down the lighted sidewalk as if on a soft blue cloud, careful not to make any ungraceful movements which might cause her to lose any of the stars in her hair. Three men sitting on the steps of an old apartment building, and a couple walking arm-in-arm, all stared at her as Doreen glided past them, totally oblivious in her dazed illusions of grandeur. If only her mother could see her now, wearing stars in her long dark hair. Her mother would see that she was as beautiful as Debbie. Doreen frowned, remembering when she had seen her mother last month, sitting in her room at the sanitarium, staring out the window. Judy Price never moved, never talked, just stared. But Doreen continued her monthly visits to see her mother anyway.

Doreen stopped at the corner waiting for the light to turn green. There was a beautiful, scintillating, green sequined gown in the window of Damion's Designs across the street, with a matching sequined and feather skull cap. Doreen didn't see the mannequin that wore the ensemble, but instead, pictured herself in that glamorous outfit standing on the stairway at the Hilton, with every head in the hotel turned her way, admiring her as she stood elegantly in the beautiful light from her stars as it radiated off the sequins of her dress. The light from those stars and from the gown would be almost blinding, she told herself.

"I went to see her today, the poor thing," the woman standing next to Doreen said to her friend, cutting into Doreen's fantasy. "She had open heart surgery last week. A triple by-pass. Can you imagine going through that?"

"No, I can't," her friend answered. "Is she all right?"

"Oh, yes. She's doing just wonderful. Especially for her age. But my goodness, Marta, you should see her scar. It starts at the neck and goes all the way down to her waist. And then, as if that isn't enough for one person to handle, she also has another scar down the back of her right leg, where they had to remove something or other to use in the operation. A vein, I think it was. God, that scar was the most hideous thing I've ever seen."

Doreen glanced sideways to look at the woman who was speaking. She was a short, fat woman in her fifties with her reddish brown hair cropped so short that part of it stood straight up, and by the dull lackluster look, Doreen could tell it had been permed and dyed too many times. The woman wore a light pink polyester pant suit which was one size too small, so her rolls of excess fat waved down her round body. She wore a large diamond on her wedding hand which sparkled every time the woman moved her hand. *She's wearing a star on her finger*, Doreen thought with a smile.

"I would rather die than have an ugly scar like that, wouldn't you, Marta?"

"Oh, my, yes. I hope I never have to have that surgery done."

"I don't know what's worse, having a bad ticker, or getting it fixed and then being a freak full of scars. Come on, Marta," the woman said, taking her friend by the arm. "The light's green."

Doreen stood where she was and watched the two women cross the street. People walked around her, giving Doreen a look as they passed. She looked again at Damion's window. The mannequin in the sequined gown stared back at her with sightless eyes. It seemed to be smiling a mocking smile.

Doreen could feel the pounding starting behind her eyes. A FREAK! The woman had said freak. The bitch! Who was she to talk about being a freak! Her and her ugly hair, and her fat ugly body! And with a star on her fat ugly finger! Who had given that beast one of HER stars?!

The light turned green again. Doreen hurried across the intersection, past Damion's pretty window, past the quiet park, and up the stairs of her apartment building. By the time she got her door open, the throbbing in her temple had turned into a full blown headache. Doreen ran to the bathroom medicine cabinet, pushing all the little bottles around until she found her prescription for Tylenol with codeine. She quickly popped two of the white tablets into her mouth, drank a large glass of water, and then went to lie down across her bed.

FREAK! A scar makes you a freak! *Why me*, her mind screamed. *Why me and not Debbie? I don't want to be the freak! That fucking doctor did it! Played God. He chose Debbie to be perfect and me to be the freak! That damned Doctor...Dr? What the hell was his name? Mc...McClain? McDonald? McClusky? That's it! Fucking rotten Dr. John McClusky!* That's the name her mother had told her. *Dr. John Fucking McClusky! I'd kill him if he weren't already dead, the old bastard!*

Doreen rolled over onto her stomach, resting her chin on her folded arms. Dr. John McWalters! Him and his jogging all the time. A jogging god! She laughed out loud. She could just see him running through the park with this halo around his head. She had seen him several times running his regular course through the park, and had decided to follow him on a few occasions just out of curiosity. Then it had become routine for her to tag along behind him. Yeah, she had the whole exercise down pat, all right.

Screw up her life, would he! Well, he'd have to pay! Everyone knew that you had to pay for everything you do in life, didn't they, so why shouldn't Dr. McWalters? McWalters? McClusky? Doreen glanced at the clock radio on her night-stand. Ten o'clock. Definitely pay time. Pay day for Dr. John McWalters. Doreen scrambled off the bed and ran to her closet. She grabbed her navy blue sweatsuit off the brown plastic-coated hanger, picked up her blue and white tennis shoes, and dashed into her bathroom.

* * * *

Dr. Lawrence Walters had thought no more

about the incident that morning with Doreen Price at the hospital. He had dismissed it immediately. Dr. Walters had always prided himself on being physically fit, and now as he stood in front of the full wall mirror in the bedroom, he decided that all the years of jogging and exercise had paid off. At fifty-three he looked and felt like a man in his early forties. There wasn't an ounce of fat on his entire five foot ten inch frame. He liked the way his body rippled when he flexed his muscles.

He smiled at himself. The teeth were great, and they were all his, not false like most men his age. His gray hair had been dyed black since he was thirty-five, and it had not thinned out that he could notice. There were minor crows feet lines by his small green-brown eyes, but he felt they gave his face character, along with the cleft in his chin.

"You good-looking devil, you," he said to his refection in the mirror. "You still got what it takes to tickle those pretty little fannies." Hadn't he constantly proved that with each cute little student nurse he came across? Sheri had been the latest conquest, a real hard case, too. A virgin. He hadn't had a ripe, ready to be picked, nineteen-year-old cherry in a long time.

She had really given him a run for his money: flowers, candy, dinner at Sardi's in New York, and still she wouldn't budge. It took box seats to see Chorus Line and the horse and buggy bit through Central Park to finally break her, but she had definitely been worth the chase. He remembered her long blond curls spread across the pillow, her beautiful mint-tasting pink mouth, her oval blue eyes wide with fear. But he was a master in the art of love-making. He had been gentle, careful and soothing until he had her moaning and squirming, then he had shown her fireworks with strong powerful thrusts.

For almost two weeks now, he had taken her to new heights of ecstasy and pleasure, but the time had come to move on to another cherry tree. When they start calling his answer service six times a day, asking for him all over the hospital, or making hints about him divorcing his wife, they became yesterday's news--history in the annals of Larry Walters.

Larry loved jogging through the park at night. He never worried about muggers. He knew that he could handle himself, having been in the army. Besides, there were no muggings in Roosevelt Park in Edison, New Jersey; at least, none that he had ever heard of. Running gave him a chance to think, to sort out problems, to plan and to dream. He especially liked to jog in the Fall when it wasn't too hot or too cold, and the changing landscape seemed to spur him on. He pulled on his red cotton jogging shorts.

"I think while you're jogging I'll soak in a hot bubble bath," his wife, Joyce, said as she came into their large bedroom. Larry watched her reflection in the mirror as he pulled his white tee shirt over his head. Joyce was a handsome woman, tall and slender. Her platinum colored hair was pulled back, curled in layers, and sprayed stiff with hairspray. He disliked hair that he couldn't run his fingers through, but the style was flattering for her. Her green eyes were heavy-lidded, giving her that sexy bedroom look.

Joyce had been an attractive registered nurse when he had married her thirty years ago, and he had always been happy with his choice for a wife. She had been loyal and faithful to him, and an understanding and patient mother to their two daughters. The gods had definitely been good to him through the years. He had a successful, thriving medical practice, a wonderful loving wife, and the two smartest, prettiest daughters any father could wish for. Larry gave his reflection one more critical look, and satisfied with what he saw, Dr. Lawrence Walters left his house.

Doreen had already left hers.

Chapter 2

Dr. Walters started jogging as soon as he came out of his large, brick ranch home. When he reached the end of his driveway, he did a U-turn and jogged back into the house. A minute later he came running out of the front door again, his headphones covering his ears, the little radio attached to the elastic waist band of his running shorts.

"Love me tender, love me long,
Never let me goooo..."

Elvis crooned into Dr. Walters's ears. Larry always had his radio tuned to his favorite golden oldies station, 101 FM.

"For it's there that I belong,
And I love you soooo..."

Dr. Walters turned east onto James Street, running past Metropolitan Hospital, where he had had to put in long, tiring hours as an intern. He glanced at the white brick hospital standing majestically in the glare from the lights in the parking lot.

"...whispers in my ear,
oooooh, sweet nothings..."

He ran under the railroad overpass, trotting on by the Parkland apartment complex, where some of the hospital personnel resided. He made a sharp right turn into the park, running through the picnic area and cutting across the grass toward the lake. The dry leaves crunched under his feet as he ran. His body was already drenched in sweat, but his breathing was good and his heart rate was steady.

Dr. Walters could see the glare from the lights which surrounded the tennis courts in the northern section of the park, shining through the large oak and spruce trees which bordered the perimeter of the lake. He lowered his head to avoid hitting a low hanging branch, proud of himself that he knew this course so well that even in the dark he could avoid its many pitfalls. *Ah, yes*, he said to himself, *I am definitely the captain of my ship, the master of my own fate, the creator of my destiny. I am my own man, a man unto...*

He caught the movement in the gloomy darkness, out of the corner of his eye, but the ebony figure moved quickly. He heard the loud crunching sound seconds before the pain registered in his brain. As he fell sideways to the cold ground, his hand automatically went to the left side of his head, where the pain seemed to radiate from, a look of disbelief on his face. He could feel something thick oozing down his face and neck, getting into his eyes. It seemed that his whole body was on fire, small explosions of sharp, stabbing pains erupting in his head causing him to vomit, but stopping him from turning his head to the side. Dr. Larry Walters knew that he was losing consciousness, and he also knew that if he did, he would die.

Doreen stood motionless over him, a cold black iron pipe hanging from one hand, and a large flashlight, its beam illuminating the prone body of Dr. Walters, steady in the other hand. She watched fascinated as the blood gushed out of the large gaping hole in the side of his head, the blood spreading, drawing crazy line patterns all over him. Blood flowed freely from his nose, ears and eyes. His chest heaved and wretched, pushing blood-streaked vomit out of his gasping mouth. Both his feet and hands twitched, and his legs jumped involuntarily. His earphones lay tangled around his neck. Doreen bent down and pulled them loose gently and listened, holding one earphone to her ear.

"I shot the sherifffff,

But I did not shoot the deputy..."

Doreen smiled. She crouched down by Dr. Walters and looked intently at his blood-stained face.

"You shouldn't have done it, Doc," she whispered hoarsely. "You ruined me playing God. Why me anyway? Why did you choose me and not Debbie? Do you hurt, Dr. McClusky? I hurt. I always hurt. All my life, Doctor. All of my miserable, fucking life!"

She listened to the gurgling sounds coming from his throat. "Can you hear me, Doc? Do you understand that you have to pay? Everyone pays for damages, Doc, even you. I'm paying and I don't even know why. Do you hear me, Dr. McClusky?" There was no answer, only that raspy, choking sound. She rolled Dr. Walters over onto his stomach.

"Are you crying, Doc?" Doreen put her ear close to his mouth and listened. She momentarily felt sad. She didn't want him to cry. She hated when someone cried, especially if she had been the reason for their pain. But that was ridiculous! She had not given the good doctor a reason to cry! It was him that had caused HER to cry! She rolled him over again. And again. And again.

"Well, here we are, Dr. McClusky. This is where we part company." She looked one last time at his dark profile. "Now we're even, Doc," she whispered, and rolled him over, face down into the lake. His hands flapped weakly at the water as his body began to slowly float out toward the center. Finally, Doreen could no longer see the dark mass in the murky water. She stayed stooped by the edge of the lake for another ten minutes before she went back to the treed area, retrieved her flashlight and the piece of pipe, and headed for home.

* * * *

Deborah had bowled a good night. A 153 average. Really not bad. She would have bowled even better, she decided, if it hadn't been for this damn headache that had started during the third game. Suzanne had given her some aspirin, but her head continued to throb. She had declined an invitation to go have a drink with the rest of her team. *Maybe I should bowl on a league closer to home*, she thought, driving past the motel area along the beach. *I could bowl on a league in Palm Coast. This half hour drive from Ormond Beach seems to be getting longer and longer each time.*

Usually Deborah liked the quiet drive up Ocean Shore Boulevard, hearing only the roar of the Atlantic Ocean as its waves broke, one by one, on the fine white Florida sand. Tonight she barely noticed the sound. Her car radio played softly, but she did not hear that either. Her temples were pounding, her eyes throbbing and burning. She felt like there was a steel band wrapped around her chest, constricting her breathing and causing her to be lightheaded.

Deborah turned left onto High Bridge. She was having trouble seeing the road. The bridge over the Intercoastal Waterway lay before her about a mile. And a mile past that, Joe waited for her at home. She seemed to be losing her ability to think, to concentrate. She drove as if in a trance, almost like the car had a mind of its own, and it knew how to get there without her help. Deborah had lost the will of her own being.

* * * *

Thomas R. Martin was a forty-eight-year-old, slightly plump accountant from New Jersey, who had finally managed to take a long overdue two week vacation in Florida with his wife, Betty. He loved Betty and their three grown children. He loved being married and the sense of belonging it gave him. He had never cheated on his wife, nor had he any desire to. He was president of a small accounting corporation which employed four certified public accountants, one junior accountant, two secretaries and a receptionist.

Betty Martin had gotten too much sun that day, trying to get as dark as possible before she had to go back up North, and she had retired to bed early. Around ten that night, Thom had decided to go up to High Bridge to do some fishing, so he made himself a thermos of black coffee, grabbed his pail and his gear, and stuffing a Macintosh apple in his jacket pocket, set off for the bridge. Thom had made one stop at Brownie's Bait Shop to get some live shrimp, and had caught Brownie closing up the store. Thom had talked to him awhile, convincing Brownie to meet him up on the bridge for some trout fishing. Brownie had said that he had to go get something for dinner, but he had promised Thom that he would meet him there around midnight.

Thom glanced down at the pail sitting on the sidewalk by his feet. There were only three small fish in the pail: two trout and a catfish. He looked out over the quiet dark waterway, at the misty glow off in the black distance caused by the neon lights of the motels and restaurants in the next town south of Flagler.

What the hell is the name of that town again, he asked himself. *Ormandy Beach? Something like that.* He dismissed that thought and picked another, more serious one to replace it- - his accounting firm. A car came slowly over the bridge, and when it reached the other side, it sped up and disappeared into the pitch black of the night. Thom watched the red glow of the car's tail lights until it was out of view, fascinated that they reminded him of an animal's eyes which he had seen in a horror movie.

"Not Brownie, I guess," he said aloud. He took his cap off, ran his hand over his smooth, bald head, and pulled the cap back on with one quick motion. *I should never have gotten that tattoo,* he decided, thinking about the small yellow rose he had had permanently etched on top of his head. Roy and Tony had talked him into it about eleven years ago by making it a bet and putting money on it. Betty had been furious.

His fishing pole jerked a little. Then again. Thom gave a yank on the line and started to reel it in. The fish pulled back and the line went taut. Thom wasn't worried about the line breaking. He had forty pound test on there. He began to reel it in again. The fish was really putting up a fight and Thom was forced to firmly hold onto the pole with all his weight, his legs spread, knees slightly bent to brace himself against the bridge wall for leverage.

He heard the car coming slowly, its lights flickering on the bridge and across the water. The fish dove deeper, pulling the line taut, causing the pole to bend in half. Thom let out some slack on the line. The car was on the bridge now, slowing to a stop across from where Thom stood. Someone got out, leaving the car running. *Must be Brownie*, Thom thought as he started to reel in again. *Wait till he sees what I've snagged!*

His head snapped forward with such force, so fast and so hard, that at first he thought that he had slipped on something, until the first explosion of pain seared through him, shooting electric jolts in all directions, and knocking the breath out of him. He felt someone grab his legs and yank them up in the air, and he was falling downward, his head hanging limply as the shock of fire in his brain was causing a short circuit in his body. He tried to call out, but even he couldn't hear it with all the pain. *Betty*, his mind screamed, *I love you! I love you...*

Thomas R. Martin hit the water with the loudest splash Deborah had ever heard. She didn't bother to look over the side of the bridge. She knew that she would not be able to see him in the dark. Instead, she picked up the pail, peered in at the fish, and then threw the pail over the concrete bridge railing. Next she threw the bait, tackle box and thermos over into the salty waters of the Intercoastal. She picked up her husband's police Kel-Light flashlight that she had dropped, and strolled across the street to where she had stopped the car on the bridge. She slid the flashlight back under the front seat where Joe kept it. Deborah slid behind the wheel of her Camaro, put the car in drive, and went home to her husband.

Chapter 3

Dave Selten always considered himself to be a fair, honest and understanding person, but this had been one hard week to be a New Jersey detective. He had had to appear in court most of the week, waiting to be called to testify on his investigation of the Nelson murder, only to be told to report back on Monday because they would not get to his testimony till then.

Murder. Absolutely senseless, he thought, as he walked down the narrow stairway to the detectives' offices located on the bottom floor of the Edison Police Department headquarters.

Nedra Nelson had been a twenty-two-year-old black girl, plain and so very thin that she appeared emaciated. The autopsy report showed that there had been grass, speed and coke in her bloodstream, but not enough for her to have been an addict or to have overdosed. Probably an occasional user, a party dabbler. But the last party she had attended had been her final one.

The coroner's report had said that she had suffered a severe beating which had resulted in her having had four broken ribs, a fractured skull, a broken jaw and massive internal bleeding. But that's not what killed her. She had been savagely stabbed thirty-four times in the neck, chest and abdomen, one of the wounds cutting an artery. Nedra's live-in boyfriend, Clyde Jones, was on trial for the brutal killing.

Dave sat down at his desk and picked up the stack of papers that were piled up in his "IN" basket: FBI reports, court reminders, inter-office memos. He glanced through them quickly, throwing away what he considered to be junk mail. Bowling league news received two full minutes of his attention, which was more than most of the papers got. Dave had decided long ago that most messages that started with the heading "MEMO" were usually not worth remembering. He stopped at a missing person bulletin.

Last seen by wife before going to jog through Roosevelt Park.

> Dr. Lawrence Walters -surgeon
> 5'10" tall, 165 lbs.
> 53 years old
> Married: wife, Joyce
> Children: 2 daughters,Mary &
> Anne
> Military: 3 years, US army
> Status: SPC5

Now what is it, Dr. Walters, Dave said to the paper in his hand, *that makes you run? Tax problems? Girlfriend pregnant? Dull, boring wife, who doesn't blow or understand you? And where do you run to? Brazil or Switzerland would be my guess. With a pretty little bleach-blond secretary with a firm ass, monstrous tits, and a "your-slave-forever" attitude*. Damn doctors. They could almost have anything they wanted: custom tailored suits, expensive cars and beautiful women, vacations in exotic lands written off as expenses by shrewd accountants. He dropped the bulletin in his file basket. "Good luck, Doctor, wherever you are."

He rifled through his telephone messages. Sergeant Tacker had called him from the road. His girlfriend Wendy: Could he make supper tonight? Please call her back. His girlfriend Arlene: Confirming their date for tonight. Wendy again: Should she chill the wine? His buddy Burke: Going fishing Saturday around six a.m. Want to come? Wendy a third time: Called again. 555-6242.

Dave picked up the telephone receiver and dialed. Why hadn't he become a doctor, he asked himself. He had no answer. He had always planned to be a cop. From the time he had been six years old, he just knew he would be one. His mother and father had told him that all six year olds wanted to be policemen, that he would grow out of the idea as he grew older. There were no other police officers in his family, so he had not followed in his father's or grandfather's footsteps.

"Hello. This is Arlene. I am not at home right now, but please don't hang up. At the sound of the tone, please leave your name and telephone number, the time you called, and a short message, and I will call you back when I return. Thank you for calling." Beeeeeeep.

"How many times must I tell you never to leave a message saying that you are not home? You won't be happy until you're robbed! It's three-thirty, and I'll be there at seven as planned. You know my telephone number, but can you guess who this is?" He hated telephone answering recorders. It made him feel inferior to a machine, as if the machine was controlling his life. LEAVE YOUR NAME! My name is Dave. LEAVE YOUR NUMBER! 555-0599. TELL ME THE TIME! The time is three-thirty. He dialed again.

"Hi. Wendy here. Please don't hang up..." He

hung up. Damn machines! Captain Caylor came walking through the door.

"I know tomorrow's your day off, Dave, but I've got two officers out sick. Can you come in?" He stood staring at Dave, one thumb hooked in his shiny, black gun belt, his belly hanging over it like an awning.

Too long in a cushy desk job, Dave decided, eyeing the captain. "Got a heavy date tonight, Cap," he answered, folding his arms across his chest.

"That's really too bad, Dave, ya' know? You can keep your heavy date and still be here at seven a.m., or you can go straight home, jack-off, and still be here at seven a.m. It's your choice, ya' know." He grinned at Dave and winked.

Dave watched him leave before he allowed himself to smile back, and shook his head slowly. He ran his fingers through his thick light brown hair.

Great! Just extend this lousy week one more day, Captain. Boy, he could sure use that fishing trip with Burke right now, but he had promised Wendy that he would take her shopping on Saturday followed by dinner and a movie. He always tried not to break a promise, but maybe this was an emergency. Maybe he should give up playing with pussy and try playing with fish. He chuckled at his own joke. He looked at his watch. Four-ten. He cleaned off the top of his desk, locked it up, and headed up the stairs. Captain Caylor was standing by the door talking to Rich Brown, a new rookie. Caylor watched Dave walk up the stairs toward him.

"Arlene, Arlene," Dave sighed when he had reached the captain. "Aaah. Such beauty. Such style. Such a nice ass!" He winked at the captain and saluted.

"Seven a.m., Romeo!" Caylor called after him, but Dave was already out the door of the station house.

* * * *

His large paw of a hand smoothed her silky hair, his lips kissed Doreen's eye lids, the tip of her nose. His hand slid down her hair to her face, stroking it lightly. His full, sensuous mouth found hers, his tongue parting her lips gently, prying into the sanctity of her warm, moist mouth. His hand moved down to her long, slender neck, her soft round shoulders, her firm breasts. He ran his tongue over her teeth, his fingers lightly pinched her nipples, the mild pain sending small electric shocks through her body. She moaned softly.

The telephone rang. He moved his body down, kissing one breast, then the other. His warm hand stroked her buttocks, her hard taut thighs, coming to rest in the moist cavern between her legs. She groaned, moving closer. The phone continued to ring. The dream began to fade. The ringing got louder. She opened her eyes slowly. It rang again.

"Hello," Doreen answered groggily.

"Hi, Dory?" Static on the line.

"Debbie?"

"Yes! Hi, how are you? Did I wake you up?"

"That's okay. Just because I was about to have the best climax of my boring life, that this call just loused up, is of little consequence when a twin calls long distance from Florida. How the hell are you?"

"Fine. Great! I've been thinking about you a lot lately. Is everything all right up there? How's Ma? Have you seen her?"

"Yes. Fine. Yes." Doreen propped herself up on one of her king size feather pillows, lit a cigarette, and inhaled deeply. She always enjoyed her first cigarette of the day. "I went to see her two weeks ago. She's still the same. Just sits there and stares out the window. Never looks at me. Never talks. It's so depressing. I hate going there, Debbie. She looked good, though. The volunteer woman had fixed her hair nice, and dressed her in a pretty housedress. But I sit and talk, and she sits and ignores me. We get along great!" Doreen and Deborah laughed. "You know Ma. She doesn't like to be demonstrative and showy. How's your cop?"

"Joe's just fine. Loving and thoughtful, as always. He's up for a promotion to lieutenant. We're keeping our fingers crossed. It would be a nice increase in pay. Your dreams sound super, but how's your real love life? Anyone I should know about?"

"Now you know I don't fuck and tell. After all, he could be married, or a prince from Saudi, an ambassador from Sri Lanka, a priest from the old neighborhood. One must be very discreet, after all."

"Oh, still a virgin, huh?" Both women laughed. "Dory, why not come to Florida for the Christmas holidays? It would be great fun. I have some vacation time left. We could walk the beach, swap work stories, find you a rich southern gentleman, and marry you off. By the new year, if we really work at it, we could have you married, pregnant and living in Palm Coast."

"We'll see, we'll see. You could come up here, too, you know. That way you could visit Mom. Think about it." The alarm went off on Doreen's clock radio. "Well, Deb, I have to run or I'll be late for work. Give Joe a kiss for me, will you? And thanks for calling, only next time, check my dream schedule before you interrupt another perfect masterpiece. Get it? MASTER PIECE!" They laughed, said their good-byes, and hung up.

Doreen laid there, listening to her radio and thinking about her mother. Judy Price had been a beautiful young girl, but finding herself the unwed mother of Siamese twins had wrecked havoc on her life. She had struggled along for ten years, working a day job as a waitress in a truck stop, and doing telephone canvassing at night from home after the twins were in bed. She rarely went out with a girlfriend, let alone a man. Getting and paying for baby-sitters had been a real chore, and she had been forced to pay one whenever she was called in to work a double shift at the diner.

Judy's parents had disowned her when they found out that she was pregnant, and had never forgiven Judy after they were born. On the day that Judy called her mother to tell her that she had had twins, Mrs. Price Senior had told her daughter that she had had Siamese twins because God was punishing her for having illegitimate children. To everyone's knowledge, Judy had never spoken to her parents again after that, and that her parents had died in a mysterious house fire the Christmas after the twins' tenth birthday, had truly seemed an accident at the time.

Judy had become more bitter, more depressed as the years had gone by. By the time she was twenty-eight, she had lost that childhood look of innocence. She had started to resent the little girls that had chained her to the miserable life she had now been forced to live. She had constantly screamed at them for every little thing, and they in turn had started to avoid her as much as possible, playing outside or in their room until bedtime.

Doreen would never forget the day that she and Debbie had come home from school, all excited that there would be no more school for the next two weeks due to the Christmas holidays. They had run up the steps expecting their mother to be making dinner. The apartment door had opened as Dory reached for the doorknob, and an older woman clad in a brown cloth coat had opened the door and greeted them with a phony plastered on smile. Two police officers had stood further back in the kitchen behind her. Debbie and Dory had stood on the steps staring up at them.

The woman had taken both little girls into the living room, and had explained that their mother was sick in the hospital, and that she was taking them to a place where they would be safe until their mother came home. Judy Price never came home again. The twins never did either.

* * * *

Joseph John Sterling had been a Flagler County Sheriff's deputy in Florida for the past five years, and he wouldn't have had it any other way. He was proud to be a deputy, and he was prouder to be Deborah's husband. Joe had grown up in Pennsylvania. His father had worked all his life in the steel mills, barely making ends meet, until one day they just closed the mills down. Joe had been in the Marine Corps at the time, and he had sent money home regularly to help his parents pay their bills. His brother, Fred, had wanted to quit school to help out, but his parents wouldn't hear of such a drastic action, so Fred had worked after school and on week-ends at the local supermarket as a stockboy. But the family's main support had come from Joe.

Joe had met Deborah in Woodbridge, New Jersey, while he was home on leave, having just returned from a one year tour in Okinawa. His buddy Frank lived in Perth Amboy, and after a week's stay in Pittsburgh with Joe's family, the two marines had gone to New Jersey to visit Frank's folks. They had started hanging out every night at the Oasis, a singles club catering to disco music, bright lights and beautiful girls. Both Joe and Frank had upheld the marine image by meeting every pretty face that entered the lounge, and then betting to see who dated which girl first. Being more aggressive, and priding himself on the fact that Italians were better studs, Frank was in the lead by one hundred dollars.

That Friday night Joe and Frank had been sitting at the far end of the long, maple bar, joking about Bootie James, one of their marine buddies back in boot camp at Parris Island. Deborah had come into the lounge with one of her girlfriends, her long dark hair hanging straight down past her shoulders, her slim body covered in a black silk jumpsuit tied at the waist with a wide, silver cinch belt.

Joe had heard fireworks go off in his head, his stomach had jumped flips, and his mouth had gone dry. He had not been able to muster enough courage to speak to her. It had been Frank to the rescue by wandering over to meet Deborah's friend, Connie. By the time midnight rolled around, both couples were getting well acquainted. While Joe and Deborah had danced slowly to the music, he had taken a deep breath and had asked her to dinner the next night. She had accepted, much to his surprise and delight, and one year later he had married her, and the newlyweds had moved to Florida.

They had been very happy these last few years. They both had good jobs, lots of close friends, and most of all, each other. *All we're missing is a child of our own*, Joe thought, tapping his pen on the desk blotter, where he now sat in his small office at the sheriff's department.

"Hey, Joe," Deputy John Woods called to Joe from the doorway. "How ya' doing?"

"John, any more on that Thomas Martin that did a vanishing act?"

"Nope. Wife's really upset, though. I have a hunch we've got a dead one. Shame, too, if that's the case. Good family man, from what the wife says. First vacation in years. Three kids. Maybe they'll be lucky and he'll show up alive with amnesia or somethin'.."

"Unfortunately I have the same feeling. But what the hell could be the M.O.? I mean, he's a god-damned tourist, never been here before, doesn't know anyone. Maybe he was mugged. Maybe he's hurt somewhere. The city boys are trying to find him checking the beaches, the hospitals, the town. If he's around, they'll find him. Shit, it could be anything. There's not much we can do but wait and see."

"And pray. I know his wife is." He picked at his front teeth with a matchbook cover. "Want to go for a brew after shift?"

"Nah. Can't. Going shopping for Deb. It's our third anniversary this week-end. I bought her a fourteen karat gold chain with a little gold heart on it."

"Sounds great. Well, I've got to shove off. Catch ya' later." John said, with a wave of his hand as he walked away. Joe grabbed his jacket and headed out the door. He watched John get into his squad car and pull out of the stone driveway. Deborah flashed across his mind again.

"Get ready, my darling," Joe said aloud. "I'm on my way to buy you lunch."

Chapter 4

"Why did I say that I would go tonight," Doreen said to her reflection in the small narrow mirror on the back of the visor. Her blue eyes stared back at her brighter than usual. She was upset at herself for having made the decision to go on the date and her eyes showed it. She tilted the mirror first downward and then up again, checking her long brown hair to be sure it had not gotten messed on her walk from the apartment to Dirk's car.

Dirk Newly opened the driver's side door and slid smoothly behind the wheel. He put the key in the ignition, turned and smiled at her. She smiled back weakly. He turned the key and the engine rolled over with a mighty roar. The 300ZX whipped into the flow of traffic. He reached over, tapped one of the many buttons on the dashboard, and soft music filled the car.

"I thought we'd take a ride down the shore and try the seafood buffet at Long John's Restaurant. Then I figured we'd try their lounge, maybe take a walk on the beach. I love the Jersey beaches in the Fall. What do you think?" he asked. Doreen stared at his profile. Wasn't too great. Not ugly, just not too great.

"Sounds fine. I've never been there, although

I've heard of the place," she answered. She reached into her purse for a cigarette.

"I really wish you wouldn't smoke in my car. There's no way to get the smell out of my upholstery. I'm sorry if it makes you angry."

"No problem," she said quickly, stubbing out her cigarette in the ashtray. "I should have asked first. I'm the one who's sorry."

"Why do you put that stuff into your system anyway? You're killing yourself every time you light one of those cancer sticks. Try a piece of gum the next time you decide you need to smoke. All you do..."

And so the talk went until they had arrived at the parking lot of Long John's Restaurant which overlooked the Atlantic Ocean off the New Jersey coast. *Dinner should help keep his mind away from his "need-to-stop" lecture*, she thought, looking out the window at the shoreline. Dirk Newly. Even his name aggravated her.

The hostess seated them at a window table overlooking the ocean, where they could look out at the pier lit up by flaming torches, their fires licking at the wind. She glanced over her menu slowly, glad to have an opportunity to bury herself away from him.

"What would you like to eat?" he asked. "Buffet or menu?"

"I think I'll have the buffet." She started to get up.

"I think I'll join you." They moved slowly down the buffet tables, picking the foods they wanted to try. Doreen had chosen a light blue silk dress to highlight her blue eyes, and the way the material draped over her willowy frame caught many glances as she passed. Doreen had the chef carve off a thick, red slab of prime rib.

"You don't want that!" Dirk said in a commanding voice.

"Yes, I do," she replied curtly, starting to move on to the lobster Newburg.

"No, you don't. That meat will kill you with fat and cholesterol," he said in a matter-of-fact tone, stabbing her meat with his fork and giving it back to the chef. He reached over, picked up the server and scooped some broiled fish onto her plate. Doreen stood staring at him in disbelief, her eyebrows raised, her mouth open, her hands on her hips.

"Just what the HELL do you think you're doing?" she asked in a sharp voice.

"Saving your life. If you don't care what happens to you, then somebody else has to, so it might as well be me as anybody." He carried their dishes down the long tables as Doreen continued to stand and glare at him. People were starting to stare at her, so she turned and stalked back to their table, leaving Dirk to do what he wanted.

As soon as Doreen sat down, the cocktail waitress appeared before her, and Doreen ordered a martini. *Why, oh why, did I tell him that I would go*, she asked herself for the tenth time that night. *He's such a...a nerd. A health nut. A goody-goody nerd!* She looked up in time to see Dirk coming towards her, balancing two plates piled high with food. He set one down in front of her. There was shrimp, fish, chicken and vegetables. His plate was identical to hers.

"Doesn't this look great!" he exclaimed, opening his napkin and placing it across his lap. The waitress was back with Doreen's drink. "What's that? A martini?"

"Yessir," the waitress answered, looking questionably at Doreen.

"What's wrong now, Dirk?"

"What's wrong? Miss, take the drink back and bring us two Perrier with a twist. Look, Doreen, I don't know how many vices you have to try to kill yourself with, but I don't appreciate you trying to do it while in my company. Cigarettes, red meats, alcohol. Jesus, you must be suicidal."

"Did it ever occur to you, Mr. Newly, that it's my body," Doreen started slowly in a low voice, leaning across the table, "and that as a full grown adult person, I may choose to smoke cigarettes if I wish, or to eat red meats, or to drink a million martinis? It's my body! My life! I do not now, nor in the future, need someone to tell me that I can't do those things, or anything else for that matter. Get the picture?"

"Doreen, are you upset that I care about you? That as your friend I should sit back and watch you destroy yourself? I'm sorry if I'm guilty of caring for someone I like. Do you understand what I'm trying to say?"

"Look. I don't care what you eat. I don't care if you smoke or drink, or don't smoke or drink. I don't care one way or the other what you, Dirk Newly, do or don't do. Do YOU understand?" She glared defiantly at him.

Dirk looked at her like a father looks at a child who has just thrown a temper tantrum. Doreen pushed her chair back, picked up her plate and marched back to the buffet tables. She reappeared within a few minutes, her dish covered with prime rib, mashed potatoes, shrimp and clams, and a stemglass filled with a dry martini. They ate in silence, except for an occasional attempt at small talk, but the air was filled with tension. When the waitress brought them coffee, Doreen took a long look at the torches still burning outside.

"Dirk, I have an awful headache starting. Could we skip the lounge and go home?"

"Sure. No problem." He motioned to the waitress for the check, and in minutes they were back in the 300ZX, heading home. The trip was made in silence, each caught up in their own thoughts, each counting the miles till they could part.

"Doreen, I'm sorry to have to say this," Dirk began when they pulled onto her street, "but I really don't think we have very much in common. You're a beautiful girl and I'm sure you're hurt, but I have to be honest with you." Dirk stopped the car in front of Doreen's apartment, but made no attempt to get out.

"Dirk, I, too, believe in being honest, but I don't agree that we have very little in common. I don't think we have ANYTHING in common," Doreen said, gathering her jacket and purse, "so in all honesty, I must say that you are the most pompous, arrogant son-of-a-bitch that I have ever had the misfortune to meet, and I cannot remember ever having had a worse time than I have had tonight. Please don't walk me to the door. I'd rather take my chances with the muggers. At the very least, it would put some excitement in my evening and make this night more memorable. Good-night, Dirk, and GOOD BYE!"

Doreen slammed the car door, and without looking back, walked briskly up the walk to her apartment.

* * * *

Slowly, slowly it reached the top until it finally surfaced. The fingers floated lazily with the movement of the water, the hand swaying gently back and forth. The arm plunged downward into the murky, dark water, appearing to be severed from its body. The lake was smooth except for the small ripples caused by the floating protrusion. The park was dark and quiet. The low murmur of traffic from the highway could be heard off in the distance. Below the water Dr. Lawrence Walters stared with lifeless eyes at the small fish swimming slowly around his head, the look of surprise still frozen on his face.

* * * *

"I love you, Mrs. Sterling," he whispered in Deborah's ear. The nightly muffled sounds familiar to Florida floated quietly into the living room, where they were cuddled up together on the sofa.

"Mmmm. And I love you, Mr. Sterling," she whispered, snuggling closer.

"Dinner was fabulous. Good thing we're married or I'd have to marry you." Joe brushed her hair back from her eyes. "God certainly blessed me when he gave me the best wife in the world."

"Okay, what are you looking for?" Deborah asked, tilting her face up toward him. He kissed her lightly on the forehead.

"Ah, my little squash blossom. What could I possibly want after such a great candlelit dinner with vintage wine and soft music? And what can I say about my gift that I haven't already said? So I repeat, what else could I possibly want?" Joe ran his finger up her thigh and began to caress her breast. "Whatever else is there?"

Deborah wrapped her arms around her husband's neck and kissed him sweetly on the mouth. He returned the kiss, more fervently than she had anticipated. Finally he pulled back, and in one swift movement he picked her up, carried her to their bedroom, and gently laid her down on the bed. He sat on the edge of the bed and slowly started to undress her. As the music continued to play in the living room, Joe and Deborah ended their third anniversary with sweet music of their own.

* * * *

High tide had been at four p.m. that day, sloshing against the banks of the waterway, and then depositing trinkets from the ocean as payment for the rape of its shores when it went out again. This day had been no exception to the daily intercourse between the land and the sea. The only difference today was, instead of jewelry or money or shells, the salty cool water of the night left behind the broken body of Thomas R. Martin, Certified Public Accountant.

Chapter 5

"Come on, Alex, row. I'm not going to do it by myself," Russ said, rowing the small boat laden with fishing gear and bait. "We'll fish closer to the center of the lake." Roosevelt Park Lake was kept well stocked with fish, which made it a favorite fishing spot in Edison.

"I'm going to ask Kathy to go to the game with me on Wednesday night. I was going to take Babs, but Kathy has finally noticed that I'm alive, so I'll give her a break and take her instead." He laughed.

"Hey! What's that?" Russ said, pointing to where ripples of water were disturbing the calm, glassy surface of the lake.

"Log, probably. By the way, we have to stop at Walt's on the way home and pick up a couple of bags of grass for next week's party. Okay?"

"I don't think that's a log. Besides, where would a log come from in Roosevelt Park Lake?"

"Who cares what it is. Did you hear what I said about Walt's? The guys are busting my ass for smoke. I need the money, Russ, ya' know?"

"Holy shit! Alex, it's a hand!" Russ yelled, peering over the side of the boat to get a better look.

"A hand? What the fuck you been smokin',

cabbage leaves?"

"Look! I'm telling you it's a hand!"

"Oh, Christ, Russ! It IS a hand!" The boat drifted closer to the puffy peeling fingers. "Don't touch it!"

"Give me the oar," Russ commanded. He took the oar and pushed at the water below where the arm disappeared. Bubbles floated to the top of the water. Suddenly a bloated, distorted face emerged, the eyes staring straight up at the two boys. "Shit! Let's get the fuck out of here!" Alex gawked at the swollen, deformed face, unable to move, frozen with fear. He had never in all his sixteen years seen anything so hideous and frightening. Things like this only happen in the movies, not in suburban towns like Edison, New Jersey.

"Row, damn you!" Russ screamed at Alex, his voice cracking from the panic that was mounting up inside him. Both boys rowed hard, their lean young bodies straining against the oars, sweat rolling down their faces despite the cold morning air that threatened snow. Hitting solid ground, they jumped out of the boat, and leaving everything behind, started to run across the park lawn.

"You stay and keep an eye on that water! I'm calling the police!" Russ yelled over his shoulder, continuing to run for the pay phone across the street from the park. Alex stopped running and leaned against a tree by the side of the lake, hands on his chest to try to stop the pounding beat that shook his body. He fixed his gaze on the spot where he knew the body was, afraid that if he took his eyes off it, it would disappear.

Dr. Lawrence Walters stared straight up at the sky and waited.

* * * *

Mamie McGee had been born and raised in Florida and she wouldn't have had it any other way. She loved the feel of the sun's warmth on her skin. Today, like so many other days, the old woman carried her long bamboo pole in one knotted, arthritic hand, and a dented metal pail partially filled with worms in the other. She squinted her ancient, jet-black eyes and scanned the sloping bank of the Intercoastal looking for one of her favorite fishing spots. She licked her deeply cracked, full black lips, thinking of the catfish she was about to catch frying in bacon grease in her big black iron skillet.

"Mamie, it sho' is gonna be a hot da'," she mumbled to herself, wiping the sleeve of her faded brown cotton dress across her wrinkled dark face. "Wha's thiz?" she asked no one in particular. She cautiously moved forward, stretching her thin, scrawny neck to get a closer look. "Oh, ma' lawd, swee' Jeezus!"

The body lay on the bank, tangled in fishing line, swollen and black, the head awkwardly twisted around. One ear was missing as well as part of the nose. The rancid smell of decaying meat reached her wide nostrils, causing her to trip as she backed away from it. Mamie dropped her pole and her pail, and as quickly as her antique body could maneuver it, she went back up the hill to find help.

Thomas Martin had caught a three foot shark that night on High Bridge, but it had not gotten away. It, too, lay dead and tangled next to him.

* * * *

As soon as the call had come in to the Edison Police Department, Detective Dave Selten had quickly left for Roosevelt Park, and now as he pulled his Trail Blazer to a stop, there was activity everywhere. Three patrol cars, the mobile crime lab unit, and the coroner's van were already parked there. Dave walked across the lawn to the edge of the lake, moving his way through the crowd of on-lookers that had gathered to watch.

"What have we got, Doc?" he asked the small, thin man stooped over the body.

Dr. Bill Daniels, one of New Jersey's best medical examiners, turned his delicate pinched face to look at Dave, and shook his partially bald head slowly from side to side. "Murder. No doubt about it. I'll have to verify it back at the lab, but I'll really be surprised if it's not conclusive. Look here," he said, pointing to the large cut on the side of the head. "See that laceration on the scalp? He's been hit with a blunt instrument, a piece of pipe is my guess. Of course, it could be a tire iron or something similar, but my opinion is pipe. His skull is depressed causing a fracture. Now whether or not that's what killed him, I'm not sure yet. I have to check the rest of him, but my educated guess is that he ended up there by someone else's doing."

"Got any idea how long he's been dead?"

"Not yet. But it has to be at least three to four days, minimum. Rigor Mortis is almost gone. With this cold temperature, it would have lasted at least three days, so it looks as though that man's been dead around four days. I'll send you my report by tomorrow afternoon." He packed up his black bag and motioned to his helpers to bag up the body for removal. Dave looked down again at the dead man.

"Was there any identification on him?"

The doctor looked at Dave and shook his head. "His keys and watch. That's it. Good luck," he said, handing Dave a set of keys and a Rolex watch.

Dave stared at the two items in his hand. There was a small silver tag on the key ring with the medical insignia on it. A doctor? Maybe a jogging doctor? He turned the wristwatch over. "To My Beloved Husband, Love Joyce" was inscribed in small lettering on the back. Dave walked over to one of the police officers.

"Anyone locate a parked car anywhere that might belong to that man?"

"No, Sir." *A jogging doctor. So this is where you went to, Dr. Walters,* Dave thought, turning the keys over and over in his hand. *Too bad. I was really hoping it was Brazil or Switzerland.* "We're looking for a possible weapon," the officer volunteered, bringing Dave out of his thoughts and causing him to look at the activity of blue uniforms all walking around searching the grounds. Dave took another look around him, and then taking one last look at the large covered mound by the lake, turned and walked back toward his car. He hated this part of his job. He disliked being the one to notify the next of kin, and in all his fifteen years on the force, he still couldn't get used to it.

Dave sighed. He stared out the front window of his car for another moment. *Who ever said jogging was good for your health,* he silently asked the body being carried to the meat wagon. Dr. Lawrence Walters had no reply.

* * * *

Less than half a mile from the park, Doreen turned first to the right, then to the left, checking herself in the full mirror. Her jeans were just tight enough to be flattering, but not tight enough to be ostentatious. Her large, knit, lavender sweater made a bulky addition to her appearance. She tied her shiny brown hair up with a lavender silk scarf, applied a light pink lipstick, grabbed her purse and bounced out of the door.

She had called into work sick today. *It's not a lie*, she had told herself that morning. *I really am sick --sick of working.* She ran to her white Corvette and jumped in behind the wheel. A day of leisurely shopping followed by dinner and drinks somewhere, maybe a good movie, had all seemed to her great reasons to take off from the normal routine of tending to the ill.

Doreen turned her car into the park, taking her normal shortcut to the Menlo Park Mall. Suddenly she spotted the police cars, the crowd milling around the lake, the flurry of animation as the cops scoured the area for clues. A tingling shock shot down her spine, followed by a violent chill. Beads of sweat broke out on her face and under her arms. She quickly drove her car away from the scene, not daring to look back in the rear view mirror, for fear that they would suspect her of having done the hideous crime.

But she had had to do it. Didn't they understand that? Someone had to make Dr. McClusky pay for what he had done to her. Her head started to hurt again, but she was afraid to stop the Vette until she had reached the parking lot of the shopping center. She sat in her car for a while, taking several deep breaths, trying to calm herself down.

Doreen slowly got out of her car. She felt as if her whole body was acting on its own, and that she was simply going through a dream state over which she had no control. She walked into the mall, past her favorite stores, and went straight into the Band Waggin Bar for a double martini. Within an hour she was back to normal, except that now she felt a little giddy and light-headed. She paid the bartender and went back out into the mall to do her shopping, the scene from the park all but forgotten.

* * * *

In Flagler Beach, Florida, Joe Sterling stood on the bank looking at the ever-changing, mysterious dark waters of the Intercoastal waterway. The medical examiner, Dr. Donald Turner, was crouched behind Joe doing a preliminary investigation on the body tangled and caught like the small shark beside him. Finally Dr. Turner stood up and went to stand by Joe. Neither man spoke. Joe watched a small white sand crab working erratically at the edge of the water. Dr. Turner was eyeing a forty-two foot catamaran cruising quietly up the waterway, wishing he could retire from all this craziness and sail off into the sunset.

"Accidental drowning?" Joe asked without taking his eyes off the crab.

"Could be," the doctor answered.

"But?"

"Oh, I'm sure that he drowned. But I don't believe that it was an accident."

"Oh?" Joe turned to face the M.E. "Why not?"

"The back of his skull is depressed in, there are definite skull fractures, and his neck is broken. Judging by the severity of the blow to the head, and by the expression on his face, he never knew what hit him. Whatever it was, it packed a wallop. I'll know more after I do the autopsy."

"Excuse me! Detective Joe Sterling?" the young man yelled, trotting sideways down the slope toward them, his jacket flapping around him.

"Yeah? I'm Sterling."

"Hello," the man said, gasping. "I'm Ken Taylor, *Flagler/Palm Coast News Journal*. Could I ask you some questions after I take a couple of pictures?" Without waiting for a reply, the reporter walked over and looked down at the body. He stood frozen for a few moments and then suddenly clutched his stomach and vomited.

Oh, Christ, Joe thought, watching the reporter. *A rookie news hound.* Just what he needed. The young man coughed several times, cleared his throat, and then composing himself, took out a small wire bound tablet and a pen.

"Sorry. Lunch must have been bad." Joe thought the reporter looked embarrassed, as well as green. "Can you tell me what happened here?"

"Nope."

"No? That's it? No?"

"Yes. That's it, no. Look. I don't know what happened here. I'm not God."

"I'm not asking you to be God. Just tell me something. You must have an idea as to what transpired here. Was it an accident? Did he drown? Was he shot? What happened to his ear and nose? There must be some little thing that you can tell me! I have a job to do, too, you know!"

"Crabs."

"What?"

"Crabs. Crabs and fish. That's what happened to his nose and ear," Joe said, looking straight into the reporter's brown eyes.

The reporter said nothing, but Joe knew the kid was about to puke again. Joe started up the bank, the coroner, his two assistants, and the body all ahead of him. He heard the reporter vomit again. He smiled and kept walking. When he had reached his car, he allowed himself to look back. The reporter sat hunched over with his head resting on his knees.

"Here's the personal effects, Joe," the officer said, holding a large plastic bag before him.

"Who is he?"

"Our missing tourist. Thomas Martin." Joe took the bag from the older man and held it up closer to his face.

"Welcome to sunny Florida, Thomas R. Martin."

Chapter 6

Detective Dave Selten had taken the keys and watch to the home of Dr. Walters, for identification by his wife. He had taken them out of his pocket, and holding them out to her, had asked, "Were these your husband's?" She had taken them into her hand and caressed them lovingly, nodding her head as she did so. She handed them back to Dave, tears starting in the corners of her eyes.

Joyce Walters had taken the news of her husband's death nobly. She had stiffened slightly, a frown creasing her brow, her beautiful green eyes glistening with tears. She had lifted her pointed delicate chin as if bracing for a punch, and had asked him how and where it had happened, and he had tried to soften his words. She had slowly lowered herself to the blue brocaded settee, sitting on the edge with her head down. When he had finished his explanation of the events as he knew them, she had thanked him, excused herself, and left the room. He had needed questions answered, but had decided to let them wait until today when the initial shock of the news should have worn off a little. He had left then, letting himself out and locking the door behind him.

Dave had next headed for Metropolitan

Hospital and spoken to several nurses, who had had a lot to say about Dr. Walters, and to a few doctors, who had very little to say about their colleague. What Dave had learned was that Dr. Walters had been a successful surgeon, a helpful and reliable associate, and the king of short lived affairs. Two of the nurses he had interviewed had been on duty the night Dr. Walters had taken his final trip to the park, but neither one had seen him.

Detective Selten had spent two hours talking to the hospital administrator, an overweight, conservative physician, who was all too happy to cooperate. Dave had requested from him a list of all hospital personnel who had been on duty the night of the murder, as well as a list of those who had been off, along with the names of all physicians that were associated with the hospital. He had finally left there, but before going to dinner with his new friend, Joni, he had returned to the park for another look around.

The uniformed police divisions had closed the park to the public and had roped off the area around the lake. Four police officers had been assigned the task of patrolling the park, keeping curious sightseers out. Dave had talked to Vinnie Marculli, one of the officers that had been guarding the area, and he had shown Dave the large area by the lake that was covered in dried blood. He had explained to him that samples had been taken and analyzed, and that the report had verified that the black, tar-like substance on the lawn was definitely dried human blood. Type O Negative. There had been a small trail of the dried substance leading to the lake, but they had found nothing that could have been the murder weapon.

When the news media had arrived complete

with television cameras, Dave had tried to leave unnoticed, but they had caught up to him. The reporters had riddled him with many questions and he had answered what he could as quickly as possible, and then had retreated to keep his date with Joni. When he had watched the news that night, he had thought that he had appeared to be an idiot, as he had not really told them anything of substance.

Now he sat in his office going over all the information that had been compiled the day before. It was obvious that Dr. Walters had been killed in Roosevelt Park, judging by the amount of blood they had found, and then dumped into the lake. The coroner's report wasn't in yet.

Dave picked up the telephone and called Joyce Walters to see if it would be convenient for him to see her around one that afternoon. She said that that would be fine if it was really important, but that she really didn't know what she could tell him that would help his investigation. He assured her that it was important, and that although it came at a stressful time, he had to attain pertinent information that might help to locate the killer. She finally relented and agreed to meet with him after lunch. The phone rang immediately after Dave hung up the receiver.

"Selten," Dave said, pulling a cigarette from the pack lying on his desk.

"Dave? Bill Daniels. I decided to call and give you my findings over the telephone. My secretary's out sick today with female problems, so it will be a couple of days before I can send you my written report."

"Great, Doc. What have you got for me?" Dave took a long drag on his cigarette, filling his lungs full of gray smoke, and then slowly exhaled through his nose and mouth.

"Cause of death was drowning. His lungs were totally filled with that dirty lake water. But the clubbing to the head immobilized him first. The laceration on the head definitely was from a piece of pipe, tire iron, something like that, judging by the elongated split of the scalp and the bruise marks around it. He was hit pretty hard, and judging by the head wound and some bone chips, he was hit from the side."

"What's the estimated time lapse?"

"I'd say he's been dead about four or five days, based on the amount of decomposition, which is slight due to the cold water, and by the post mortem lividity."

"Post mortem what?" Dave asked. He hated when someone talked over his head in technical jargon which he didn't understand. He flicked the ashes off his cigarette into the Sands Casino ashtray sitting on his desk.

"Post mortem lividity is when the heart stops beating and the blood settles to the bottom of the body and stays fixed there. If I can't move the blood around, it means the victim has been dead over ten to twelve hours. Understand?"

"Sure." He didn't really, but it wasn't his problem to know how the coroner did what he did or knew what he knew. Only the final answers that the doctor found interested him.

"The victim was in excellent health, so I really don't think he saw it coming or he would definitely have been able, physically, to put up quite a struggle, and there was no evidence of that. There were some scratches on his face, but they may have been caused when he hit the ground."

"Or from being rolled from where he was hit to the lake," Dave said, remembering the trail of dried blood leading to the water.

"Rolled to the lake? Why would the killer ROLL him to the lake when he could have dragged or carried him?" the doctor asked. "Unless the perpetrator was physically unable to do so, which means you're looking for a small person, or a person who may be handicapped, because Walters was no lightweight."

"Or a person who is female," Dave said, tapping his pen lightly against his chin, thinking about what he had just said. Maybe one of Dr. Walters's little flings got angry. Maybe the good doctor was breaking off an affair and the lady was unwilling.

"True. A female, unless she was very large, or a very strong woman like an athlete, would definitely have had a problem moving the body, especially because Walters was still alive when he hit that cold lake. By the way, Dave, is someone coming to identify the body for positive verification?"

"I'll bring Mrs. Walters over this afternoon, if she's up to it. I'm going over there after lunch." Dave stubbed out his cigarette in the ashtray. "By the way, Dr. Daniels, what was Walters blood type?"

"O Negative. Somewhat rare. Anything else?" Dave answered no, thanked the medical examiner and hung up. He dialed an extension number.

"Sergeant Tacker? I'd like you to bring in Miss Sheri Touter for questioning. You can get the information from the hospital, or the Lowman Nursing School. She's a student nurse, assigned to Metropolitan for training, so someone should have her home address on file."

"Got something, Dave?" Sgt. Tacker asked.

"Don't know, but she seems to be the doctor's latest playmate according to the gossip around Met. I just want to talk to her. If she scares, let her. Be easier for us if she does. She'll be more willing to help if she thinks her ass is grass and we're going to be the mower. Also, check the doctor's answer service for all calls made to him in the past month. Tell them I want it as soon as possible. You can find out the name of the service by calling his office number. The service should answer it. I also want the names of all nurses, receptionists and secretaries who worked in his office in the last five years." He thought a moment, "See if his nurse can tell you who his patients were, if he's had any problems with anyone lately, if he screwed up somewhere. Maybe there's a malpractice suit or something."

"Sure. I'll put men on it right away. Anything else?"

"Meet you in an hour at Stokes for a hoagie and beer?"

"Sure. You buying?" Tacker asked, laughing.

"Only if you have all that information by then."

"You cheap son-of-a..."

Dave hung up, quietly placing the receiver back on its cradle, so Tacker would not know right away that he had been cut off. Dave smiled, knowing he had edged Tacker once again.

* * * *

Doreen had awakened that morning with a severe hang-over. It had been an effort to go to the medicine chest to get some aspirin, but she had somehow managed it. The aspirins were quickly followed by a large cold glass of tomato juice, two cups of steaming black coffee, and a cold shower. She had arrived at work ten minutes late for patient briefing before the shifts changed. Mary Dubronchek, the head nurse on the midnight shift, had had to reiterate to Doreen what she had missed regarding Mr. Seaver, who had suffered another heart attack during the night, and she had not appreciated having to do so. As she told Doreen stiffly, when her shift was over she just wanted to get home, not stay and brief late personnel. Doreen had ignored her.

"Isn't it awful about Dr. Walters?" one of the nurses commented, fixing morning medications on her cart.

"Really," another nurse agreed. " I wonder who could have done such a thing."

"What's wrong with Dr. Walters? His wife catch him with some young thing?" Doreen asked, setting down Mr. Seaver's chart.

"You mean you haven't heard? They found Dr. Walters dead in Roosevelt Park Lake," the nurse responded, excited to be the one to relay the news to someone else.

"Roosevelt Lake? Dr. WALTERS?" Doreen asked, confused. *There must be some mistake*, she thought. *That's not Dr. Walters, it's Dr. McClusky!* Maybe McClusky's body hadn't turned up yet. So that's what all the excitement had been about yesterday in the park! She smiled to herself. She had panicked for no reason. Dr. McClusky was still in the lake. But then, what had happened to Dr. Walters, she wondered. "Did he drown?" she asked the nurse.

"Don't know yet. Police aren't saying, but they were here yesterday asking questions. In fact, a lot of questions about him. Poor guy."

"Poor guy, my Aunt Tillie! Probably a jealous husband or boyfriend killed him!" one of the nurses exclaimed, smirking.

"Or his own wife!" another said. The women all snickered. Except Doreen. She was totally perplexed about the news. Doreen sighed and felt herself relax. *I thought that they had found*

McClusky, and then almost gave myself away by losing control, she admonished herself. With a little luck they would never find the body.

"Who's on call for Walters's patients?" the nurse asked. "Mrs. Bollen is requesting something stronger for pain."

"Ah, let's see," the other nurse said, looking on the change order sheet. "Oh, some new doctor, name's Sweeter. Hey, that's cute! Dr. Michael Sweeter. I wonder if he is." All the nurses laughed. "Hey, girls, I wonder if he's single. I'll have to check it out." Doreen had already tuned out their idle gossip. Her head ached and her stomach felt sour. She needed to lie down. She took two Tylenol tablets out of the large bottle, told the others that she was going to the cafeteria for a cup of coffee and a cigarette, and pushed the button for the elevator.

"What's wrong with her?" one of the nurses whispered.

"Who knows. Monthly, probably," the other one whispered back. "With Doreen it's hard to say, you know what I mean?" They smiled secretly at one another, glancing over at Doreen as the elevator doors closed.

* * * *

Joyce Walters opened the door and stood staring at Dave for a moment. She appeared as composed today as he had seen her yesterday, her hair curled in place as if it were a wig, her expensive navy blue pantsuit giving her a conservative look. It was her eyes that gave her away. They were a dull green today, sad, anxious and red from all the tears she must have shed. Mrs. Walters motioned him inside.

"Can I get you some coffee or tea before we start?" she asked.

"No, thank you," Dave answered politely. Mrs. Walters showed him once again into the living room. Dave sat in one of the formal arm chairs, she again sat on the edge of the settee. Dave took his notepad out of his jacket pocket.

"Mrs. Walters, I know this is hard for you right now, but please tell me about your husband."

"Like what, Detective."

"What kind of man he was; how long you've known him; who his friends were." She stared at him for a while, mulling the questions over in her mind. Dave waited silently, watching her. She told him what type of loving, caring relationship they had had with their thirty years of marriage, their two daughters, his successful practice, and about his closest friends. When she was through with her analysis of her husband and their life together, she stopped, staring down at the plush, thick carpeting, lost in her memories.

"Did he have any enemies that you know of?"

"No. None."

"Were there any malpractice problems? Any angry patients?"

"Not that I'm aware of." Short guarded answers, not wanting to say anything negative about her dead husband.

"Mrs. Walters, I'm sorry to have to probe like this, but anything you can tell us may help." Her green eyes were defensive. Dave decided to push harder. "Did you know your husband was having affairs with other women?" He thought he saw her flinch.

"Yes." He waited for further comment, and when she offered none, he pressed for more.

"Did he ever discuss them with you?"

"No." She stared at him, hands folded in her lap, head held high. Why did these women protect their cheating husbands, he asked himself.

"Did he ever mention a Miss Sheri Touter?" Dave watched her expression closely, but there was no change. She only shook her head.

"How often did your husband jog, Mrs. Walters?"

"Almost every night. Unless he had a meeting or an emergency. Sometimes if we had plans to go out, or had guests coming, he would put off his running, but on the average, I would say he jogged five or six nights a week. He was very dedicated to being physically fit."

"Did he always run the same route, and always to the park?"

"As far as I know, Detective Selten. I did not jog with him, so I can't be positive." She took a deep breath and sighed. "I'm very tired, Detective. I did not sleep well last night, so if you have enough information, I would like to lie down and rest for a while." She started to rise.

"Mrs. Walters, can you prove what you were doing that night while your husband was jogging?" She seemed startled, as if she could not believe he was considering her suspect.

"Yes, Detective Selten, I can. I took a hot bubble bath, and then my daughter came over for coffee. Ask her." She was more than unhappy with the digging into her private life and the fact that she could be considered a possible murderer.

"I'm sorry, but we need you to come down to identify the man we found, to be sure that it is your husband. It's routine, even though we're sure it's him." Dave saw her pale, her eyes frightened. "Unless there is someone else in the family, or perhaps a close friend, that you prefer went instead."

"No. That's all right. I'll go myself." The emotion disappeared as fast as it had come. "I'll just get my coat."

Dave drove her to the morgue, trying to make small talk along the way. She said little, but preferred to stare out the front window, obviously caught up in thoughts and memories which Dave could not know. They entered the hospital, took the elevator to the bottom floor meeting Dr. Daniels at the office door. Dave introduced the doctor to Mrs. Walters and they proceeded into the cold, white tiled room. Dr. Daniels ushered them to a wall of large drawers, which resembled safety deposit boxes at a bank, only much larger. He opened one of the drawers and pulled back the cover sheet. Mrs. Walters let out a gasp just before she fainted.

Chapter 7

"Oh, my God! Oh, nooo, nooo!" Betty Martin wailed, one hand on her chest, the other holding onto Joe for support. "Thom! Thom!" Deputy Joe Sterling held her tightly, pulling her away from the table while the coroner covered the face of her dead husband. It had been a macabre sight for her to see, but identification had to be made. Joe knew for certain that it was the missing New Jersey accountant, but he had to follow procedure.

"I'm sorry, Mrs. Martin. I wish there was something I could do. Would it help if I gave you a Valium injection to help you calm down?" Dr. Turner asked her. She continued to cry, but shook her head. Joe gave her his handkerchief.

"Why? It's so senseless. So, so..." She couldn't finish the sentence. The two men could do nothing but stand there and wait for her to get over the initial shock of seeing her husband's face so mutilated by sea creatures and decomposition. Dr. Turner moved her to the sofa in his small trailer-office, and she collapsed, crying. The doctor decided to let her cry it out, and walked back to where Joe still stood helplessly watching.

"I can't understand why Martin was killed. There's absolutely no motive for it. He had money in his wallet and his watch and wedding band were still on him, so we can rule out a mugging. Unless someone tried and he put up a fight. But you tell me he never knew what hit him." They both glanced over at Mrs. Martin sitting quietly on the sofa now, sniffling into a hanky. "Well, I'm going to take her back to her motel and check some details with her. By the way, Doc," Joe said sheepishly, "I'm going to be a father come January."

"Hey, congratulations! I hope it's a boy. Girls can be so hard to raise."

"I don't care what it is. Deborah and I have wanted a child for so long now. Maybe it will be the first baby born next year." Joe walked over to the sofa where Mrs. Martin waited. "Mrs. Martin? If you're ready, I'll take you back to your motel." She slowly stood up with Joe's help. "See ya', Doc."

Dr. Turner watched them leave and then turned back to the body lying in the other room. *Some die while others are born*, he thought matter-of-factly. *It's just the way it is.*

* * * *

Deputy Joe Sterling had talked to Betty Martin about her husband's actions prior to his having gone fishing that night, and had learned that Thomas Martin had walked to the Flagler bridge, and that being in need of bait, he would have had to have gone to Brownie's Bait Shop. It was the only place within walking distance of the motel and the bridge to get bait.

Mrs. Martin had filled Joe in on her husband's background, friends, acquaintances and associates. She had assured him that her husband had been a quiet, gentle and kind man with many close friends. He had been a precise orderly person, who had liked everything neat and in its place. Very seldom, she had confided to him, had he ever said something bad about someone, even if he had been angry.

He had been a church going man, who had a strong faith in God, and worked one day a week for the church in which they were members. His hobbies had been photography and coin collecting, and although he was not a very physical person, he had on occasion enjoyed playing golf or going fishing.

She had also informed Joe that her husband had never been an impulsive person to do things without thinking it over at least twice before he actually did it, with a few exceptions. Like the time his friends had talked him into getting that tattoo done on the top of his head, so that he would not be just "plain" bald like other men. Thomas Martin was usually not the type of man who could be easily talked into something. Why, Betty Martin had asked Joe, would someone kill a good man like her husband? Deputy Sterling had not had an answer for her.

Joe had dropped Mrs. Martin off at her motel, and was now parking his squad car diagonally in front of Brownie's Bait Shop. A few people were sitting on the hard wooden park-like benches on the water's edge, talking and watching the large boats cruise majestically up and down the horizon of the Atlantic Ocean. The inside of the small store looked like almost any other bait shop with live shrimp in large water basins, packages of lures, sinkers and hooks, and a barrel of all different size bobbers, the circular red and white plastic decorating the center of the room.

There were fishing poles of varying sizes lined up against the side wall. A large box of brightly colored, plastic worms sat on the counter, and stacks of crab nets and lobster pots were piled up by the one window. Casting nets were suspended from the ceiling, giving you the slight feeling of possible entrapment. Joe browsed around the store while Brownie waited on a customer. He flipped through a book on fly casting until the transaction was completed. Finally Brownie looked his way.

"Hello, Detective Joe," he said, his auburn hair curling down his forehead toward his small dark brown eyes. "What can I do for you? Going fishin', are you?" he asked, looking at the book in Joe's hand.

"Kinda," Joe answered, putting the book back in the rack. "I'm doing some checking to verify some information regarding ..."

"Regarding that tourist that was murdered, right?" His eyes opened wide, and his stubby freckled fingers stroked his bushy mustache, the color of which matched his unruly hair. "Saw it on the news last night. Terrible."

"Right. Anyway, did Thomas Martin come in here last week, around say, 9:30, 10 o'clock at night to buy bait? It was probably Thursday or Friday night." He watched Brownie's eyes. Joe had learned that people could mask expressions and actions, but a person's eyes could tell another story.

"Yeah, he came in here just as I was closing up for the night. We talked for a while. We both came from Cherry Hill, New Jersey, ya' know. Said he was going up to the bridge to do some fishin' cause he couldn't sleep, and he was going home two days later. Practically begged me to go fishin' with him."

"Did you?"

"Yes. No." Brownie corrected himself. Joe

thought the big man looked suddenly nervous.

"Which is it?" Joe leaned on the counter with his elbow. He had had some other run-ins with Brownie over drugs, but he had never been able to gather enough evidence to make any charges stick.

"Yeah, I went up there after I grabbed some chow. No, I didn't fish with him cause he wasn't there." Brownie seemed to be getting defensive and agitated.

"What time would you say you got there?" Joe tossed one of the bobbers in the air and caught it.

"Around midnight. I drove to the bridge, parked my car, and fished till around two a.m. The guy wasn't there, Joe. That's the truth." Joe studied him, his eyes.

"Was there anyone here or outside when you closed up?"

"No."

"Did you see anyone loitering around the bridge?"

"No, but I'm beginning to wish I had," Brownie answered, staring at him, arms folded across his chest. A man came in the shop followed by a boy of around ten. "Is there anything else, Detective?" he asked formally.

"No, Brownie, thanks," Joe said and smiled. "I'll be in touch." He threw Brownie the bobber he had been playing with, turned and left the store. Brownie watched him get in the patrol car and pull away before he turned angrily to help his customer.

Chapter 8

"Good morning, Miss Price. Come to see your mother today, have you?"

Doreen smiled at the plump, homely nurse. "Good morning, Nurse," Doreen said, continuing quickly down the green corridor toward her mother's room. She didn't bother to knock. Her mother wouldn't have answered it anyway. Doreen stood fixed just inside the door glancing around the neatly decorated but drab little room with its single bed, two gold cloth arm chairs, maple dresser with mirror, and matching nightstand. She wrinkled her nose in distaste. Never, she promised herself, never would she ever end up in an awful place like this. Never!

The Oakville Institution in Matawan, New Jersey, was a privately owned sanitarium which Doreen managed to pay, difficult as it was to do. As soon as she had turned eighteen, Doreen had spent three years searching for her mother. She found Judy Price in the Marlboro Hospital in Marlboro, New Jersey, a state hospital which housed many patients with psychological problems. Doreen had then investigated other hospitals and, although Marlboro was cheap, had finally had her mother moved to the Oakville Institution.

Now Judy Price sat facing the window, her back to her daughter. If she was aware that someone was in the room, she made no acknowledgment of it. Doreen walked quietly up behind the chair, and stared out the window for a moment trying to see what it was that held her mother's concentration there.

"Good morning, Mother," she said finally. Judy Price did not move, nor did she answer. *Oh, Christ*, Doreen thought, *why do I bother coming here?* She moved around the chair to face her mother.

"How are you feeling?" Nothing. "Oh, I'm feeling better, Doreen dear, and how are you today? Oh, I'm just fine, Mother. Thank you for asking," Doreen said in a mocking tone. No movement, except for an occasional blink of her eyes. "Ma, won't you please talk to me?" Doreen pleaded.

Judy Price continued to stare out the window. The morning sun streamed in through the glass, showing thousands of tiny dust particles, all floating erratically in space, reminding Doreen of minute snow flakes.

"Look at me, Mother. It's Doreen, PLEASE!" She took her mother's face between her hands and gently turned her head, so that Judy had no choice but to look at her, but the blue eyes that stared her way were blank. Doreen was exasperated and angry.

"You want to know something, Ms. Price? I come here every week since I can remember, and you ignore me. I send you flowers, bring you candy, nighties, books. I tell you everything that's going on in my life and in Deborah's, so that you know that we're all right, so you don't worry about us. But you know what, Ma? I don't think you care whether I come here or not! So why do I bother? Huh? Can you tell me, Ma, why I bother to come and talk to a vegetable that won't talk back? Can you tell me if I should come back? Do you like when I come here? Do you really care one way or the other?"

Judy Price did not respond.

"The doctors tell me that there is no reason why you won't talk to me, to the nurses, or to the doctors. So why won't you? Will you at least tell me that much? What have I done that you refuse to say even a lousy hello? Why do you hate me? What the fuck did I ever do to YOU?! Or is it because I was born? I didn't have anything to do with that, Ma. You did! I love you, but you treat me like a stranger, an unwelcome stranger. A volunteer visitor. TALK TO ME, DAMN YOU!" Doreen screamed.

Judy Price physically flinched as if she had been struck, but her eyes showed no emotion, no sign that Doreen was getting through the iron door surrounding her mother's mind. Doreen took her hands away from her mother's face, and Judy turned back to the window, almost automatically, like her head was on a spring.

Doreen took a deep breath and sighed. "Look at yourself. You look awful. You're letting yourself turn into an old, shriveled up shell of a woman, that's what you're doing. And why? Because you're too much of a chicken-shit coward to face life, to face reality!

"Well, let me tell you something, MISS PRICE! I don't need to be treated this way, by YOU especially, so I won't be coming here to see you anymore! You have my number, if and when you ever decide to become human again, if you still remember HOW. Should you decide that you're going to talk to me, you can call me, or have one of the nurses do it. I can play your game, too, you know. As far as I'm concerned, I no longer have a mother! My mother died when I was ten!" Doreen stood up and glared down at her mother. "Maybe you really should have," she whispered, and then turned and stormed out of the room.

Tears slowly found their way down Judy Price's face, and her lips formed the words, but the gray fog which clouded her mind prevented her from uttering a sound.

* * * *

Judy Price pushed her way through the heavy fog, searching. She was trying to remember something, something important, but what that was, she had no idea. All she knew was that it was urgent that she remember it. She had to help Doreen. Or was it Deborah? Or both? There was a danger, just as real, as vicious as the gray wet mist that kept pulling her down, down into the depth of her soul, and kept her safe there. Down to where no trouble could follow.

She extended her arms, palms up, trying to feel her way through the clouds. Her foot hit something. Their kitty, Mew-Mews, was dead, lying stiff and cold at her feet. Judy bent down to get a closer look, to be sure that's what it was. What had happened to the cat? Suddenly the dead animal dissolved and was gone.

Her hands reached out again as she continued to wander in the darkening mist. A red glow! Fire! It was a fire! She saw the large old Victorian house where she had grown up loom up before her, flames devouring the wood with an appetite straight from hell! The fog was being burned off by the heat. She looked at the upstairs window and saw her parents standing there, and although she could not hear the actual sounds, she knew that they were screaming, their faces twisted and distorted. Then they were melting before her eyes, their skins slimy, wet and gooey, their eyes pleading with her to save them, accusing her of it.

The fog was returning, sealing her off from them, so that she could no longer suffer the hurt and the guilt, but it did not conceal the little girl who was standing by the side of the house, a small fiery torch clutched in her tiny fists. Her daughter! She was sure that it was one of her daughters, smiling her impish, evil grin! Anger began to well up inside her. She reached out for the child, but the fog was thick again, too heavy for Judy to get through. The child was dissolving. Judy was falling back into the darkness from where she had come, the heat from the fire burning her face and the palms of her hands.

Chapter 9

Doreen sat studying him from two tables away. Mathew Parker, M.D. She had accidentally bumped into him and one of his associates in the Dragon Lady Restaurant about two hours ago, and then had followed them to the Bounty Lounge, where they now sat.

Dr. Parker was a handsome man with black curly hair, big oval brown eyes, and a dimple in each cheek. She knew he was divorced and had been for a year, but he was still in love with his estranged wife and he made no bones about it to everyone. Some of the other nurses had tried to get close to him, but he would not give them any of his attention unless it had to do with a patient. Doreen had not bothered to make a play for him, paying him even less notice than he had given to her. Doreen preferred older men, and Dr. Parker was only in his early thirties.

Doreen glanced around the dimly lit lounge. There was a group of people standing by the curved bar laughing, while some couples sat at tables quietly talking, and still more people were dancing slowly on the small circular dance floor. She brought her gaze back to rest on Dr. Parker.

After about an hour, Dr. Parker's friend finally

had gotten up to leave. Doreen pulled out a five dollar bill and threw it on her table. She watched him until he was out of the line of vision, and then turned her gaze back to Dr. Parker, who was finishing his drink. She got up and slowly walked toward where he was sitting, keeping her eyes turned away, pretending not to notice that he was there.

"Doreen?" She snapped her head toward the voice, deliberately looking over his head as if trying to locate the caller. She was surprised that he knew her name, but it made her feel good inside. When her eyes met his, she reacted with surprise and then with delight upon seeing him there.

"Hello, Dr. Parker. I don't remember ever seeing you here before," she said, as if she had always frequented that nightclub. "I know I would have noticed you."

"Matt. And I don't know how you could have seen me here. It's the first time I've ever been to this lounge, so your memory is not failing you. My friend suggested this place, so we came here for lack of a better spot. How are you?"

"Fine, thanks. I was just going home, so please don't let me intrude on you and your friend."

"My friend has already deserted me, so you're not intruding. Besides, why go home? It's early. A pretty woman like you should be partying all night somewhere."

She laughed, flattered by the comment. "Don't know of any all night parties, Matt, do you?"

"As a matter-of-fact, I do. I was just going there. Do you know where Spruce Street Apartments are?"

"Yes. Is that where the party is?"

"Uh-huh, that's it. It's at 118 Spruce Run Way, just off Spruce Street. You'll have a great time, I promise. Coming?"

"Maybe. But suppose those people don't want me there. I mean, they don't even know me. They may not want you to just invite strangers."

"Take my word for it, you'll be more than welcome. Please come. There will be plenty of good food, drinks, music and fun people. I'd really like you to come." His eyes seemed to melt her usual icy detachment.

"I just might do that. Well, if I don't see you at the party, I'll see you around the hospital." She smiled and walked out of the bar. She got in her car and waited. He came out before long, and starting his car, pulled out of the parking lot. Doreen waited a few minutes before leaving, and then having made her decision, headed her car across town toward Spruce Street. Why not, she had asked herself, but now she was having second thoughts. Her headache was beginning again, and she was afraid that it would turn into one of her migraines before too long.

By the time she had argued the question in her mind, Doreen found herself on Spruce Run Way. She drove slowly down the street looking for number 118. She spotted it almost right away and pulled her car into a parking spot near the apartment. It had started to drizzle, so she ran for the door and rang the bell. She could hear no loud music, no noise of any kind. Dr. Parker answered the door.

"Doreen, Sweetheart! I'm so glad that you decided to come after all. Come in," he said, opening the door wider.

"Where's the party? she asked, looking around the ultra-modern living room.

"Right here," he said, disappearing through the swinging door and returning with potato chips, onion dip and a blender full of martinis. "Make yourself at home. See," he said, putting the tray on the glass and chrome coffee table, "food, drinks, and now some music." He clicked on the stereo and soft music poured out of the large wooden speakers. "And me, the fun people." He bowed before her.

Doreen laughed. "Why, Dr. Parker. You tricked me!"

"Did I not give you everything that I promised you? Food, drinks, music and me? An all night party? I have all night, Sweetheart, do you?" he said in his best Humphrey Bogart imitation.

"Yes, I have all night," Doreen said softly, lowering her eyes to look at the floor covered in thick plush pile carpeting. Her head began pounding again. "Do you have some aspirins? I'm afraid that I'm getting a headache."

"I have a cure for a headache, Sweetheart," he said grinning. "Or I can go ahead and give you some aspirin." She laughed, taking a sip of her martini and then lighting a cigarette.

"I'll take the aspirins for starters. Thank you." Dr. Parker went to his bathroom and returned with two white tablets. They sat and talked and drank martinis. Doreen's headache continued to get worse.

"Care to dance, Doreen?" Matt Parker asked, his words beginning to slur together from all the alcohol he had consumed so far that night.

"Sure, John. I'd love to."

"John? The name's Matt, remember?" His voice was thick with liquor and he had trouble getting to his feet. He swayed slightly as he stood over her.

"Huh? Oh, did I call you John? I'm sorry. I don't know why. I don't even know anyone named John." He took her clumsily into his arms, and started swaying awkwardly to the music. *Why am I doing this*, she asked herself. *Dancing with Dr. John McParker.* That was impossible! She couldn't be dancing with him. He was dead! She had killed him! He HAD to be dead.

"Yourra great little dancer, Sweetheart," he mumbled, nuzzling her ear.

Maybe he had lived, her mind reasoned. Maybe he hadn't drowned. But of course not. How could he have drowned and be here dancing with her now? She was dancing with the man who had made her ugly, for Christ sake!! Her temples were really pounding now. Fear began to spread throughout her entire body. Would he tell the police that she had tried, unsuccessfully, to kill him in the park?

He was kissing her neck, her cheek. His hands caressed her back, but were slowly moving down to her buttocks. *Run*, her mind screamed, *run while you have the chance!* But run to where? There was no place that she could run to that he would not find her.

Maybe he's not going to turn me in, she reflected. Maybe he was going to ignore it. *Not on your life, Doreen, you jerk! Would you ignore it if someone had tried to kill you? Face it! He's up to something. Blackmail! That's it!* He was pressing his body closer and closer to her and she could feel the hardness in his groin. Sex! He wanted her. *Good*, she thought smiling. She remembered something that she had read somewhere that said that a man was at his gentlest and most vulnerable state while making love. *Okay, Dr. John McClusky, sex it is!* She tilted her head up to him, and he kissed her mouth hard, bruising her lips. Her pain continued to strike heavy blows to her temples, causing her to be nauseous. The scar! He would see the scar if she got undressed! So what, she reminded herself, he had put it there!

Dr. McClusky was leading her down the hall to the bedroom, staggering and bumping against the walls as he went. The large bedroom was elegantly furnished, with a large round bed in the center of the room. A small crystal chandelier hung directly over the bed, and he dimmed the light so only a warm glow filled the room. He kissed her again, roughly undressing her and throwing her clothes on the floor. She sat down naked on the bed while he fumbled with his own clothes, almost falling when he stepped out of his expensive knit slacks.

Doreen found his love-making lacking, and performed in an extremely selfish manner, but she went through the act of climax, playing the role like it was a matter of life and death. *If I was an actress*, she decided, *I'd win an Oscar for this performance.* She stifled a laugh, afraid that he might have heard, but he only pounded her harder. *Enjoy yourself, Dr. McClusky*, Doreen said silently, watching his face contort with the passionate shudders he was experiencing. *I want you to enjoy your last fuck on earth. Hey, that's ironically funny.* He had fucked her when she was born, and now he was fucking her again before he died.

"God, Sweetheart," he whispered hoarsely, panting, "that was great."

"How about another martini then?" she whispered back. When he went to get the martinis, Doreen followed him into the kitchen. It was a small, compact kitchen, complete with microwave and dishwasher. They stood there naked, talking idle chatter while Matt made them each a ham and cheese sandwich and another container of drinks. He took the tray back to the living room, which was richly decorated in beige and browns.

Soon after they had polished off the last of the martinis, Dr. Matt Parker made the deadliest mistake of his life --he passed out on the large sofa. Doreen sat very still in one of the modern swayback chairs and stared at the unconscious naked body lying face up.

"Had enough, Doctor?" she whispered. She got up and walked to the kitchen door. She looked back, and satisfied that he was still out, went into the kitchen. She returned within a few minutes. She stopped and stared at the body. He had not moved.

"Thought you could out-smart ME, Doc? How very naive of you," she said, almost to herself. "You knew I'd find you again. You probably even planned it. Thought you'd have me right where you wanted me, didn't you?" She took a step toward the sofa. Her right hand firmly held a large, steel butcher knife. "Why won't you leave me alone? Why are you tormenting me? Why did you hurt me? Why did you pick me and not Debbie?" There was no sound except for the soft music which still played in the background. "Doc? You must stay dead, you know. It's not fair for you to come back. Dr. McClusky? Are you sleeping?" She inched closer.

"Answer me, Doc!" No answer. Closer still. "Hey, Dr. John McClusky, QUACK! Why don't you ever answer any of my questions?" she asked louder. Closer. "Are you willing to say you made a mistake? That you FUCKED up!" she screamed at him, fists clenched at her sides, knife pointed away from her. Again no answer, no movement.

She pulled the knife up slowly till it was suspended above her head. "Admit it, damn you! ADMIT IT!" She brought the knife down with such sudden force that Dr. Parker's body slammed into the cushions as soon as the blade went into his chest. Blood ran down his chest and arms. He tried to open his eyes, but they wouldn't focus. He was confused, couldn't remember where he was or with whom. He moved his arms to his chest which burned like fire, but the knife caught them and the pain made him cringe.

"ADMIT IT!" He felt the blade again pierce his flesh, the sound reminding him of his father's butcher shop in Newark. "ADMIT IT, DR. MCCLUSKY! ADMIT IT! ADMIT IT!" She brought the knife down again and again. He no longer heard the gushy sound, or felt the burning heat of the blade. Dr. Mathew Parker, General Practice, no longer felt or heard anything.

Doreen stood over him, knife still in her hand. "And don't come back this time!" she hissed at him. "Hear me?" She went to the kitchen, rinsed the blood off the knife, dried it and put it back in the kitchen drawer where she had found it. She glanced at the bloody, ripped body lying on the couch as she made her way to the bathroom. She showered under extremely hot water, and brushing her hair, went to retrieve her clothes from the bedroom floor. When she had reached the door of the apartment, Doreen turned back to the body.

"Oh, by the way, John, darling," she said, smiling, "you're the worst piece of ass that I have EVER had!" She blew him a kiss. "Good-night, SWEETHEART!"

* * * *

He staggered out of the High Corral Bar which was the only bar for blacks in Bunnell, Florida, carrying a bottle of Maddog wine, and leaned against the wall for support. He opened the bottle, guzzled down another long swallow of the harsh tasting liquid, then burped loudly. His head was spinning and his stomach felt sour. He heard a car pull into the stone parking lot, but he paid no attention. It did not concern him. What did concern him was his bladder that told him that it needed to be emptied, and soon. He cupped a scrawny black hand over his groin pressing hard against his bladder to try to hold back the pressure he was feeling.

He tried again to focus his eyes, but it hurt his head. Lights. Where were the bright lights coming from at this hour? He blinked his tired old eyes, trying to see a spot where he could take a leak. He pitched forward, stumbling into an old rusty pick-up truck which was parked there by the door. He couldn't hold the urine back anymore.

He started to unbutton the fly in his dirty, shabby coveralls when a sharp pain cut through his back and he tottered forward, his skeletal, sickly frame crashing against the truck, his face sliding slowly down the truck door, the rust scratching his face. He pushed against the truck with his hands, trying to stand upright, but his legs wouldn't hold him and he fell onto his back. He could feel a cool hand push his forehead down. He relaxed. Someone had come to help him home. Maybe it was his momma, he thought.

The searing pain started at his right ear and moved quickly across his throat to the other side. He tried to breathe, but the air would not fill his lungs. He grabbed his throat and felt the ragged gap, as the blood ran down his neck and shoulders. Another stab in his chest and abdomen. What was happening? Where had his momma gone? His hands flew to his stomach, and his body jerked. The old black man's blurry, partially blind eyes rolled to the top of his head, as his bladder finally emptied itself.

Deborah wiped the knife off on the sleeve of the old man's brown flannel shirt, and then snapped it shut. She threw the knife back in her purse, where Joe had made her carry it for protection when she went out alone. She quickly got back into her car and drove out of the parking lot onto Route One, without so much as a backward glance in the rear view mirror. Deborah went home, took a shower, and slipped into a pretty powder blue negligee, and pouring herself a rum and coke, sat down to wait for Joe to come home from work.

Chapter 10

Detective Dave Selten stood next to Medical Examiner Dr. Daniels, in Mathew Parker's plush Edison apartment. Both men stood staring down at the prone, cold body, stiff with rigor mortis. Dried blood covered most of the upper part of the torso, with black streaks down the abdomen, groin and legs. The light colored sofa was also drenched in blood, as well as the light tan carpeting. There were footsteps of blood leading to the kitchen and then back again, proceeding down the hall to the bathroom.

Police officers and detectives were everywhere, like ants at a picnic. Some were photographing the scene and marking outlines, so that the body could be removed, while others were dusting everything for fingerprints, or just hunting for clues of any kind.

"What's happening, Dave?" the coroner asked, running his slight hand over his face in exasperation. "What is this with doctors?"

"Damned if I know, Doc. Somebody obviously has a grudge, but I think this time we may have some evidence that will help us identify our killer. If we can just get enough to put a name on him," Dave said, looking around the room, "or her."

"Well, I think we'll find that our victim has had intercourse before this happened," the M.E. said, waving his hand toward the sofa, "seeing that he's naked, the two empty glasses on the table, the bed being in disarray. There should be some personal evidence on him to prove it. I'll go over him totally when we get the body back to the morgue. I figure he's dead about two days. I gave the maid a mild sedative to calm her down," he said, looking over to where two officers were taking the statement from the pretty young Cuban girl, who sat sniffling into a tissue. "Bag 'em up, guys," Dr. Daniels said to the two young black men who were standing by the door talking between themselves.

"Excuse me, Detective Selten," a young policeman said, coming into the living room. "It seems that the perp may have taken a shower. We found blood stains in the tub and on the tiled wall, along with one good bloody fingerprint on the faucet and another on the shower door. I took a sample of the hair stuck in the drain, too." He stood there erect, beaming like a puppy who has just brought its master his slippers and is waiting for a pat on the head.

"Thank you, Officer...?"

"Davids, Sir."

"Officer Davids. Mark the evidence and give it to the sergeant." Dave went into the kitchen. Two more officers were going through the drawers and cabinets. All the fixings for martinis were still on the counter.

"Anything?" he asked them.

"Yes, Sir, this," the black cop answered, holding up a large thick carving knife, which had been carefully placed in a plastic bag. "Been washed off, but I believe there may be blood in the crevice by the handle. Of course, it could be from carving animal meat, but I'll have the lab check it out. Other than that, nothing." Dave did not answer, but took another look around the cluttered kitchen and again at the footsteps on the white linoleum floor. Small feet, he observed. A woman's size?

He walked back through the living room, down the hall, and into the elegant bedroom. Another officer was there, taking hair samples from the sheets and putting them into another plastic bag used to protect evidence. The man looked up briefly and then went back to what he was doing. After a quick look see, Dave retraced his steps stopping long enough to look around the bathroom. He left the apartment then, and headed back to Metropolitan Hospital to do some more interrogation of the hospital personnel. There had to be a link, and Dave suspected it had to be there. Gut feelings. He had learned many years ago to follow his hunches, and right now, everything told him to start there.

* * * *

Metropolitan Hospital was almost filled to capacity, what with the flu and bronchitis season here again, not to mention automobile accidents, heart attacks and the usual necessary surgeries. The hospital was alive with activity, and Doreen's station was no exception. They had had ten patients scheduled for surgery of one kind or another that day.

Yesterday had been the same way, but it had been her day off, and she had spent her entire day at the beauty shop getting her hair cut short and then body-waved into large soft curls framing her delicate face, giving her the appearance of an eighteen-year-old girl. She had been pleased with the result. She had been busy all morning getting caught up on what she had missed the previous day. Mrs. Porter's light came on.

"Would you go see what Mrs. Porter wants now, Shasta?" Doreen said to one of the student nurses, who was sitting at the nurse's station talking to an intern. *Shasta! Sounds like a God-damned soda drink*, Doreen thought, watching the pretty young girl take her time getting up as ordered. "NOW!" The girl jumped up, and giving Doreen a disgusted look, walked casually down the corridor to Mrs. Porter's room.

"Doctor," Doreen said to the intern, "I would appreciate it if you would allow my nurses to do their jobs. Especially the students. They're here to learn about patient care, not about doctors." Before he could protest her remarks, she stormed down the hall to change Mr. Hershal's dressing.

"Excuse me, Doctor," Dave said to the same intern a minute later, "but the administrator told me I could find the head nurse, a..." Dave stopped to consult his notepad. "A Miss Doreen Price, at this station. Is she here?"

"No," the intern replied hotly. "I mean, this is her station, but Her Holiness is down the hall in four twenty-one. Who are you?"

Dave ignored the obvious hostility. "Detective Dave Selten, Edison P.D. And you are?"

"Dr. Arrons. Can I help you with something, or is this a personal visit?" he asked Dave, hopefully. He wanted it to be personal, so he would have an excuse to give it back to the bitch for talking to him that way.

"Business. By the way, did you know a Dr. Mathew Parker?"

"No. Should I?" the intern asked. Dave shook

his head. He watched a beautiful nurse walk toward him, a frown wrinkling her pretty face. The doctor hissed at Dave, and getting his attention, pointed to that nurse.

"Miss Price?" Dave asked. Doreen turned and stared at him dully, with the most beautiful, clear blue eyes that Dave had ever seen. "Do you have a minute?"

"I'm very busy right now. If you have a question concerning a patient here, I suggest that you speak to the doctor that's involved," she retorted.

"My name is Dave Selten. I'm a detective from the Edison Police Department, investigating the murder of two doctors associated with this hospital, and this wing in particular. Can we talk someplace a little less busy?"

Doreen said nothing, just stood there, her mind racing a mile a minute. Had they found McClusky already? She led him to the nurse's lounge. It was empty. She sat down at one of the round tables, and pulling her cigarettes out of her pocket, lit one. She waited. "Did you know Dr. Lawrence Walters?" he asked her, taking a chair across the table from her. Doreen took another drag on her cigarette. Dave watched her. She was absolutely beautiful, tall and slender, her mouth full and sensuous. Dave decided that he wanted to taste it.

"Yes, I knew him. All of my nurses knew him, as they know all the doctors who specialize on the surgery ward. I heard he was..." She hesitated.

"Murdered? Yes, he was. What can you tell me about him?"

"I don't know anything about his murder!" she said, almost too quickly. Had her eyes shown fear, he wondered. Those beautiful, crystal blue eyes with the long black lashes curling just enough to be sexy instead of cute. Dave disliked cute.

"I never said that you did, Miss Price. I asked you about Dr. Walters, not his murder. How well did you know him?"

"Oh. Well, about the same as any of the nurses. He was a by-the-book type, but he had a bedside manner that wouldn't quit. For his patients anyway, but not so with the nurses. To the nurses he was callous, demanding and chauvinistic. He thought, or at least acted, like women were strictly playthings or servants. Very antiquated thinking." Doreen thought for a moment and then added, "But if I had required surgery of any kind, he would have been the doctor I would have chosen to perform the operation. He was a good surgeon." She fell silent.

"Were you aware, as some of the other nurses were, that Dr. Walters had been having an affair with one of the student nurses, a Miss..."

"Sheri. Yes, I had heard that," she answered. "And there had been rumors of others. Mostly all student nurses. I think most of them enroll in nursing schools to major in 'Doctor Husbandry'. But what a doctor does is his own business, not mine, Detective."

Very defensive, Dave thought. *Hmmm. Interesting.* "Tell me about Dr. Mathew Parker." *Maybe I should get sick,* he thought. *She could be my nurse.* He liked the idea.

"Dr. Parker? Why Dr. Parker? Did he have something to do with Dr. Walters's death?" she asked, stubbing out her cigarette.

"He's dead, too. Murdered in his apartment about two days ago. His maid found him this morning when she went to work there." *Maybe I should ask her to dinner.*

Doreen blinked twice, then swallowed. Her mouth was getting dry. She got up and walked to the coffee pot, pouring herself a cup. "Would you like a cup?" He shook his head no. What was this man talking about, she wondered. "Dr. Parker? Dead?" He had to be wrong! It was McClusky, not Dr. Parker! Had he escaped death again? That was absurd! Impossible! *They must not have found McClusky yet*, she decided.

"Yes. He'd been stabbed to death." She paled noticeably. "Were you a friend of his? If so, I'm sorry I had to be the one to break the news to you." She didn't answer. She seemed genuinely confused, disoriented, even frightened. "Miss Price, are you all right?"

What had she done wrong? First at the lake, now at his apartment. How could she have missed? He had to be a demon, a devil! He had to be! How else could she accept it? God-damn him! Oh, God, what if he decided to come after her?

"Miss Price?" What was wrong, he wondered. Had they been friends? Lovers, maybe? He decided that he had better wait on the dinner invitation till he found out a few more things, like what this nurse's relationship had been with Dr. Parker.

"Huh? Oh, I'm sorry. I didn't know about Dr. Parker. It's just such a shock. First Dr. Walters and now Dr. Parker." What if he did come after her? Would he kill her the next time he saw her? Her head was beginning to hurt. *Dr. McClusky! Damn you to hell!* "I'm sorry, Detective, uh..."

"Selten. Dave."

"I have to get back to my patients," she said, ignoring his attempt at familiarity. "I really didn't know Dr. Parker very well. You may want to talk to some of the other nurses. All these killings are really upsetting me. Could any of us be in danger, do you think?"

"I don't know, Miss Price. I sure hope to hell not."

She excused herself, and practically fled from the room. Dave stared after her. *What a beauty,* he thought. *I've definitely got to get to know her better, and I will,* he decided, writing her name down in his little notepad, larger than it was already written there.

Chapter 11

Judy Price had loved her twin daughters. Yes, they had been a burden, but not of their own doing. She had never doubted her decision to have them out of wedlock. They had been the driving force in her life, the reason that she had kept going, struggling, trying to make a life for them and for herself. She had been proud when they were born. Proud that for the first time in her life she had someone who needed her. It had upset her that her parents had disowned her, especially at a time in her life that she had needed them most, but she felt that it had been mostly their loss because they would never know the happiness that grandchildren could give.

But then those awful things had started happening. The dead kitten hung on a clothesline by a shoelace around its neck, until it was dead; the parakeet whose neck had been broken, found lying dead and stiff in its cage; the little girl Mary, whose mother had come complaining of a knife cut on her child's neck; the fire that had destroyed the home in which she had been raised, resulting in the death of her parents. Oh, there had been more, much more. Put that all together with the strain of the two jobs, the responsibility of raising twin girls alone, and the secret knowledge of a psychotic child, and no-one would have been able to stand the mental strain. Anyone's mind would have snapped.

But now she was aggravated. She was tired of the fog that kept her eyes clouded and weighed so heavy on her mind that she could not think, could not remember. She knew she had to. Someone's life may depend upon her getting through the mist, out into the sunlight.

Debbie and Dory. God, she loved those little girls. Dory occasionally tried to find her through the heavy wet clouds that surrounded her. She could hear Doreen's voice, but she couldn't see her. She had tried each time that she had heard the sound, but Doreen never appeared out of the mist. The voice sounded different, older than she remembered. The tiny shrill sound that she had known as Dory's voice had matured to a huskier, deeper note. Could she have been in these clouds that many years?

Judy Price stopped her struggle to think, and listened. Had she heard something moving in the fog, or had she imagined it like so many other times? She turned her head slightly. There it was again. She strained her mind's eye, trying to see what could be causing the tiny vibration her ears had picked up, but her vision would not clear.

The nurse set down the breakfast tray and looked at Judy. *Funny*, she thought to herself, *I could have sworn she heard me, that her head had moved. Must be a muscle twitching, poor thing.* "Okay, Judy," the nurse said, "someone will be in to feed you shortly." She left the room, closing the door quietly behind her.

Chapter 12

"What have you got on the knifing victim?" Deputy Joe Sterling asked, pointing to the sheet covering the old black man's body.

"His throat's been cut and he's been stabbed about eight times in the back, chest and stomach," Coroner Turner stated, indicating the areas with two fingers. "There are also several cuts to his hands and arms, but that's from trying to ward off the attacker. Alcohol content was 2.9. No I.D. anywhere on the body. No keys, no name, no address. In fact, no wallet. Guess is, he's one of the migrant workers in town for planting season." The doctor lowered his voice, as if the old man on the table could still hear.

"What the hell is going on around here, Joe? First Mr. Martin, now the old man."

"Think they're related, Doc?"

"Nah. Not even close. Martin was clubbed and then drowned. The old man was stabbed. The only similarities are that they were both killed violently, and both killed at night. Hell, they were even killed in two different towns: Flagler and Bunnell. I doubt if they were done by the same person, although it's possible, but not probable."

Joe left the medical examiner and decided to

find out who the old man had been. He felt that he owed it to the dead man to put a name on him, so that his death would not be ignored in passing. No one should be dead without identification on the grave. He drove west on State Road 100, to the small quiet town of Bunnell. When he reached Route 1, he turned left heading south. He passed the High Corral Bar, which had already been cordoned off with yellow tape with the words "SHERIFF'S DEPT. CRIME SCENE/ DO NOT CROSS" stenciled on it in black lettering.

Joe had interrogated George Washington Black, the bar's owner, the night before when he had found the body in his parking lot, dead by his truck. According to Mr. Black, the victim had come in very much drunk already around 10:30 p.m., had purchased a bottle of Maddog 20/20, and then had staggered back out. Joe had no reason to disbelieve him. If the owner had wanted to kill the old man, and there seemed to be no earthly reason he should have, he certainly would not have done it on his own property, and then left the body there.

Joe drove to several farms to see if anyone recognized the dead man from the photo the coroner had taken of the victim's face. No one had. He had saved Bob "Buck" Tyre's farm for last. It was the largest of the cabbage and potato farms, and employed the most workers. Joe drove his green and white squad car up the long dirt road leading to the main house of the Bucking T Ranch. Acres of land surrounded the roadway, with large planting tractors moving slowly across the dirt, while men, sitting on the long planting planks, dropped small cabbage plants into the mounds of moist soil streaking the landscape.

He didn't look to either side; he had seen it all before. Whenever it was planting season, the calls came into the station house faster than deputies could be dispatched. There were many reasons for the numerous calls, but fights over women and wine, and disorderly intoxication, were the most frequent causes. These people lived in deplorable living conditions, and all were extremely poor. No matter how hard they worked, they always seemed to be indebted to the "Bossman". Borrowing from the farm boss in order to buy meager food and lots of cheap wine was a standard practice. After the long hot hours in the sun planting or sowing, they would spend their nights sitting around campfires talking, drinking and arguing.

Most farms housed their workers in small shanties with many men to one shack. There were usually no bathrooms, only one or two outhouses. The Bucking T Ranch had two long concrete buildings with ten small rooms in one and twelve smaller rooms in the other, with a centralized bathroom with showers in a separate building. Several men crowded together in each room, with each man occupying one cot with a single army blanket for warmth. This particular farm at least supplied minimal heating.

Most of the migrants had no families, and even for the small number of men who did, their kin usually had no idea where the worker had wandered off to in search of work. The workers would find their way to Bunnell, Florida, every fall in time for cabbage planting, and most would stay until after potato season ended.

Joe pulled the squad car up to the large bi-level, brick and frame house. A big, shaggy black dog sauntered clumsily over to him, head down, bushy tail brushing the dirt causing a small dust cloud to rise as it went. Joe patted the dog's head, and the animal gave a slight wag of its tail, as if the effort was too much.

"Mornin' depety," Buck said, coming down the front porch steps, his cheek bulging with Red Man Chew tobacco. "What brings ya' out here? Boys bin actin' up agin?"

"No more than usual," Joe answered, leaning against his car fender, arms folded. "But we have a body at the freezer. Old black man. Migrant worker, for sure." He reached into his shirt pocket and pulled out the photo of the dead man. "Do you recognize this man?" Buck stared at the picture before him, but never took his hands out of his jeans pockets.

"Looks familiar. Hard ta sey, tho', ya' know whatta meen, Depety? Those nigga' boys awl look alike." The burley man spit through his teeth, almost hitting the old dog, and then began chewing again.

"You saying he doesn't work here, Buck?" Joe pressed, giving the man a hard, stern look. Buck stared back, hooking his thumbs on the back pockets of his jeans.

"Naw, I didn' sey that. The ole nigga's worked for me before, on occasion."

"Is he working for you now?"

"Nope. Ain't seen 'im his season. Musta picked 'nother farm," he drawled, rubbing the toe of his western leather boots on the back of his pant leg. Joe hated this combative communication, but he understood that the farm boss did not want to get involved in any possible homicide.

"Know his name? Or did you forget it since the last time he worked for you?" Joe asked sarcastically.

"Willie." Buck spat again. "Willie Thomas Baines."

"Are any of your men friends of Willie Thomas

Baines?" he asked. Joe decided that he did not like this backwoods redneck very much.

"Dunno. Ain't my job to keep their social calendar for 'em, Depety."

What's the sense, Joe thought in disgust. "Well, thank you for your time, Buck. If you think of anything later on, call me."

"Sho' will, Depety. I always try ta hep the law when I kin."

Joe looked around the farm, bringing his eyes back to Buck. He said no more to the uncooperative farmer, but got back into the car, spinning his wheels as he gunned the motor, the tires kicking up sand and gravel, causing the farm boss to jump back, his clothes covered in grit. Joe looked in the rear view mirror and squinted his eyes.

"Eat dirt, shitkicker!"

* * * *

Joe had had to call Deborah's supervisor that morning before going to work to inform her that she would not be in today because she was experiencing severe morning sickness. Her supervisor had been sympathetic about her feeling under the weather, but had explained to Joe that sometimes women had worse morning sickness towards the end of pregnancy than in the beginning, as had been the case with herself. He had listened sympathetically until the woman had stopped her discourse.

Joe had given Deborah some crackers and tea to settle her stomach, and then had left for work. He had come home very late the night before due to the investigation into the death of the tourist from up north who had been murdered, he had told Deborah, and then had received a call to go to the High Corral Bar in Bunnell as there had just been a stabbing.

People can be such violent animals, Deborah thought to herself, putting a load of dirty towels into the washing machine. *Why can't everyone just get along, live and let live? What could have been so important in someone's life that they had to kill over it?* She made the bed, and having straightened up the bedroom, pulled the dirty clothes out of the hamper.

A baby! They were going to have a baby in less than three months. It was all she could think about. Joe had loved the things that she had bought for the baby: tiny undershirts, kimonos, blankets, teeny soft white shoes. The lady in the store had looked at Deborah approvingly when she had learned that this was Deborah's first child, like it was a big accomplishment or something. *But of course it was a big accomplishment,* she thought proudly, smiling. She sorted the whites from the colors, picking up the maternity shirt and slacks that she had worn the day before.

"What's this?" she asked aloud. Her beige slacks and brown knit blouse were full of blood stains! Amazed and confused, she stood there in the small laundry room, staring at the outfit she held up in front of her. How had that happened? She mentally retraced her footsteps of the day before, trying to figure out if she had cut herself, or had been somewhere where she may have gotten blood all over her. She remembered having gone shopping at the mall in Ormond, eating dinner at a local fast food steak house, and then treating herself to a movie.

Deborah was perplexed. *This isn't a little blood, like a person would get from a cut finger or hand,* she told herself, *it's a lot of blood.* She could not think of anything that could account for it.

She began to remember the nightmare she had had last night. She always had nightmares after one of her black-out spells, and she was sure that she had had a spell last evening. She must have, because she did not remember anything after she had come out of the movie. She could not remember driving home, or arriving at their small two bedroom house. She could not even remember taking a shower or dressing for bed. The last thing she did remember was waking up from that awful dream and finding Joe beside her. She had forgotten the dream and started showing him all the wonderful baby things which she had bought, including a few more maternity tops and slacks.

But now, thinking about it, she could remember that in the nightmare she had been driving down an extremely dark, deserted road, and had heard her sister, Doreen, screaming for help. But as in most dreams, Deborah had been unable to find her in the dark. Everything was in slow motion, and no matter how hard she tried to move faster, she had not been able to do so. She had tried to call out Doreen's name, but the sound would not escape her lips. And then she had spotted them in the parking lot of a local tavern in Bunnell.

A very dark, evil-looking man had had Doreen pinned up against a truck, and he was cutting her with a scalpel. Doreen was screaming and screaming, blood running down her scar side, the muscle tissue open wide, her ribs showing white in the light from Deborah's headlights. She had watched for a while from her car, too frightened to move, and then remembering the sharp knife in her purse, she had all too slowly gotten out of her car and killed the man, stabbing him over and over.

When she had looked up again, Doreen had disappeared, and in her place sat Joe, kissing her over and over again lightly on the mouth, and she had realized that it had all been a dream. A horrible nightmare. She was home, safe and sound. No Doreen. No evil, dark man.

But if it had been a nightmare, where had all the blood come from? Deborah shook her head sharply, trying to clear her vision. The migraine had started, and nausea swept over her again. She threw the stained clothes behind the dryer, shut off the washer, and went to lie down on the bed.

Chapter 13

Miss Doreen Price. Nurse Price. Doreen. He couldn't stop thinking about her, saying her name, dreaming of her eyes. Detective Dave Selten had always prided himself on being a lady's man, not a man to fall head over heels like a damned school boy of sixteen. But she was gorgeous, he reasoned to himself, especially dressed in her whites, with her short dark hair in soft curls under her nurse's cap, her fair, clean, wholesome look. Every boy's girl next door.

She had sparkle, intelligence and compassion. He wondered about her age, sure that she would probably think he was too old for her anyway. *I mean, think about it,* Dave said to his reflection in the mirror over his bathroom sink. He was thirty-eight years old and she was maybe, MAYBE, twenty-two, twenty-three tops, if that.

His eyes scanned his reflection, first focusing on his thick, light brown hair, moving to his deep set brown eyes, and stopping at the dimples in his cheeks that were noticeable even when he didn't smile. He grinned at himself, showing large, straight white teeth. On the whole, not too bad for an old man. A few lines by his eyes, and a few minor surface frown lines on his forehead between his eyebrows, but really not too bad. For the first time, Dave realized how much he resembled his father, Bernie.

Bernard Selten had grown up to be a bus driver much to his parents' dismay. He had not cared. He had been his own person, doing what he wanted when he wanted. After graduation he had joined the army, where he had met and married Barbara Sue Landon. Two sons and one daughter later, Mr. and Mrs. Bernard Selten were comfortably settled in a small white frame, two-story house in Haverhill, Massachusetts. It was there that David Selten was born, and after him, Darlene, Paul and Louis.

When Dave was four years old, his parents moved them to Linden, New Jersey. Dave enjoyed his childhood years there with all his brothers and sisters, but his favorite companion was Dottie, the oldest of the now seven Selten children. They had a great rapport. Dave had always been comfortable with her, confiding in her, sharing his feelings, fears and dreams, trusting her enough to divulge his deepest hidden secrets. Dottie had never, not even once, ever made him feel like a child. She had listened as well as talked to him, had teased him when she was irritable, and had counseled him when he was out of line. He had adored her.

Dave had married Victoria Dennis when he was twenty-two, but it had not been a marriage made in heaven. Victoria's parents had definitely not been delirious about the wedding and it could not have been more obvious if they had put a full page notice in the Sunday newspaper. Dave did not care what they felt. In fact, he had felt a little power high on the fact that their daughter had ignored her parents and married him anyway.

But Victoria had listened to the constant chant

coming from her parents after the wedding. At first she had fought them, stood her ground, but slowly they had verbally beaten her down. Victoria had been torn between her parents and her husband, and the tug-of-war had finally stopped when she had filed for divorce. Dave had not fought to keep her, but just let her go her way. He now wondered if he had taken Victoria far away from her parents, if they would have made it together.

Dave noticed that he was again frowning, causing deepening creases in his forehead. He made a mental note to stop frowning so much, but then it came with the job. He rubbed his large hand over his chin, deciding he needed a shave. But why bother? He had no plans for tonight, except all those reports that he had to go over before he could rest.

Captain Caylor had been all over his ass today. Answers, that's what he had said he wanted, needed, NOW! Something, anything, he could tell the commissioner, the reporters, the public. A lead. "Just one lousy lead," Caylor had said with his teeth clenched, lips pulled back in a sneer. Doesn't he realize that he'd give him one if he had one to give? God-damned jerk!

Dave walked over to the refrigerator, yellow with age, grabbed a cold light beer, and snapped the can open, throwing the thin metal lip into the garbage. He unwrapped the submarine sandwich he had brought home from the Pickle Barrel Deli, and took a huge bite. Police politics, he mused, taking a big gulp of his beer to wash down the sub. Right down the line to him! Everyone knew that the heat would be on. After all, the victims were doctors! Good, law-abiding, upright, steady citizens. The pillars of society. The owners of many businesses and the backers for others, not including their own practices.

He sat down at the small round wooden dinette table, and rifled through the folders he had stacked there. He picked up the coroner's report on Mathew Parker. It was a lengthy report, type written with concise headings and neatly formed paragraphs. Dave took another bite of his sub, followed by another gulp of beer. He started reading, jotting down notes on a white, blue-lined pad of paper.

He made two headings, one marked L. Walters and the other M. Parker. Under each heading he listed all pertinent facts relating to each victim, hoping to find similarities between the two. There had to be a link, and he was determined to find it.

He finished both autopsy reports from the medical examiner, and went on to the crime lab's findings. He reread his own notes on the interrogations of Mrs. Walters, Dr. Parker's maid and all the hospital personnel he had already talked to. He scanned the reports from Sergeant Tacker concerning all of Dr. Walters's office personnel and that of Dr. Parker's that Tacker had gone ahead and gotten on his own volition.

Tacker's report on Walters was almost worthless. It told Dave nothing which Dave didn't already know, but the report on Parker revealed that he had had dinner and then drinks with an associate prior to going home to his rendezvous with death.

Dave finally looked at the round, butcher block style clock hanging on the kitchen wall. Eleven o'clock. He walked over and switched on his portable color television to catch the late news, and then glancing back at the screen every few moments, went back to get another cold beer and the open bag of potato chips sitting on the counter, before he dropped his six foot three inch frame into his big, overstuffed brown leather recliner. He rubbed his eyes with the balls of his palms, until the burning stopped and his eyes felt better.

It was hard to concentrate on what was being said. His mind floated between daydreaming about Doreen, and picking apart the bits of data he had learned about Dr. Walters, Dr. Parker and the possible killer. There was really not too much to go on as far as Walters was concerned, but he had gathered plenty on Parker, and some more on the killer.

Dr. Mathew Parker, according to all evidence, had entertained a female friend in his apartment that night. He had also had intercourse, probably with the same woman. They had found dark pubic hair, not matching Parker's, on his body and his bed. Also, the woman had long brown hair. There were strands of it on the pillows and in the drain in the shower.

They had also obtained plenty of fingerprints from the bathroom, off the glasses which had contained martinis, and on the cigarettes they had found in the cut-glass ashtrays. Whoever she was, she smoked Virginia Slims brand, but then so did a lot of people. The killer also had size seven feet, a woman's size seven he was sure. The knife that they had found had had no fingerprints on it that could be distinguishable, but the blood found on the knife matched Dr. Parker's: O positive.

No one that Tacker had talked to knew of anyone that Parker had been seeing on a social basis. According to all who knew him, he had still been in love with his ex-wife, and had been hoping desperately for a reconciliation. Dave had set up appointments for tomorrow with several people whom he needed to question, and one of them was Patty Parker, the victim's estranged wife.

Dave gulped his beer. Could it be just coincidence that two men were both murdered in Edison, within two weeks of each other, and that both men had been physicians associated with Metropolitan Hospital? Dave doubted it. He felt that unless he could quickly put a name on the killer, more doctors would die. He was also convinced that the murderer was a female: the long brown hair, the small foot size, the inability to move a body, the brand of cigarettes. Everything pointed to it.

But who was she? Obviously both doctors knew her. Or was it just bad luck that they both had encountered her along the way? If she was the killer of both men. But Dave found it hard to believe that there could be two women doing the killings.

Dave rubbed his temples, and throwing the reports into his briefcase, retired for the night to dream about a much more pleasant subject. A nurse named Doreen Price.

* * * *

Doreen stood staring at the two new dead-bolt locks which she had had installed. She didn't feel safe and that upset her. Maybe shutters on her windows would help, or iron bars. Her apartment was on the second floor, but that fact didn't seem to make a difference. Her gaze moved around the room, mentally checking her living room, with its immense green velvet pit-group sofa, large brown velvet chairs, and its glass and cork tables in assorted sizes. There were plants dotting the room, giving it a comfortable homey atmosphere, and a fifty gallon fish tank filled with Angelfish, Neons, Butterflies, Guppies and a special fish with elephant type trunks, occupying a corner of the room.

She walked over, clicked off the light on the small end table, and immediately turned it back on. Better to leave it lit, she decided, in case she had to get up in the middle of the night, for some reason. Any reason. She scuffed her way down the hall, her slippers caressing the highly polished oak wood floor. She flipped the switch and two small boudoir lamps came on, casting a warm glow around the bedroom. She stood there staring at her reflection in the dark window. Was he out there looking for her? Watching her?

"Are you out there, Doc?" she whispered, walking toward the window. "Can you see me?" She put her palm against the cool glass and peered out into the darkness. "John? Where are you now?" Her breath sprayed a warm, foggy mist on the glass. She pulled the cord, closing the floor to ceiling drapes, and without taking her eyes off them, backed up till she was seated on the edge of her bed. Could he get in through there, she wondered, nibbling on a ragged cuticle. She slowly pulled back the blanket and top sheet and, deciding to leave the bathroom light on, crawled naked between her percale flowered melon sheets, pulling them up around her neck.

She wished that she could have bought a gun, but the man at the pawn and gun shop had told her that a license was required. She had then gone to the police station to get her gun permit, but the application asked for the reason for buying a gun. She did not know what to write down. How could she tell them that a man was trying to kill her because she was trying to murder him? She told the officer that she would fill the form out at home, and had crumbled it up as soon as she was out the door of the station house.

Maybe a baseball bat would help her. She could

pick one up in any toy store. Or her tire iron from the trunk of her car. She suddenly jumped out of bed and ran to the hall closet, returning shortly with the piece of black iron pipe, and set it upright by the headboard. She had meant to get rid of it, but now she was glad that she hadn't. It made her feel better. But she really had to get rid of it as soon as she bought the bat. Tomorrow.

* * * *

Deputy Joe Sterling had also spent the night pondering the facts in the cases of Martin and Baines. There was no way to go on Willie Baines. But Martin? Why him? Brownie. Would he lie? In a heart beat, Joe decided, in a heart beat. He had Deputy Jack Green checking something out on the bait shop owner. He went down the hall to the bedroom and peeked in. Deborah slept peacefully curled up in a ball, her long dark hair spread out behind her on the pillow like a wild mane. He smiled again, and quietly closed the door. He went to the kitchen for a cola and a piece of cold southern fried chicken. The telephone rang and he scrambled for it, knocking his drink over.

"Hello," he barked into the phone, grabbing up the bottle and reaching for the roll of paper towels.

"Joe? Sorry to bother you so late, but I've got that info you wanted on Brownie." Deputy Greene hesitated, waiting for Joe's reply.

"That's okay. What did you find out?"

"You were right. We had the narcotic guys get a search warrant and check his boat. He had a lot to be nervous about. Ten cement bags full. Pure Columbian. Narcs and DEA picked him up about an hour ago, and he's being booked now."

"Good. Lean on him and then drop in the

murder. Break him. If he's guilty, he'll slip up. Anything else?" Deputy Greene said no and hung up. Joe knew Brownie was guilty of running drugs with his boats, but he prayed that he was guilty of murder and that he would confess. That would settle the Martin case and end the possibility of another body being washed up on one of Flagler's beaches.

He walked over and sat down on the large brown and gold print colonial couch. He lay down on his back, hands under his head, and stared up at the ceiling, waiting for the answer which he knew would come soon. Confess, damn it! Sure, and there really was a Santa Claus.

Chapter 14

In Edison, New Jersey, Dr. Bill Daniels yanked his small brown Samsonite week-ender out of the storage closet and wiped the dust off it with an old towel. He carried it back upstairs, coming into the sunny kitchen where his wife, Lucy, stood at the stove dressed in her fluffy pink bathrobe and mule pump slippers, making him link sausage and fried eggs.

"Did you find it?" she asked him without turning around. Dr. Daniels walked over and kissed the back of her neck.

"I sure did." He wrapped his arms around her waist and kissed her behind the ear. "Why don't you put that on the back burner for a while? There's something I want more than breakfast, if you get my drift." She turned around to face him.

"You have to get packed or you'll miss your plane," she reminded him.

"Then I'll catch another one later. Or I won't pack. I'll just buy clothes there or go naked." He laughed and kissed her again, this time on her mouth. "Atlanta can wait an hour. The coroner's seminar can wait an hour. I, on the other hand, cannot wait an hour." He turned off the stove, put the skillet on the back burner, and holding his wife's hand, started up the carpeted stairs to their bedroom.

Bill and Lucy Daniels had been married for almost twenty-five years, and that union had produced a daughter, now twenty-three and in college studying to be a psychiatrist. Bill was a modest, old-fashioned man, conservative with his clothes as well as his ideas, but thoroughly modernistic with regard to the methods used to determine the cause of death of a person.

He had grown up in Princeton, New Jersey, and had chosen to attend the University of Pennsylvania instead of his hometown college. He had finally decided to become a forensic pathologist and had enrolled at Columbia Medical University in New York. He had never once regretted the decision. The manner in which a person had died never ceased to be a fascination for him. It was like a puzzle, and the more pieces to that puzzle he found, the more he learned about that person, and people in general. Each time he was able to help the police identify a killer, the satisfaction he felt was a natural high which he would ride for as long as he could.

But now he needed to get away and relax for a while, and the medical examiner's seminar being held at the Peachtree Plaza Hotel in Atlanta was just the excuse he needed. It would take his mind off the "Medical Exterminator", as the media had labeled this new serial murderer. He would make his plane on time. He always did. For now, he just wanted to concentrate on Lucy, the warm body lying next to him.

* * * *

Sheri Touter came into Detective Dave Selten's office scared and angry. Dave had expected her to be hostile. "Why was I brought here?" she asked hotly. "I didn't have anything to do with Dr. Walters's death. I hardly knew the man." Dave watched her shift her weight from one foot to the other, hands on her hips. He motioned for her to sit down in the straight back wooden chair across from his desk. She glared at him for a few moments longer, and when he made no attempt to move or speak, she plopped herself down.

"I guess a woman could be a man's lover and hardly know him," he said quietly. He watched her face turn bright pink. A girl who blushes. Good. An easy thing to read.

"Who told you that?"

He could barely hear her. She seemed to be easily intimidated, so he decided a harsh approach would work best. "What? I can't hear you," he said gruffly.

"Who told you that I was his lover?" she repeated, head up.

"Weren't you?" he asked, ignoring the question. She lowered her head again. "I asked you a question, young lady. Please answer it."

"Yes." A whisper.

"What?"

"Yes! Okay? Yes!" she shouted at him, tears filling her blue eyes. "But I loved him. I wouldn't have hurt him. I couldn't."

"How long were you two lovers?"

"About a month. Maybe less."

"And you loved him? After less than a month? Kind of fast, wouldn't you say?" She didn't answer. Dave pointed to her blond curly hair. "Natural?"

"No, it's permed."

"I mean the color."

"Of course! What has that got to do with Larry's death?"

"Can you tell me where you were on October sixteenth and seventeenth?"

"The sixteenth and seventeenth? How am I supposed to remember where the hell I was? That was over three weeks ago."

"Better try." He watched her slim, ringless fingers nervously smooth out the folds of her tan poplin skirt.

"The sixteenth was what day?" She took a pocket calendar out of her purse and started flipping through the pages. "A Thursday. I have dance class on Thursday nights and then I usually go with some of the other girls for a bite to eat. Maybe a drink or two. Friday nights, if I don't have a date, I usually go to the library to study. Nursing school usually keeps me pretty busy with homework."

But not too busy to fuck a married man, Dave thought.

"I can prove where I was if needed."

"What size feet do you have?" She seemed confused.

"Five and a half. Why?"

"Do you smoke?"

"What, like grass?" She seemed alarmed. *Must be a toker,* he mused to himself.

"Cigarettes."

"No. Never acquired the habit. Can I go now?"

"Where have you been for the past couple of weeks?"

"Institutional training. In order to complete my schooling, I have to have so many hours of training in different types of institutions. This time they sent me to Bellevue Hospital."

"I can check that," Dave responded.

"Go ahead and check."

He studied her for a full minute, then decided

to let her go on home. There was no way to pin it on her, no way that the evidence fit her.

"You can go, Miss Touter. Thank you for coming in and answering my questions." She seemed surprised to be released. At the door she turned back to Dave.

"I hope that you catch him, Detective. Short time or not, I really did love Larry."

I'll catch her Miss Touter, he said to himself. *I definitely will.*

* * * *

"Debbie! What a nice surprise! Two calls in the same month. How are you?" Doreen babbled into the telephone. "Why do I get honored with a call here at work?"

"Am I interrupting something?"

"No, not at all. Wait a minute! Is something wrong?"

"No," Deborah laughed. "In fact, everything's great! I called to tell you that I'm going to have a baby!"

Doreen couldn't believe her ears. Debbie was going to be a mother?

"Dory, are you there? What's wrong?"

"Nothing. I'm just so...surprised! How wonderful!"

"Oh, Dory, I'm so excited! And I want you to be the baby's godmother. Oh, say yes, please!"

"Yes, of course I'll be the godmother. I'd be honored! When is it due?"

"The beginning of January. I would have told you sooner, but, well, time just seems to get away from me. Dr. Brenner says I need to take it easy, but everything should be fine."

Dr. McClusky? Did she say Dr. McClusky? Doreen was confused.

"Isn't it wonderful, Dory? Joe's so excited, he's been talking to everyone about it."

Was McClusky trying to get to her through Debbie, Doreen wondered. Or was he after her, too? "Debbie, I want you to stay away from him. Do you hear me?"

"Stay away from Joe? Why?" Deborah was bewildered.

"No, not Joe. The doctor! You don't know him like I do. He can do nothing but harm! Maybe you should come up here and stay with me till the baby's born. That way I can protect you from him."

"What are you talking about? The doctor wouldn't hurt me! You met him when you were down here. He's my friend as well as my doctor. You know that!"

"Then do what you want. You will anyway. Only don't come running to me for help when you realize I'm telling you the truth! I'd die before I help you now! I wash my hands of the whole thing!" Doreen slammed down the receiver, and looked up to see everyone staring at her. "Don't you people have any work to do?" They began to go about their business, whispering among themselves. Damn fool! As soon as McClusky got the chance, Debbie was in for it. But she had tried to warn her, hadn't she? Well, it would serve her sister right if McClusky killed her! And her baby!

* * * *

Deborah sat looking at the telephone, shock still written on her face. What had happened? What was Dory talking about? Why would Dr. Brenner hurt her? God-damn her sister! It was just like Doreen to spoil her good news. She had always been jealous of her! Jealous of every good thing that had ever happened. Jealous because she had

had no friends! Jealous because she had had no
boyfriends, no husband, no baby!

That's why she had not told her sister sooner
about the baby. She knew this would happen. Well,
if that's the way her sister wanted it, then that's
the way it would be! As far as she was concerned,
she no longer had a sister!

Chapter 15

Brownie did not confess to murder. In fact, he totally cleared himself. According to him, and his witness who corroborated his story, he had shown up on the bridge that night to fish, and Thomas Martin had not been there. What Brownie had forgotten to tell Deputy Joe Sterling was that he had had a friend with him, a lawyer named Carl Stiles, who was in Florida on vacation from New York. Deputy Greene had verified Brownie's story and it had checked out okay. Deputy Joe Sterling found himself back at square one.

Two unsolved murders and no clues, no motives, no nothing! Exasperated, Joe poured himself a cup of coffee and stared out the window of his office. One possible suspect and he turns up with an alibi. Brownie should be glad his friend is a lawyer, cause he sure was going to need one with the drug charges. If he could just solve the Martin case, Joe thought. It would look better on his record, not to mention better to the sheriff. A clubbing and drowning, and a stabbing. What was next, a shooting?

"Deputy Sterling? Can I talk to you a minute?" Joe turned to see the young reporter standing in the doorway.

"What can I do for you, Mr. ahhh..."

"Taylor. Ken Taylor. Ken," the reporter said, fidgeting, one hand in the pocket of his jeans. Joe continued to stand where he was. The man was dressed in a light blue sport shirt with a thin yellow tie with small black specks on it, and faded denims. "I was hoping you could tell me what progress there has been on the Thomas Martin murder since I last saw you? Do you have any suspects?"

Joe thought for a moment. He motioned the man to a chair by his desk. "I wish I did. It's a real baffler, I'm afraid. There is really nothing I can tell you right now."

"Are we going to go through that again, Deputy?" He glared openly at Joe, not bothering with politeness this time. He had come for answers and he was not about to let this deputy put him off.

"Look, Mr...Ken, I'm leveling with you. We have found no clues. We have no witnesses. We're hitting a dead-end everywhere." Deputy Gatton came into the office.

"Joe, shooting in Bunnell," he said, getting a form out of his desk.

"What?" *Here we go again*, Joe thought, exasperated.

"White male. Been shot through the head by his girlfriend. City police are already there. They have her in custody now." *Well, at least it's not connected. For a minute there*, Joe thought, *it looked bad.* He sighed. He was beginning to get paranoid. That's all he needed -- especially with the press sitting here -- was another murder left up in the air.

"Check to see if there is any connection between her and the other two killings, just to be sure."

"Can I go with you, Deputy?" Ken asked, the eyes pleading as usual. "I'm not getting anywhere

here!"

"Who the hell are you?" Gatton asked harshly, eyeing the man.

"Ken Taylor. *Flagler Palm Coast News Journal.*" Gatton looked at Joe, who nodded his head. At least that would get rid of him.

"Come on," he answered, not at all happy about it. Joe smiled as they left the office. Thank God.

He read through some interoffice memos. A blood drive. All personnel were expected to donate the gift of life to refill the blood bank. According to the memo, there was a decrease in donations due to the fear of possibly contracting AIDS while giving blood, and the blood bank was beginning to run seriously low.

He made a note on his desk calendar of the time and place. He hated needles, and having a pint of blood taken from his arm made his stomach queasy. The feeling embarrassed him. A full grown man, a sheriff's deputy, afraid to give blood. Well, he wasn't really afraid, just squeamish. He felt stupid.

"Excuse me. I would like to talk to someone about that New Jersey man who was killed about three weeks ago." Joe's head jerked up.

"Come in, please. Sit down," he said, watching the boy nervously approach him. He appeared to be no more than seventeen or eighteen years old. Maybe he was about to get a break. But from a boy? "I'm the deputy in charge of the investigation. Joe Sterling's the name."

"My name is Bill. Billy Dunn." He sat down and folded his hands in his lap, as if prepared to get a lecture from a school principal for smoking in the boy's room.

"Okay, Billy, what did you want to see me about?"

The boy hesitated, and then clearing his throat, stated, "I'm not so sure it's important, or even if it was him..." his voice trailed off, uncertain if he should continue.

"Let me decide," Joe prompted.

"Okay. I was coming home from...a party, and when I came across High Bridge there was this guy fishin'. I didn't pay him too much attention, just kinda checked him out as I went by." He paused.

"What did he look like?"

"An old...older guy, wearing a cap. He was just fishin', like I tole you."

"What time was this?"

"About eleven-thirty or so. At night. Maybe a little earlier or later. I'm not sure. I was in a hurry to get home." He seemed embarrassed. "I was late. I was supposed to be home by eleven o'clock that night. It was a school night, and I knew my parents would be pissed when I got home. My mom worries if I'm ten minutes late."

"How old are you, Billy?"

"Sixteen, last month," he answered proudly. Joe tried not to smile. He could remember when he had been that age, and the memory was pleasant.

"Do you remember anything else about him?"

"Well, he was a little fat. You know, like older people get at that age. Around the middle, I mean. He was wearing a baseball type cap, like I tole you. There was a pail on the sidewalk by his feet.

"He was just kinda standin' there starin' out over the water. He looked at me as I drove by, like he was expectin' someone. I just kept goin'. That's it. I tole you it probably wasn't important."

"Billy, think hard. Did you see anyone else around or by the bridge?"

Billy thought for a moment. "No, no one. In fact, there was only one other car on the road, behind me aways. Other than that, it was especially quiet that night. Sorry."

"Why did it take you so long to come talk to me?" The kid again looked embarrassed.

"Well, I didn't figure it was important information, and..." He stopped. Joe waited quietly. "And I was afraid to get involved. My parents didn't know that I had come home late, 'cause they had been out. I figured if I came here, they would find out I had been late and I would be grounded. We had our Homecoming dance coming up. I just couldn't be grounded or I would miss it. I mean I already had promised to take Summer...my girlfriend, to the dance. If I got grounded, how would I tell her?"

"So your conscience bothered you and you decided to make it right by coming here?"

"No, Sir. Not exactly. I mean, Yes, Sir, my conscience bothered me," the boy said quickly, blushing. "That, too, but..." He looked away.

"But?"

"My kid brother told my parents, so I figured, why not? I had nothing to worry about now." Billy stood up. "Well, I better be goin'. My girlfriend is out in the car." Joe took his name, address and telephone number.

As he was leaving, Joe asked, "By the way, Billy, how was the dance?"

The boy grinned sheepishly. "I wouldn't know, Sir. I missed it. I'm grounded for a month." Joe smiled at him.

"Well, it can't be too bad. I mean, if Summer is out in the car, I guess she took missing the dance better than you expected."

"Oh, no, Sir. Summer went to the dance with

someone else. That's Shannon in the car." The boy grinned back at Joe, and with a wave of his hand, he disappeared out the door.

Joe laughed. He picked up the telephone and called the hospital, checking with Debbie to see if she was feeling all right, and then left for High Bridge. He was about to do some pail and cap searching.

* * * *

The Flagler County coroner, Dr. Donald Turner, sat at his desk in St. Augustine, Florida, jotting down notes on his preliminary findings concerning the shooting of the young man, now lying stiff on the autopsy table in the other room of his trailer/office. His assistant had just brought the body in, much to Don's dismay. He had called the travel agency as soon as the sheriff's department had notified him, telling the agent to change his flight to Atlanta to the next day.

Always something, he thought, angry that he could not get to the seminar ahead of schedule, so that he would have had time to relax awhile over some drinks with his associates from other states. He had run out to Bunnell to the scene as soon as he had notified the travel people. Now he placed a call to his wife, Joan, to let her know that he had had to change his plans and would be catching an early morning flight out.

He ran a hand through his full head of silver gray hair, and then bringing his hand down, absently stroked his gray mustache and finally his neatly trimmed beard. *Might as well get started*, he decided, picking up his gold rimmed, tinted glasses, and headed for the next room.

Whole place is going nuts. People dying all over

the county. The tourist, the migrant worker, a heart attack victim found in his home, a lady killed in an auto accident on the interstate, the little girl who had drowned in her backyard swimming pool. Didn't anyone die of old age anymore?

His mind went back to the drowned girl of five, and then floated to his own son of six. Donnie Junior was the highlight of his second marriage of eight years. The boy was active and full of vitality. They had had him checked for hyperactivity but he had tested normal. He pulled the sheet back from the body. Thank goodness he was going away for a few days. He needed a break from everything around him, from death itself.

"Okay, pal," he said to Al Montgomery, lying dead on the table, "this won't hurt a bit. I promise."

Chapter 16

Detective Dave Selten spent the morning talking to Dr. Walters's office staff and then to Dr. Parker's people. Walters was most definitely a womanizer according to the testimony of his nurses and his private secretary, Nancy Willis. She had a lot to say about her deceased boss, ranting on about all his sweet young admirers and his many conquests of those ardent fans. Dave had not understood her hostility, until she had finally admitted to being one of the notches on his bedpost. Only, her affair with the amorous surgeon had continued on and off for almost three years.

Yes, she had known about his wife. Yes, she had known about all of his affairs. After all, she had told the detective, it was her that had had to buy his wife's gifts, and had had to send the flowers and candy to whomever was his latest passion partner and flavor of the month, not to mention the many hotel reservations she had had to make for his afternoon "luncheons".

Oh, yeah, he had been good to her in other ways: paid for and furnished her luxurious apartment (he had retained the extra key, coming and going as he had pleased, unannounced), made sure that she was paid an exorbitant salary, so she would have plenty of money (he had made her buy plenty of gourmet food to keep on hand, so that she could fix him dinner whenever he decided to spare her a few precious moments of his valuable time), bought her new cars every year (he had used them on many occasions in case his wife had hired a private eye to follow him). She was especially bitter now that her benefactor-lover was dead and she was responsible for her own financial load.

Dr. Walters had his share of business problems, though. He had currently been involved in a malpractice law suit due to the death of a sixteen-year-old boy named Sammy Dunlap. The teen-ager had required a simple emergency appendectomy, but the appendix had burst before they had prepped him for surgery.

Mr. and Mrs. Dunlap claimed that their son had had the pains in his right side for over a month, and that Dr. Walters had originally misdiagnosed the problem as being a stomach virus. Dr. Walters had also told the Dunlaps that Sammy was in no real danger and that his surgery could wait. Dave made notes from the data in the boy's folder, deciding to talk to Sammy's parents. Maybe Mrs. Dunlap had decided an eye-for-an-eye was the solution.

Dr. Matt Parker's personnel, on the other hand, had only good things to say about him: he was a quiet, conservative and compassionate man; he was a very dedicated and caring physician; he was a loyal husband, even though he had been separated from his wife for a while. No one knew of any possible enemies, nor were they aware of any other women in his life besides his wife, Patty.

Dave had looked around Dr. Parker's private office just as he had done at Dr. Walters. Everything was unduly neat and organized. Dave had checked through the doctor's appointment book. There had been only one entry written on October 29th, the day he had been killed: Dinner with Jason. Dr. Parker's secretary had told Dave that Jason was Dr. Jason Kaufman, director of the surgical teams at Metropolitan, and Matt Parker's closest friend. He had then called Kaufman and made an appointment to see him.

Dave was now driving west on Oak Tree Road, through the town of Iselin, then past Oakwood Plaza. When he reached Grove Avenue he turned left. The homes in this section were each different, yet the same: neat clipped lawns, gardens well tended now going dormant for the winter. He turned left onto James Street. Suddenly Metropolitan Hospital loomed up on his right. He pulled into the parking lot and parked his navy blue and white Trail Blazer.

* * * *

Doreen had walked the urine samples down to the lab for testing, and had been waiting for the young lab technician to get off the telephone for over five minutes now. Her patience was wearing thin. Finally the girl hung up.

"Miss, I have some samples here from ..."

"Excuse me, Nurse, but I'll be right back," the technician said, heading for the door.

"Miss, I can't..." Too late. She was already gone. Doreen was furious. She set the samples down on the white counter and scouted around the lab rooms looking for someone else to help her. The entire lab was devoid of human life. Now what? She couldn't just leave the samples on the counter. Maybe a note. Suppose the note blew off, or was just plain missed. No, she'd have to wait for

someone to come back or take the samples back
upstairs till after lunch. It was her own fault for
coming down here at noon. Now she'd be late for
her own lunch!

Doreen walked along the cabinets, peering at
the labels on the many bottles sitting on the
shelves, reading little notes stuck on the counters,
and touching some of the vials of different liquids.
Her eyes read it, passed it, and then returned their
gaze on to one large white bottle. She picked it up
with both hands and reread the label carefully:

CAUTION! POISON!
CYANIDE POWDER
DO NOT TOUCH
UNLESS AUTHORIZED!

Doreen did another quick scan of the room.
Still no one, no sounds. She walked over and took
a paper towel from the counter and set it out
smoothly, and quickly opening the bottle, dumped
some of the white powder onto it. She recapped
the bottle and set it back in place. She twisted the
towel into a small ball and hurriedly stuck it into
her pocket.

"Can I help you with something, Nurse?"

Doreen jumped slightly, and abruptly turned
to face the girl who had disappeared earlier. "Well,
it's about time! Did you think that I had all day to
stand around down here? Is this lab supposed to
be left unattended? Who is your supervisor, Miss?"

"I, ah, I'm very sorry, Nurse, but I had to relay
an important message to a doctor across the hall
and his phone was busy. I didn't mean to keep
you waiting. I'm really sorry."

"Never mind," Doreen stated flatly. She walked
over to where she had left the samples. "These
samples are STAT for patients on four east." She
fixed her stare on the girl's soft, light brown eyes.

"Yes, Nurse. I'll get to them right away," she said, picking up the plastic containers. Doreen started for the door. "I really am sorry about the wait." Doreen didn't bother to look back.

* * * *

As he walked to the hospital door, Detective Dave Selten replayed from memory his earlier conversation that morning with Patty Parker, wife of the second victim. She had cried, claiming that she had loved her husband, but that they had been unhappy being married and living together and that she would never have wanted to see him hurt, let alone dead. She had told him that her husband had been a very quiet, very alone type man, and that had been part of the problem which had caused the divorce.

She informed Dave that her husband had been a movie buff, had enjoyed playing eighteen holes of golf on his days off, and had been an avid reader of mystery novels. She had not believed that her husband had picked up a strange girl that night, as it would have been out of character for him, but agreed that he may have a girlfriend, although she had no actual knowledge of that fact. Dave had believed her.

He walked into the modern lobby of the hospital and stopped at the information desk. The receptionist directed him through two large swinging doors and to the first door on the right. Dr. Jason Kaufman, Director, was stenciled on the door. Not knowing whether to knock or not, Dave simply opened the door and walked in.

"I have an appointment with Dr. Kaufman," he said to the secretary. "My name is Dave Selten, Edison Police Department." The heavy-set woman smiled, her fleshy pink face radiating warmth. She picked up the telephone receiver and informed the doctor that Detective Selten was there. Still smiling, she told Dave to go on in.

Dr. Kaufman was an attractive young man in his early thirties, sitting authoritatively behind a massive mahogany desk. His green eyes seemed to dissect Dave as he stood before him. "Detective Selten, come in, please," he said, pointing toward a dark green leather chair.

"Thank you, Doctor," Dave said, surprised at how comfortable the chair felt. "I'm sorry to interrupt your day, but I have a few questions I'd like to ask you."

"It's no bother, but I don't know what I could tell you that I haven't already told the other detective."

"Was there anything that you may have noticed the night you went out with Dr. Parker for dinner and drinks?"

"Like what? I don't know what you're getting at."

"Anything. Someone who may have talked to him, was flirting with him, maybe. Did he pick up a girl that night?"

"Not when I was with him. And that really was not Matt's style. He was kind of quiet, reserved. He didn't even speak to anyone except the waitress and the hostess at the restaurant, and the waitress at the lounge." He sipped his coffee. "Cup of coffee, Detective?"

"No, thanks. Did you know of anyone he may have been dating? Someone from the hospital possibly, that he may have been seeing recently?"

"Sorry. Not that there weren't women around who wanted to date him. Matt was an eligible, successful surgeon -- young, handsome and rich.

Get my point?" Dave nodded. The green eyes watched him, reminding him of a cat waiting to see which way the dog was going to turn.

He suddenly brought his palm down hard on the desk blotter. "There was something that struck me as coincidental that night. I'm sure it's nothing, though."

"Try me," Dave said, hope mounting in his chest.

"There was this girl. A beautiful girl. Long dark brown hair, big blue eyes, nice figure." The description made Dave think of Doreen, and he decided to stop up and see her before he left the hospital. Maybe he'd even ask her to dinner tonight. "Anyway, I spotted her at the Chinese restaurant. She was sitting alone, and she kept looking at our table. Finally we left and went to the lounge. We weren't there ten minutes when in comes this girl."

"Are you sure it was the same girl?"

"Oh, I'm sure. I'm telling you she was gorgeous! You don't forget a looker like her that easy."

"Then you would recognize her again if you saw her?"

"You bet I would. In fact, if you find her, call me. I want to take her out." He laughed.

"Did she talk to either of you?"

"No, just sat there. But I caught her looking at Matt every once in awhile."

"She never spoke to either of you at neither place?"

"No."

"Did you and Dr. Parker leave the lounge together that night?"

"No. I left first. Matt stayed to finish his drink. He had tried to talk to his wife, Patty, that day, but she had hung up on him and he was really upset. He was really knocking down drinks."

"Was he drunk when you left him?"

"Pretty close. He assured me that he was all right. I had asked him if he could drive and he said he was fine, that I should go ahead and leave. So I did."

"Could you help a sketch artist put her on paper?"

"I'll sure try, but I can tell you in advance, it won't do her any justice. Just let me know when."

"I will. Thank you, Dr. Kaufman. You gave me more to go on."

"Do you think that she did it?"

"We're just checking everything we can. It may be nothing, but it won't hurt to find out who she is. Besides, if she's that good looking, I want to meet her myself!" Dave grinned. "Thanks, Doctor."

Dave went upstairs to the four east wing. As he got closer to the nurse's station, he began to feel stupid and awkward. Maybe she would think he was out of line. Maybe she had a boyfriend. Probably a doctor. Nurses always went for doctors. At the very least, an attorney. What chance would a cop have?

"Can I help you?"

"I was looking for Nurse Price," he said, trying to act nonchalant, not caring whether she was there or not. His eyes checked all the faces behind the counter.

"I'm sorry. She's on late lunch today. I don't expect her to be back much before two. Did you want to wait? There's a lounge down the hall."

"No, thanks. I'll try and stop by later."

"What's your name, so I can tell her?"

"Never mind. I want to surprise her. Thanks again." He dashed into the elevator, feeling like a jerk, not to mention the feeling of disappointment for having missed her, but glad just the same to escape without making a fool of himself. He'd be patient. After all, it had been fate that had caused him to meet her in the first place, hadn't it?

* * * *

"Oh, Doreen. There you are. There was a good-looking gentleman here to see you about a half hour ago."

"Oh? Who was he?" Doreen asked, throwing her purse in the back cabinet.

"I don't know. He wouldn't leave his name. Said he wanted to surprise you."

Surprise her? Oh, no! McClusky! Had he escaped death again? So it had to be him! It had to be! Who else would be coming to see her at work? Few people knew which hospital she worked for, and they certainly would not know where to find her if they did.

"What exactly did he say?" Panic was rising in her throat.

"Just that he would try and stop back later, and that he didn't want to leave his name because he wanted to surprise you. Doreen, are you feeling okay? You suddenly look very pale. Is there something wrong with this guy? Are you in trouble?"

"No. No, I'm fine, thanks. I've been having some trouble sleeping lately and I guess it's just catching up with me. I appreciate your telling me." *Warning me is more like it!* Where could she go? She'd have to face him. *Wait, that's it! That would be great,* she decided. *Get it over with, once and for all.* She didn't like the way things had changed. The way McClusky had now become the hunter and she the prey. Well, it had to come to a head sometime.

She had to find out what he wanted. She felt the small bulge in her pocket and remembered the white powder. *Okay, McClusky*, she said silently, *ready when you are.*

Chapter 17

"Debbie? What's wrong?" her husband, Joe, asked, watching her sit there staring at her reflection in the darkness of the window pane.

"I'm homesick, Joe. I guess I miss my mother. My sister," she said without turning around. "I want to tell my mother about the baby, you know. Maybe it's because of the baby that I need to see my mother. I know it's crazy. My mother wouldn't even hear me, wouldn't know what I was talking about even if she could." He listened to her soft, almost child-like voice.

"Do you want to make a trip home? It might do you some good to see Doreen and your mother. It's been what now? Three years, maybe four? I think you're long overdue for a visit. Don't you?" There was no response. Joe got up, and walking to where she sat, wrapped his arms around her from behind. He watched their reflection. "Well? Doreen made the last visit. Why don't you call and tell her you're coming?"

"No. I really want to surprise her. Are you sure you don't mind?"

"Of course I mind! I'll miss you! But I want you to go. Besides, I'm up to my ears with these murders, so I won't be around much anyway. I'll even help you pack."

"Are you trying to get rid of me, Mr. Sterling?" She smiled at him in the glass. He turned her around slowly and kissed her mouth.

"Never," he whispered hoarsely. He stared into her ice-blue eyes. She smiled sweetly and kissed the tip of his nose. He took her hand. "Come on. I'll prove it."

* * * *

Doreen had raced home after work, just like yesterday and the day before. She was convinced that he was out there, waiting. Waiting for the right moment, that one time when she would let her guard down, becoming more vulnerable. She walked around the apartment, turning on all the lights as she went. She had already locked all the doors. It had become routine. They had come and installed the black wrought iron bars on all her windows just yesterday, and that had relaxed her some.

Where was that son-of-a-bitch? She peered out of the living room window, straining her eyes. She clicked the light off and waited for her eyes to adjust to the darkness. "John? Come on out and let's talk this over, just you and me," she whispered to the distant sounds of traffic. "Do you want me again, Johnny?" Her whispers floated over the surface of the glass, clouding it up in a lopsided circle of mist. She'd find him. She found him last time, didn't she? When he couldn't get to her when he wanted to, he'd have to come out in the open, and she'd be ready. Oh, yes! Good and ready.

* * * *

In the Peachtree Plaza Hotel in Atlanta, Georgia, there were people everywhere: in the lounge draped around the bar like animals at a watering hole, in the restaurant quietly talking, and at the reception/check-in counter trying to get their rooms. Medical Examiner Donald Turner was glad he had decided to attend this seminar. He would learn some new techniques, swap war stories with his colleagues, and see old friends.

Atlanta was a good place to host a seminar, with its bright lights, happy people and all night madness. But for the immediate future, his plans only included a quiet dinner, a relaxing hot shower and a comfortable bed. With all the craziness back home, he had not been able to leave until after supper and had to call his travel agent again. She had sounded exasperated on the telephone.

"Don?"

He turned to see Coroner Dr. Bill Daniels, dressed in a blue blazer and off-white slacks, waving at him from the lounge door. "Hey, Bill, how are you doing?" he said, extending his hand to his long time friend from New Jersey. "I was hoping I'd see you here."

"Almost didn't make it. There's nothing but craziness up North, not like your quiet little territory. Come on, I'll buy you a drink, so I can cry in it." They maneuvered their way through the crowd in the bar, greeting other associates along the way, till they found an empty table in the corner of the semi-lit room. A waitress appeared almost immediately and took their order.

"My 'quiet little territory', as you call it, is anything but quiet these days. Take my word for it. Flagler County, Florida, may not be as big as Middlesex County, New Jersey, but we have our share of crime."

"I honestly don't know what's happening lately. In the past several weeks, bodies have been turning up everywhere. I don't know if the news from up there filters its way down to the sunshine state, but we have some nut killing off our doctors, and what's worse, we have no possible suspects."

The waitress returned carrying a tray filled with a large assortment of glasses, each filled with a different colored liquid.

"How are they being murdered?"

"That's one of the problems, Don. Each victim, so far, has been killed in a different way. The first doctor was a jogger. He was clubbed with a piece of pipe of some kind, and then apparently rolled into the park lake, where he consequently drowned. The next one was found stabbed to death in his own apartment. Multiple stab wounds, so it may be a crime of passion on that one. The victim was naked on his couch, and we found all the usual evidence that indicates a romantic interlude had transpired before his death. Our killer, at this point, seems to be female."

Dr. Turner stared without speaking, absorbing every detail that his friend related to him, like a recorder saving the words for some future playback. "Bill, this may sound weird, coincidental at best, but we had a tourist from New Jersey, an accountant, who was in Flagler on vacation, and while he was fishing on one of our Intercoastal bridges one night, was clubbed, tossed over the bridge railing, and drowned. No motive, no clues, no witnesses. A couple of days later an old black migrant worker was attacked and stabbed to death, also multiple stab wounds, in the parking lot at a local tavern in the black section of Bunnell. Again, no motive, clues, or witnesses."

"Do you remember the date of each one? As close as you can."

"Well, the first one had to have occurred around

the sixteenth of October. The second one around the twenty-ninth. Both apparently done at night. Correspond to yours, or am I way off in my analysis?" He took a big gulp of his Scotch, feeling its bitter warmth all the way down to his stomach.

Bill Daniels said nothing. Could they be related, he wondered. But if the four murders were related, then it would have to be the work of a group. Or at the very least, two people. But if there were only two people involved, what could be the reason, and why did they pick New Jersey and Florida as their target areas? It just didn't make any sense.

"Bill? It does parallel your cases, doesn't it?"

"Except our victims are physicians. Surgeons, in fact, and the victims down there were entirely different, almost like yours were picked at random. In the wrong place at the wrong time type of thing, whereas ours seem to be hand picked. The dates and the methods by which they were both killed seem to be the only common ground.

"If they were connected, there are many questions which arise. The murder of doctors, particularly surgeons, indicates a vengeance of some magnitude. It's hostility with a direction. The Flagler killings seem to be an after-thought, a type of copycat situation, except the fact that they happen on the same day. There would have to be a link between the two perpetrators, but then why aren't the victims ALL doctors? I would guess that our killer is much more of a burden due to the fact that he knows why he is killing, and because he has a focal point. Probably has accessibility to doctors more so than the one in Flagler."

Both men stared down at their own drinks, oblivious to the talk and laughter around them. "If the two are connected, the imagination brings forth some horrendous images of what's to come."

Chapter 18

It had been a sunny morning, unseasonably warm and balmy for November in New Jersey. Just the kind of day which made Dr. Jason Kaufman feel alive and energetic. He had accomplished a tremendous amount of work, work that had been cluttering his desk for days. He felt great! Indian summer in Edison. He loved it.

Without lifting his head, his green eyes checked the small digital clock built into his marble desk set. Twelve forty-five. Might as well break for lunch, he decided, closing the report folder in front of him. Wondering what was on the cafeteria menu for the day, he reviewed his daily desk calendar to see what appointments were scheduled for the afternoon. There were no notations anywhere on the page. His day was free. Maybe he ought to take the rest of the day off for some long put-off holes of golf. The fresh air would do him some good. His intercom buzzed loudly.

"Yes, Helen?"

"Detective Selten is on line one."

"Thank you," he said, pushing the lighted button on the telephone. "Detective, how are you?"

"Fine, Dr. Kaufman. I was wondering if you would have time to stop by headquarters some time today to sit with our artist and help him do a composite of that girl. Do you think you can fit it in, or are you booked up?"

"No, as a matter-of-fact I'm not. I'm totally free for the afternoon. I was about to grab some lunch, clean up my desk and leave. I was going to hit a few balls around the fairway, but it can wait. How's three o'clock sound?"

"Great. I'll let him know you're coming. When you get here, just tell the sergeant at the desk to call me and I'll meet you upstairs."

"Sounds good. I'll see you then." This was different, Jason Kaufman mused. Should be an interesting afternoon after all. He picked up a folder, and dropping it on his secretary's desk, headed for the cafeteria.

The hospital cafeteria was all but empty. Not as bad as during the twelve to one lunch. Jason picked up one of the large brown plastic trays and stopped dead in his stride. There she was! That gorgeous brunette whom he was about to try and describe to an artist was coming straight toward him! He couldn't believe his luck! Her hair had been cut short, but he was positive that it was the same girl. His pulse quickened but he was paralyzed, unable to do anything but stand and gawk at her.

"Well, hello there," he finally managed to say when she reached past him for a tray.

Doreen turned to gaze at him, fear sparkling in her blue eyes. So she was right, she thought, her throat constricting. She knew he'd come out into the open looking for her! Doreen's hand went slowly down, fingers touching the pocket of her crisp white uniform slacks, feeling the bulge of the small bottle of powder she now carried at all times.

"How have you been?" she asked in a low hushed voice.

"Okay. But now I'm great. I have been trying to locate you everywhere and here you are right here at the hospital!"

"I figured you'd find me, so I just waited for you."

Jason couldn't believe his ears! So she had noticed him at the restaurant and lounge. He must be as attractive to her as she was to him, or she wouldn't have been waiting for him. Jason couldn't comprehend his good fortune.

"Well, I'm glad that you did. Can I buy your lunch?" He motioned to the plump black woman behind the counter and she scooped mashed potatoes onto his plate.

"Gravy, Sir?" she asked him.

"Yes, thank you, just on the roast beef." Jason looked back at Doreen's profile, his eyes memorizing every detail of her delicately chiseled face. The long dark lashes feathered around big blue eyes, the full pouty lips, the small pointed nose. "So is lunch on me?"

"No, thank you, Doctor. I'm only getting a yogurt and a cup of tea to take back upstairs. Thank you anyway."

What would he do next, Doreen wondered, pretending to be occupied with her yogurt selection. Would he try to get her out of here? Damn McClusky! How long was this going to go on? Would he chase her forever? She watched the dark woman hand him his plate. Her hand reached into her pocket, her fingers closing tightly around the small capped bottle.

"How about dinner then? Tonight, maybe?" Jason reached for a Styrofoam cup.

Doreen took the bottle out of her pocket and set it on her tray.

"Well?" he asked, turning toward the large industrial coffee pot.

Doreen glanced around, taking note of everyone in the area. Except for the two of them and the counter woman who had her back turned to them, the counter area was empty. Swiftly and nimbly she sprinkled the powder over his mashed potatoes.

"I'm sorry, I really can't make it tonight," Doreen answered, stuffing the bottle into her pocket. "Maybe another time, John."

"Jason. By the way, what's your name?"

"What? What's the matter with you? You know my name's Doreen!" What was he trying to do? Play games with her? "I'm sorry, I have to get back to my floor."

Doreen walked briskly up to the cashier, and paying for her yogurt and tea, turned back to the doctor. "Bon appetit, Doctor," she said, giving him a wink.

Jason smiled, his green eyes shining. He'd get her. He knew he would. He had to. She was the most beautiful girl he had seen in a great while. *Easy, Jason*, he admonished himself. She could get under your skin and then walk right through your mitral valve and into your heart.

He set his tray down on an empty table. Now he wouldn't have to do the police sketch. He knew who she was. Or did he? Doreen. Doreen who? Why didn't I look at her name badge? That's all right. She worked there as a nurse. She'd be easy enough to find. He'd call Detective Selten and notify him that he had found her. He took a bite of roast beef. Jason tore open a packet of sugar and poured it into his coffee. Glancing at the other tables to see who was there, he scooped up a forkful of mashed potatoes.

"Hi, Jason. Mind if I sit with you? I hate eating alone." Barbara Lickman was standing above him, her lunch tray in her hands.

"Sure, sit down. I'd be a fool to turn down an invitation such as that from such a pretty nurse," he said to the young redhead. She set her tray on the table and sat down opposite him. "In fact, you're doing me a favor. I hate eating alone, too."

Jason shoveled the mashed potatoes into his mouth, and after he had chewed for a few minutes, speared another piece of meat.

"God, we've had such a busy morning on maternity. I think everyone decided to have their baby today. I guess there must have been a blackout or something nine months ago."

Swallowing, he asked, "You work on maternity? I should think that's a very rewarding area to work in."

"Oh, it is. I just love it there. All those new, tiny human ..." she stopped, suddenly alarmed. Dr. Kaufman's face had turned a bright cherry red, his eyes bulging. With his hands clutching sporadically at his chest, he fell forward, his face crashing into his plate of food.

"Jason? Oh, my God! Quick! Somebody! Code Blue! CODE BLUE! HURRY!" she shouted, running around the table. Quickly wiping the food off his face, she laid him gently down on the cold linoleum floor and loosened his tie, shirt and belt. She pinched his nostrils together and filled his lungs with her breath as she blew into his mouth. The cardiac arrest team was there in short order, followed by doctors and nurses from all over the hospital, but it was too late for Dr. Jason Kaufman, Director and Surgeon.

* * * *

Deborah had eaten her lunch in the courtyard of the hospital, soaking up some of the sun's warmth. She loved Florida in the fall with its air getting cooler after the hot summer. She had eaten slowly to prolong going back to the lab, but finally she had had no choice and returned to her desk.

"Deborah, we ran out of sugar. Would you happen to have any here in your department?"

"Huh?" Deborah seemed confused. Her head was once again striking powerful shots of pain against her temples. "I'm sorry. I didn't hear what you said."

"Deb, aren't you feeling well?"

"No, I'm sorry. I have an awful headache. I get them once in awhile. What can I do for you, Millie?" She tried to focus her eyes on the older woman, but it made her head hurt even more.

"Sugar. Do you have any we can borrow? I'm dying for a cup of coffee and there's no sugar over there in personnel. I only need two teaspoonfuls."

"Sure, Millie. I'll get you some. Watch the phones for me, will you?" Deborah took the cup from the pudgy woman and disappeared into the back room. Walking blindly, her fingers pressing against her forehead, she stopped at the counter where shelves of different bottles were stacked neatly, each label clearly marked in large black letters informing everyone of the contents inside. She reached up, took down a large white bottle and spooned some of the fine powder into the steaming cup of coffee. Screwing the cap back on, she replaced the container on the shelf.

"That was fast, Deborah, thanks. I'd just die without my coffee," Millie said, taking the cup from Deborah's hand. "How have you been feeling lately, dear?"

"I, uh, have such a migraine," she answered, wishing the old woman would just go back to her own office. Deborah felt horribly nauseated.

"Probably due to your pregnancy. I remember when I had my son, Charlie. I was so sick for the whole nine months," Millie said, blowing on her coffee. When Deborah didn't respond, she commented, "You do look awful, dear. You should lie down for a while somewhere. Well, I'd better be getting myself back across the hall or my work will never get done. Thank you again." When Deborah continued to sit at her desk with her head down in her hands, the woman quietly left the lab.

What's wrong with me? Debbie wondered, her headache finally beginning to subside. Maybe a psychiatrist would help. She would have to stop by Dr. McIntyre's office later and see what he thought. There had to be a reason. Something was causing these spells, as Joe called them, and she decided to find out once and for all what it was. She was concerned that whatever was behind these attacks might just affect her unborn infant, and that worried her more than anything else.

"CODE ONE, PERSONNEL! CODE ONE, PERSONNEL!" the hospital loudspeaker blared, the voice trying to remain calm yet firm. Deborah only half listened to the message. She was used to hearing that voice all day. She could hear people running down the hall. She'd ask Millie later what had happened. Her fingers continued to massage her temples. The noise in the hall grew louder. She tried to stand, but waves of dizziness swept over her. Grabbing onto the desk for support, she lowered her head, her legs suddenly starting to tremble, the muscles losing control.

"Hey, Deb, come on! Millie's just had a heart attack at her desk! Deb? What's the matter?"

Deborah raised her head slowly, her face white, lips moving but no sound emanated. Her blue eyes slowly rolled upward, the eyelids suddenly closing, and Deborah collapsed in a heap.

Chapter 19

Detective Dave Selten had been watching the clock since two-thirty. It was now three forty-five and still there was no sign of Dr. Kaufman. The police artist was getting antsy to leave. Maybe Kaufman had had an emergency, or his car may have broken down, or shit! Probably just plain forgot, gone to the golf course with his cronies like he had wanted to do. Dave placed a call to the doctor's office.

"Dr. Kaufman's office. May I help you?"

"This is Detective Selten. Is Dr. Kaufman there?"

"Is this the detective that was here the other day?"

"Yes, it is. I had a three o'clock appointment with Dr. Kaufman today and he hasn't shown up yet. Would you happen to know if he's on his way here?"

"Detective Selten, Dr. Kaufman died of a massive heart attack around one-thirty this afternoon," the woman said, her voice beginning to break with emotion. Dave was stunned. Him and his damned luck! It sucked! Of all times for the doctor to have a heart attack

"Miss, wasn't he kind of young to have a massive heart attack? Has anyone requested an autopsy?" His mind searched. Gut feeling again. Another dead doctor, a possible witness to the identity of a female killer. Too much coincidence.

"No, Sir. I don't think so. It was just a heart attack," she replied defensively.

"Where's the body? In the morgue?"

"Yes, Sir. I guess so. We have already notified his parents. They're sending someone for the body."

"NO!! I mean, that body's not to go anywhere till I get the M.E. to check him over. Can you put me through to the morgue physician?"

"Yes, Detective Selten. One moment, please." There was a click, then total silence until there was another click and a male voice came on the line.

Dave informed the morgue attendant that Dr. Kaufman's body could not be released until the coroner gave his okay. He explained that there was an official investigation going on and the body needed to be examined, that someone would get back to him, that he should contact the family and explain.

Dave put in a call to Dr. Daniels and was informed that the doctor was at a medical examiner's seminar and convention in Georgia. After an explanation of who he was and why he needed to contact the doctor, he was told that he could find Dr. Daniels registered at the Peachtree Plaza Hotel in Atlanta. Next Dave placed a call to the hotel. After the hotel operator had rung the doctor's room about six times, she came back on the line and took a message from Dave.

He leaned back in his chair, his hands clasped behind his head. Coincidence? No way. That meant that if this turned out to be another murder and not a heart attack, the killer was probably associated with the hospital, for very few, if any, knew that Dr. Kaufman had seen a mysterious female who matched the description of the suspect.

Did she work there? A nurse? Maybe even a doctor? That could be it. A girl goes through med school, harassed and jeered at by her male peers maybe, extra pressure and embarrassment from the professors. Maybe something happened, something bad that she couldn't forget, and now she was a doctor with a built in hate that was burning out of control. Possible, but not very convincing. This was the 1990s after all. The time of sexual harassment suits.

A nurse maybe? Sgt. Tacker had talked to most of the nurses, including a few who had had affairs with Dr. Walters. Of the few only one was a brunette who had a size seven foot, but the fingerprints found in Dr. Parker's apartment were conclusive that she had not been the woman. At least not in the Parker murder. Also, she did not smoke, and she had had an airtight alibi for the time that Walters was killed.

But someone at that hospital was committing murder, and so far, getting away with it. All hospital personnel would have to be checked, probably fingerprinted. Doreen! She sure fit the description and she smoked cigarettes, but he could not remember the brand. She was also very defensive when he had talked to her. But she had been shocked about the murder of Dr. Matt Parker. Would she had been if she had killed him? Unless she was a good actress.

Dave thought of her expression when he had told her that day. He thought of her blue eyes. No, she had honestly been surprised about the murder, and she had short curly hair, not long and straight. He dismissed the idea and felt a twinge of relief flow through him. But she might have an idea of who it could be, and that would give him an excuse to take her to dinner. He decided to go over to the morgue to view the body and at the same time he could drop in on Doreen's floor first. All in the line of duty, he told himself. All in the line of duty.

* * * *

"Deborah's fine, Joe, just fine. Sometimes women faint while pregnant. Expectant mothers are prone to dizziness; stress, body changes, not enough rest, are all some of the reasons," Dr. Brenner explained to Joe Sterling.

"But it could be something else, right? Something worse?"

"It's possible. Anemia, fatigue, illness. We're going to keep her a day or two and check her over, do some tests, just to be sure. She claims to have had a migraine again accompanied by nausea. She'll be just fine, and so will your baby. Don't worry." Dr. Brenner rubbed the corners of his eyes with his fingers.

"Tired, huh, Doc?"

"Yes, you bet I am. I lost a good friend today. Millie Jepper. Worked in this hospital thirty-two years. She would have retired in less than two years. Just became a grandmother for the sixth time. I'll miss her. She was a wonderful woman."

"I'm sorry to hear that. How'd she die?"

"Massive coronary. Millie was one of the sweetest ladies you'd ever want to meet," the doctor said, shaking his head slowly.

"I'm really sorry," Joe said, putting his hand on the older man's shoulder. "Can I see Debbie now?"

"Sure, go ahead. Tell her I'll see her later this evening."

Joe walked down to room 4B and peeked in. Deborah lay with her eyes shut, her long dark hair highlighting the whiteness of the pillow and sheets. She looked so small and helpless lying there. He had never seen her sick before, not even a cold. Only those damn headaches. Joe moved one of the chairs closer to the bed, sitting at his wife's side, waiting for her to awaken. He wanted to tell her how much he loved her.

* * * *

"Hello. I'm Dr. Daniels, room 617. Someone's been paging me?" the coroner asked the hotel clerk.

"Yes, Doctor," the handsome young man behind the counter replied in his thick Georgia drawl. He handed Dr. Daniels a note. The doctor read it, and scowling, crumpled it up. He walked across the lobby and picked up the telephone, placing a call to the airlines. The next call was to his wife, then his office, and the morgue at Metropolitan Hospital. Finally he called Detective Dave Selten's office and left a message telling Dave that he would be back in New Jersey that evening, and went up to his room, packed up his belongings, left a message for his friend Dr. Donald Turner, and checked out of the hotel.

Any other time a doctor having had a heart attack would not be so circumspect, but in view of the circumstances over the past month, an autopsy was definitely in order. Dr. Daniels, seated in the first class compartment of the DC-10, silently prayed that it had been a coronary and not another act of vengeance.

* * * *

Detective Selten had changed his original plans

and gone to the morgue before going to see Doreen. That way he could just come right out and ask her to dinner. If she said yes, he would take her tonight before she changed her mind.

"You were my link to the killer, Doc," Dave said softly to the body on the gurney table. "Why now? Why did your heart decide to stop now?" Dave stared at the cherry red coloring still around the hands, fingers and lower extremities. Was it high blood pressure that had caused it? Where had the redness come from? "Or did you find her, Jason? Is that it? She works here and you, unfortunately, found her?"

"Did you say something, Detective?" the attendant asked, coming into the room.

"No, just thinking out loud."

Dave turned and headed out the door for the elevator. He pushed the button for the fourth floor, and as the elevator took him closer to Doreen, he mentally reviewed his dinner offer approach. What if she turned him down cold? This was ridiculous! She was only a girl, for Christ's sake! A beautiful girl, but still just a female. He hadn't ever had too much of a problem when he wanted a date with someone.

The elevator was coming to a halt on the fourth floor. He quickly took two deep breaths, and sucking in his stomach, stepped into the corridor across from the nurse's station. Doreen sat alone behind the counter, her head just barely visible from where he stood. He took another deep breath and stepped closer.

"Hi," he said as brightly as he could. Doreen looked up.

"Hello, Detective." She stared at him, her expression blank.

He leaned on the counter with both elbows,

smiling his sexiest smile.

"Can I do something for you?" she asked him.

"Yes, as a matter-of-fact. I have some more questions concerning Drs. Walters and Parker, and I thought, maybe, you and I could discuss them over dinner after you get off work tonight."

She did not answer. He waited her out.

Why her? she wondered. She had no knowledge regarding the murders of those doctors. Or was he baiting her? Had they found out about McClusky? Did someone see her sprinkle his food with the cyanide? *Stay calm*, she warned herself, *stay calm*. Deciding that she could handle this cop, one way or the other, she said, "I'd like that, Detective Selten. Say, around sevenish?"

"Seven is great. Do you want me to pick you up here?"

"No. I get off at four-thirty. I live at the Parkland Apartments. One twenty-two Cherry Tree Circle, apartment B. Upstairs."

"Terrific. Do you like Italian food?"

"Yes, I do." She watched his expression. No hint of any kind. Nothing showed that could give her a clue as to what he really wanted. He was playing with her, she was sure. But he was underestimating her and he'd find out the hard way. She was nobody to screw around with.

"Good. We'll go over to Mama Maria's for some great food and chilled vino. Can I have your phone number? Just in case something comes up. With this investigation I never know what's going to happen," he said, his brown eyes staring deep into her clear blue ones.

She thought for a moment, considering if there might be an ulterior motive for his wanting her number, but then decided that it didn't matter. It was in the telephone book anyway. "555-8680."

He wrote her number in his notepad, realizing that he had never seen her smile, not once. "Okay. See you at seven then. Come hungry," he said grinning. She gave him a weak smile in return.

She continued to stand where he had left her, totally absorbed in her thoughts. He was attractive, in a rugged austere way, but was his attentiveness genuine, or was he trying to implicate her with McClusky's death? She turned away from the elevators doors, her icy-blue eyes moving to the bulletin board attached to the wall behind her. She folded her arms, leaning against the white Formica counter. What did it matter? It was just a dinner date. She had never dated a cop before and the idea intrigued her. He reeked of authority and machismo, but she found that somehow very masculine, giving her a heady feeling. Her eyes focused on a large white sheet of paper with the word "bulletin" stamped across the top in large red letters.

"ATTENTION ALL SURGEONS!!!
You are cordially invited..."

They were always "cordially invited" to everything, she thought bitterly. Nurses did all the work while the doctors had all the benefits.

"You are cordially invited to attend the Bembbar Seminar Dinner to be held at 7 P.M. at the Emerald Restaurant in Rahway on December 27th..."

All surgeons invited. Who cares, she told herself. *ALL SURGEONS INVITED!* Doreen's mind screamed it again. *ALL SURGEONS INVITED!* They would all be there, or at least a good amount of them. December 27th, Emerald Restaurant, Rahway. ALL SURGEONS INVITED!

Chapter 20

The little nurse's aide stood by the bed lathering up the thin washcloth till it was good and soapy. She hated her job. Every day it was the same thing: wash the patients, feed the patients, dress the patients. Then it was change the beds, scrub the bedside tables, not to mention the crap she had to take from the patients and the nurses.

The doctors weren't too bad. They just ignored you. But for some reason unknown to her, the nurses treated the aides like second class citizens. Maybe even third class. If it wasn't for people like her, the nurses would have to do all the dirty work themselves. She soaped Judy Price's arm, starting at her shoulder and moving down to the elbow. Damn vegetables, that's what they were!

Why bother to keep them alive anyway? They were no good to society, no value to anyone, including themselves. Take this one for instance. She couldn't do anything for herself. She didn't even talk or move. Just lays there on her bed staring at the ceiling, or sits in her chair staring out the window. Euthanasia. It should be legal, and they should start here. She dried Judy's arm, and after rinsing and resoaping the cloth, started on Judy's other arm. Judy Price blinked.

College. Maybe she should take some classes and learn something that would take her out of this miserable place. Back to civilization and normal people, where people you worked with talked to you, said hello when you came on duty, knew you were there. She began methodically soaping Judy's chest and stomach.

An R.N. No. She wanted out of this line of work completely. A secretary? That definitely sounded better. She'd learn to type, take dictation, maybe even learn to use a computer. She'd work in a large corporation. Executive secretary to the president of AT&T, IBM, General Motors. She liked the title. She liked the whole idea! Judy Price blinked rapidly several times.

Oh, yeah. She could picture herself bringing her boss coffee in his favorite cup, talking to big deals who had appointments to discuss critical decisions which needed to be made, wearing fancy clothes instead of the thin blue nylon uniforms she now wore, filing her nails at her desk. The aide studied her hands, concentrating on the short nails with their chewed cuticles.

"Come on, Zombie," she said harshly to Judy Price. "Time to put on your nightie so you can go sleepy-bye. Not that you're ever awake. Girl, you're always sleeping." She pulled the flannel nightgown over Judy's head and arms.

"D...Dory?"

The aide froze. She turned quickly to glance at the small frail woman whom she had been dressing for bed. "Did you say something?" she asked Judy nervously.

Judy's sunken blue eyes stared straight ahead, the dark purplish circles beneath them very prominent. "Dory? Debbie? Are you girls here? Please answer me."

The aide slowly backed away from the bed, keeping her wide-eyed gaze on Judy Price's face as if she were watching a corpse coming back to life. Suddenly she turned and bolted from the room.

"Nurse Durfmier! Hurry! NURSE DURFMIER..."

* * * *

"I'm almost ready," Doreen said, closing the door behind Dave. "Please sit down. I'll be right back."

Dave watched her slim, willowy body glide confidently down the hall, her high heels clicking against the wood floor. Dave wandered around the living room looking at the furnishings, the plants, the fish, trying to absorb the human side of this beautiful girl. He had learned through the years that a person could learn many things about people by seeing how they lived, and judging by this apartment, Doreen lived very well.

Something was missing, though. What was it, he wondered, studying the room. Nothing personal in the room. No family pictures, no knickknacks, no personal items. The room looked like it belonged in a furniture store, set out for display, but not really belonging to anyone in particular. Cold. Sounds of struggling followed by some banging floated to his ears from the back room.

"Are you all right?" he called to Doreen. "Something I can help you with?"

Doreen jumped at the sound of his voice. "No. It's all right. I'm just closing a stuck window. I got it already, thanks."

Dave walked over and looked out the window in the sterile living room. "Why are there bars on all your windows?" he asked loudly over his shoulder.

"I live alone, Detective. I sleep better knowing I'm safe and secure," Doreen answered from the bedroom. She checked her face in the large mirror. She checked her hair again. Her shiny brown hair swirled in soft curls, the front forming ringlets which surrounded her china-like face and highlighted her dark-lashed blue eyes. Her bare ear lobes were hidden behind large blue star earrings.

"Feel safe tonight, sleep with a cop," he said quietly, remembering his T-shirt with that slogan.

"I'm ready, Detective Selten," she said, coming toward him.

"Dave," he said, barely speaking above a whisper. She was radiant! Her eyes sparkled brilliantly, reminding him of blue sapphires set in an ivory statuette which he had seen while he had been stationed in Korea. "And you look gorgeous!" He started toward her.

"Ready to go?" she asked, turning away from him. "I'm starved."

* * * *

In the morgue at Metropolitan Hospital, Dr. Daniels made a clean straight cut down the chest and abdomen, stopping at the groin. A distinct odor of bitter almonds filled his nostrils. He stopped, taking another sniff of the air. There was no doubt about it. He knew the smell from his intern days. His very first autopsy, if his memory served him correctly. He went to the office, placing a call to the Edison Police Department, only to learn that Detective Selten was off duty. He left word with the night sergeant for Dave to return the call no matter what the time, and then gave the officer his home telephone number. Next he called Dave's home direct. After three rings a recording came on.

"This is Dave. You know what to do at the sound of the beep." Beeep. *Short and to the point*, Dr. Daniels thought. Also brash.

"I thought you didn't like answering machines! Dave, this is Bill Daniels. Better call me as soon as you can. We've got another one for sure. Try me first at the lab, then at my home. I don't care what time it is." Dr. Bill Daniels hung up and went back in the other room to finish his autopsy on Dr. Jason Kaufman.

* * * *

It had been a momentous evening for Dave, filled with countless surprises. He had been amazed by the number of facts and interests they had in common.

When having told Doreen that he was an enthusiastic and devoted bowler, a sports and outdoors man, he had been delighted to hear that she was into the same things. He was born in Massachusetts, raised in New Jersey, and so was she; he had four brothers and two sisters, and so did she; his father was a bus driver, and her father had been a truck driver before he had died of a heart attack; he loved children and animals, as did she.

He was thrilled. He would have to take her backpacking and camping very soon before the temperatures dropped to freezing. Yup, everything had gone great: the Fettucini Alfredo had been a gourmet's dream, the conversation stimulating, and the movie delightful. He had made another date with Doreen for Friday night, for dinner and dancing. It would be a long two days. For him anyway. He couldn't wait to see her again.

Dave fumbled with his keys, and finding the right one, unlocked his apartment door. Removing his gun, which he carried tucked in the back waist band of his slacks under his jacket, he walked over to the small plastic table he used to hold his answering machine, to check his messages. Without listening to the entire tape, he clicked the machine off as soon as he had listened to the first message, and called Dr. Bill Daniels at the coroner's lab.

"What have you got for me, Doc?" he asked as soon as the doctor had answered the phone.

"Dave?"

"I'm sorry. Yes. How did this one fall?"

"Cyanide poisoning. The food in his stomach was loaded with it."

"The guy at the morgue told me that Kaufman had had a heart attack while eating in the hospital cafeteria."

"First of all, cyanide poisoning does look a lot like a massive heart attack. Similar symptoms: redness of the skin, inability to breathe, body freezes as if in shock. Without the autopsy and testing for cyanide traces, there would have been no way to distinguish between the two. Second, it had to have been put directly onto Kaufman's food, because no one else died, or even got sick in the hospital, that had eaten there. I already checked the records. With cyanide it happens quick.

"There's one more thing..." he said, pausing long enough to give the air some tension. "Where did the killer get it? It had to come from inside the hospital. It's usually kept in the labs." There was no response. "Dave, did you hear what I said?"

"I heard you, Doc," Dave said, evaluating the information. "Who would have had access to it?"

He rubbed his forehead with his large thick fingers. So Kaufman had probably found her! Right there at the hospital after all. Dave's adrenaline was rapidly spreading through his bloodstream.

"Lab technicians, doctors who work in there. Maybe even a lab secretary. That's about it." Both men fell silent, lost in their own analysis and conclusions.

"Better call the hospital in the morning and notify them to trash all of yesterday's food, just in case, but for them not to do it till my lab crew gets over there to get some samples. But under no circumstances are they to serve any of it. I'll be there early in the morning talking to all of the cafeteria personnel. I'll let you tell his family."

"That's big of you, Dave."

"I'll probably have to interview and fingerprint everyone who works at Met," Dave said, ignoring the doctor's remark. "It will be time consuming, but I don't know what else to do. Do you?" It suddenly hit him just how tired he was.

"Administrator is going to object. It will put a scare into everyone, especially the killer. What if she bolts?"

"Have to chance it. Besides, I don't think she will. She's obviously aware that we're getting closer, but I don't think she cares. She may even be toying with us, trying to see just how far she can go until we catch up with her."

"Or she's truly psychopathic and isn't thinking rationally. Maybe she's driven by fear. It could be a lot of things. Are you sure that you want to chance it?"

"Don't have much of a choice, as I see it. The killings will just continue unless we track her down quickly. By the way, Doc, does cyanide come in powder or liquid?" Dave lit a cigarette and inhaled deeply.

"Both. Just depends on which type Met uses. They may even have both forms, but the powder is easier to store."

"And to use? Thanks for the info, Bill. I'll get on it first thing in the morning." Hanging up the receiver, he turned on the recorder to hear the rest of his messages. He kicked off his shoes and wriggled his toes.

"Dave, this is headquarters. The M.E. called and needs to talk to you as soon as you can. Sounded important. Said he didn't care what time it was. Also, a Mrs. Alice Smiley, a neighbor of victim Dr. Matt Parker, called and said she wanted to speak to the detective in charge of the investigation of his death, that she has info that might help. Number's here on your desk. Hope you got lucky tonight!"

Dave clicked off the laughter that followed.

* * * *

"Judy? Can you hear me? This is Nurse Durfmier." There was no response.

"I'm telling you she talked to me! She was looking for a Dory or Debbie. She thought I was them," the aide persisted, rubbing her scrawny thin hands together.

"Judy? Please try to talk to me. I want to help you," the nurse continued, ignoring the hysterical aide. Judy Price's eyes blinked rapidly. "Are Dory and Debbie your daughters? Do you want me to call them for you?" Judy's mouth opened slightly and a small pink tongue appeared licking her lips. "That's it, Judy. Try."

Dr. Norman DeLeon, the sanitarium's house doctor, came into the room, his suit crumpled, the dullness of sleep still in his old brown eyes. "What's all the excitement about, Nurse?"

"Doctor, this aide claims that Miss Price spoke to her while she was getting her ready for bed. She has not talked to me yet, but she does seem to be trying to respond to my voice. Almost as if she can hear me."

The doctor bent over the bed and with his thumb and forefinger opened first one eye as far as he could, and then the other, peering deeply into Judy's pupils. "Miss Price?" he asked loudly. "Can you hear me?"

"M...m...my babies. Where are my girls?" Judy whispered, her voice raspy and cracking. The doctor and nurse exchanged glances. The nurse, as if by cue, hurried from the room to check the chart for family contacts.

* * * *

"Yes?" Doreen answered abrasively, trying to hold the receiver to her ear, keeping her eyes shut against the lights she now kept on all night.

"Miss Price? I'm sorry to awaken you. This is Nurse Durfmier at the Oakville Institution. We thought we should call you right away. There's been a change in your mother's condition and we thought you should be notified immediately."

Doreen hurriedly pulled herself up to a sitting position, leaning against the headboard of the bed, and reached for a cigarette. "Are...are you trying to tell me my mother's dying?"

"Dying? Oh, no, Miss Price. Just the opposite. Your mother is calling for you!"

Doreen's hands began to tremble, almost dropping her cigarette. "Call...calling for me?" It had been almost fourteen years since she had heard her mother's voice. "Are you sure, Nurse?"

"Oh, yes, ma'am, we're sure. She said your name and your sister's. Called you both 'Dory and Debbie' and asked where you were. We thought you would want to hear the good news right away. The doctor's with her now."

The DOCTOR! *Oh, no,* Doreen thought. *Not again!* He wasn't dead! Dr. John McClusky had found her mother! "I'll be right there!" she said, slamming down the receiver.

* * * *

Deborah slept restlessly, tossing from side to side, softly moaning in her troubled sleep. Her husband, Joe, snored softly next to her. Her suitcase was packed and ready by the front door in the living room. Her plane ticket was in her purse. In the morning, the large 747 would fly her north, bringing her forward in time only to face her past.

Chapter 21

"Mrs. Smiley?" Detective Dave Selten asked when the woman answered the telephone. The bright New Jersey morning sun sprayed light into the small office that Dave shared with two other detectives.

"Yes?"

"This is Detective Dave Selten of the Edison Police Department. I understand you called yesterday regarding information you have about Dr. Mathew Parker?" Dave toyed with his pen, rolling it back and forth across his desk.

"Yes, Detective. I don't know how important it is, but I thought I better call and explain something which I found unusual." She sounded old.

"Yes, ma'am, and what was that?"

"Well, a few nights before Dr. Parker was found, well, found in his apartment, I had heard yelling coming from his apartment. I live next door, and have lived here for five years now. Usually it is very quiet in this complex, especially this building, so I was surprised to hear someone yelling at that time of night."

"What time of night?"

"Around eleven, I think. I had been dozing in front of the television set. The screaming woke me up."

"Was it screaming or yelling? There's a difference."

"Yelling. Yes, definitely yelling. I guess a scream would be just a sound, not words. Especially angry words."

"What exactly did you hear, Mrs. Smiley?"

"A woman. She was yelling what sounded like 'admit it, admit it.'"

Admit it? What the hell was that all about? Dave wondered, suddenly getting more interested. A lover's quarrel, maybe? A jealous girlfriend? Or wife? "What else did she say?"

"That's it. That's all I heard until about twenty minutes later when I heard his front door shut."

"I don't suppose you saw who left, did you?" he asked, doodling little circles on a scratch pad.

"Oh, yes. I mean, I don't normally snoop, or pry into anyone else's business, but because of the hour and the yelling, I was curious, you understand. So I went to the window to see who it was." She hesitated, waiting to be asked, liking the attention she was receiving with this conversation.

"And?" Dave asked, getting impatient. He hated it when someone beat around the bush. *Get to the facts, lady, get to the facts.*

"It was a woman, all right. I couldn't really see her face because it was dark, but the lights from the parking lot lit up enough for me to see she had long dark hair."

"Was she thin, fat, short, tall? What?"

"Well, let me think a minute. She was fairly tall, taller than me. And thin. Like a model. She was probably very pretty."

"Why do you say that?"

"She carried herself well. Confidently, you know?"

"Did you see her get into a car? Do you remember what she was wearing?" Dave was jotting down notes now; his small handwriting scribbled across the pad.

"I'm sorry. I watched her walk down the steps, but I can't see the whole parking lot from here. I really don't remember what she was wearing. I was very tired," she apologized. She had nothing more to add.

Dave took her name and address, explaining that another officer would be out to see her and to go over her story again. She sounded pleased. The phone rang immediately after Dave had hung up.

"Selten."

"Dave, better get over here. I spoke to the cafeteria people, and one woman who had served Dr. Kaufman yesterday said that he had been talking to a nurse while he had been in line, and that she had noticed him eating with another one," Sgt. Tacker stated, unable to hide his excitement at having learned something important.

"Could she give you their names?" Dave asked, quickly putting his cigarettes in his shirt pocket, ready to head for the door.

"No, but she gave me a partial description of one and a good description of the other, and Dave, the one in line comes close to matching our mystery girl."

* * * *

Doreen sat by her mother's bed, watching the woman she no longer knew, sleep. They had to tranquilize her mother, Nurse Durfmier had explained to Doreen when she arrived at the hospital, because she had gotten hysterical and started screaming. They were afraid that her mother would have disturbed the other patients, or so she said, Doreen thought dryly. But she knew better. Her mother had probably been screaming for help, had probably recognized Dr. McClusky and had known what he was trying to do to her daughters, had probably remembered what he had already done to them at birth.

So for the time being anyway, he had quieted her. After all, he wasn't really after her mother, only her. McClusky had known that Doreen would come to her mother's defense, even if it meant her own life. Doreen understood him, just as McClusky must also understand her. They knew each other well. Too well. They were two of a kind, her and Johnny, and she understood that, too.

She realized that she was more than a little disappointed at having missed him, that he had had to leave before she could get to the hospital. He was just making her wait. What was happening to her lately? All she could think about, dream about, was him. She feared him, she hated him, yet she also respected his ability to elude her attempts to kill him.

She stood up and stretched, arms pulled backwards at the shoulders. Rubbing the back of her neck, Doreen crossed to the windows, staring out at the large shrubbed garden which seemed out of place at this loony-bin. Was he here somewhere at the hospital, hiding from here? Wearily she sat down in the armchair by the window, turning it so she could face her mother's bed and keep an eye on the door at the same time. Her eyes felt gritty and heavy.

She glanced at the gold Seiko watch on her wrist. Almost noon. Had she really only slept two hours since yesterday? Maybe she should call Debbie and tell her -- what? That their mother had finally screamed at the top of her lungs? That McClusky had found their mother? After the last unpleasant phone conversation between them? No. Better to keep her out of it as much as possible, Doreen decided.

There was nothing that Debbie could do anyway. It was up to Doreen to stop him, to save them all from whatever McClusky had planned. Besides, she WANTED to do it, to be close enough to feel his breath on her face, to smell his masculinity, to experience the thrust of power she would have over him. But where? And when?

She thought of the seminar bulletin, reminding herself of the meeting where most of the surgeons would be learning new procedures to ruin someone's life. Doreen's eyes burned and her head ached. Would Johnny be there, too? Would he dare show up again? She slowly closed her eyelids. Oh, yes, she resolved. John McClusky was hers and hers alone.

* * * *

Joe missed Deborah already. He had taken her to breakfast at the coffee shop in the Jacksonville Airport, sat with her till she boarded her flight, and had watched until her plane was out of sight. It left him feeling empty and alone. The long two hour drive home again had given him a chance to think about what his life would be like without Deborah, without her smile and laughter, and the thought had brought tears to the surface. Blinking rapidly several times, he had cleared his throat, and forced himself to think of other things.

For the past several hours, he and two other deputies had been walking the banks of the Intercoastal, still searching in vain for a baseball cap and a pail, both of which had belonged to Thomas Martin.

A large water moccasin slithered into a hole in the mud on the east slope. He shivered as a chill ran up his spine, causing the small hairs on his neck and arms to stand up as his skin prickled. Snakes were a necessity of nature, he knew, but he wished they didn't have to come up on land. Like alligators. Snakes and gators. Two of God's obvious mistakes, if He made mistakes.

A glint to his left caught his eye, but it turned out to be a little girl's silver locket. He picked it up, and placing it in a plastic bag, continued to walk northerly up the waterway. He looked across the water. One of the other deputies was engrossed in something he had come upon and was busy inspecting it. Joe turned toward the Route 100 bridge which loomed up ahead. The patrol car sat parked on the east side of the metal expansion, the other deputy leaning against it smoking a cigar. He waved at him. Joe did not acknowledge, but went back to his quest for clues and answers.

By the time they had reached the bridge, the hot sun had turned to its hazy late afternoon glaze.

"Find anything new?" he asked the tall deputy walking across the bridge.

"A thermos bottle, a gold bracelet, and..." the officer hesitated, smiling, "a baseball cap."

"Let me see that." Joe turned the cap over and over in his hand. Then he looked at the thermos, and the bracelet. He'd have to call Jersey and talk to Mrs. Martin. But even if it did belong to her husband, so what? It means they have someone that saw him before he was murdered, but still no suspect. He was frustrated. It looked like the search was over. Another unsolved crime. He looked at his watch. His shift was over. Joe glanced up at the Bridgetender Inn.

"Buy you guys a drink?" he asked, starting across the street toward the large wooden building. "I need one."

* * * *

She stood in the doorway surveying the room. Her mother, who lay sleeping peacefully, had turned old-looking since she had last seen her years before. Doreen was also asleep, sitting upright in a chair by the window, her head laying to one side. She moved to the side of the bed and stared down at her mother. *So pale*, Deborah thought. She was frail looking, her eyes dark shadowed and sunken. Her jaw hung slack, showing some missing teeth, and her hair was stringy and had a lackluster look. *Oh, Mom*, she said silently, *I need you.*

"Mom?" Deborah said softly out loud. "Mom?"

"What are you doing here?"

Deborah jumped, snapping her head toward Doreen. She did not answer, only stood staring at the girl whose mirror image was her own. She had always been fascinated at being able to look at herself while looking at her sister. It also gave her an uncanny feeling. "Hello, Dory. Nice to see you, too."

"Who called you?" Doreen asked, ignoring her sister's obvious sarcasm.

"Called me? No one. Why should someone call me? Is there something happening to Mom?" she asked, again looking down at the withered human sleeping quietly.

"They claim she came out of her comatose state, that she talked to them. But they sedated her, so I can't say with any certainty that it's true.

If no one called you, then why are you here?"

"Why? Does it bother you that I am?"

"Don't you realize how dangerous it is to come up here right now? Do you want to jeopardize your baby's life as well as your own?"

"What are you talking about?" Deborah was truly confused, and becoming very alarmed. Doreen's eyes had taken on a wildness she had not seen since they were children, and it upset her to remember that things -- bad things -- had always happened after it.

Like the time Cindi Lee had overheard them talking in the school gym locker room about Alan Levy. Dory had had such a crush on him and he had finally asked her to the Senior Prom. She had been beside herself, raving about what she would wear and how she would fix her hair and make-up. Debbie had been so happy for her, laughing at her enthusiasm. They had had to hurry. Alan was to have met her outside the gym by the cafeteria, but when they entered the hall they overheard Cindi Lee telling Alan that she couldn't believe that he was so hard up for a date that he had had to ask "the freak".

Those that had been standing around them snickered. When Alan had walked off with his friends, Cindi Lee and her companions had sneered at the Price sisters. That awful look had washed over Dory's face. She had said nothing, but Cindi Lee had been killed that night when the car she was driving had lost both front tires as she had turned a sharp curve coming down a steep incline in the Watchung Mountains.

It had been a closed coffin funeral, as the body had been so mutilated. A freak accident is what the police report had stated. *Boy, was that the truth*, Deborah thought, and then felt guilty for having thought it.

"...and he's after me. I've tried everything to stop him, but to no avail," Doreen was saying. "Now he's going after you and Mom. You've got to go home, Debbie. For your own sake and Mom's."

"Who's after you?"

"John McClusky! Aren't you listening to me?" She was pacing around the room now.

"D...Dory? Debbie? Are you girls there?"

Both women turned toward the bed. Judy Price sat staring straight ahead with sightless eyes, her bony arms stretched out before her.

Chapter 22

In the Metropolitan Hospital cafeteria, two police officers, Detective Dave Selten and Sergeant Tacker, stood with the woman who had served Dr. Kaufman lunch the day before. Each watched the cafeteria activity.

"She's obviously not coming to the cafeteria for lunch today, Dave. Maybe we ought to call it a loss and try again tomorrow."

Dave's eyes searched the large room, studying each female face, hoping to locate a possible suspect. "Do you see her?"

The black woman shook her large head, her huge cow brown eyes surveying the cafeteria. "She ain't here. Sorry."

"Do you think you could describe her to a police artist?" *Here we go again*, he thought.

"Well, I could try, but I only saw her for a second. I have work to do. I don't have time to study everyone who comes in here. Besides, you'd have to clear it through my supervisor first. I can't be losin' my job. I got five kids to support."

"What's your supervisor's name?"

"Belinda Carter," she said, nodding toward another tall black woman. "The one givin' me the evil eye for not doin' my work."

Dave walked over to the tall attractive black woman who stood by the kitchen door, a scowl distorting her classic Jamaican features. He explained to Belinda Carter the necessity for the composite drawing, how vital it was that her employee Alma Browne be allowed to take time off to go to police headquarters, and that other lives might be saved.

Dave assured her that it wouldn't take more than a few hours, but made it clear that he would take the matter to the hospital administrator if necessary. Miss Carter reluctantly agreed to let Alma Browne have the time off, without pay, the next afternoon after lunch had been served. He decided not to argue the pay deduction. He would take it to the comptroller and have Mrs. Browne paid by the police department.

Dave told Sgt. Tacker to stay with Alma Browne in the cafeteria for the afternoon just in case the woman made an appearance. She may have just been tied up and not able to take lunch yet. Or she could have brought her lunch today. Maybe it was her day off. Possibly have called in sick. If she didn't show up today, Sgt. Tacker and Mrs. Browne would have to repeat the watch every day until the nurse again went to the cafeteria.

Dave figured as long as he was at Met, he might as well stop up and say hello to Doreen. Passing the hospital gift shop, he noticed a single red rose in a small white milk glass vase in the cooler window. Although he was not normally inclined to romantic actions, especially on the spur of the moment, Dave bought the flower for Doreen.

He felt ridiculous standing before the nurse's counter with the rose in his large paw of a hand, especially with Doreen no where in sight. His feelings suddenly turned to disappointment when he learned that she was off for the day. He left the vase with the nurse along with a note, and went to the pay phone.

She did not answer her telephone, and Dave was forced to give up. He knew very little about her, he realized, so there was no way to track her down. He'd try again later. Maybe stop by her apartment and offer to take her for an ice-cream cone in the park. A walk around the lake at dusk. A kiss in the moonlight. Was there a moon? Dave couldn't remember.

He had wanted to kiss her the night before when he had taken her home, but she had kept aloof, letting him know without words that he had better not try. Probably had had a bad love affair and she was just cautious about becoming involved again. This would have to be handled delicately, Dave decided, with flowers, candy, candle-lit dinners -- total romance. Gain her confidence and trust. He wondered if she could cook. He'd have to hint around and find out on Friday night.

* * * *

Judy Price could hear them calling to her through the fog, begging her to keep trying, telling her that they were there. But where? She couldn't see either one of them. She had fumbled through the heavy fog, come out into the clearing where the house of her childhood stood burned and ashen, only the brick fireplace and chimney still standing. The mist was lifting, her vision clearing. Light was coming from somewhere, burning off the heavy fog and warming her face.

"Dory! Debbie!! Where are you?" she called out, straining her eyes to see.

"Mom, we're here. Can't you see us? We're here,

right next to you."

What did they mean, next to her? Judy Price looked around her. The mist was getting thinner and thinner, rays of sunshine filtered lightly through the darkness. She kept walking toward the warm streams of sunlight, searching for her two little twin girls. She passed the dead kitten, but she refused to look down at it, instead concentrating on the hazy light that seemed to guide her out of the fog and away from the horrible things that lurked hidden in it.

"Girls? Please don't hide from me. Where are you? Come out this minute! Do you hear me?"

"Keep coming, Mom. Please! Keep coming."

"Toward the light? Should I walk to the light?"

"What light? What is she talking about, Dory?"

"Sssh! Yes, Mom, the light. Walk toward the light!"

"Are you there in the light? Dory? Debbie?"

"Yes! Please, Mother! Come to the light!"

Judy Price mentally walked faster now, afraid to stop. Afraid the fog would envelope her again before she could reach the sunlight. Afraid she would lose her daughters once more.

"Girls?"

"We're here, we're here."

The light was getting brighter, stronger, the heat on her face a welcome sensation. Her arms still reached, her hands suddenly touched something -- something warm and familiar, something small and smooth. Strength flowed into her. She held fast to the object as if to let go would be the end of her existence. She knew that if she didn't hold on tight, she would perish and cease to exist. And so Judy Price held on with all her might as she continued to walk closer to the light.

Doreen held fast to her mother's hands, even

though Judy Price's fingernails dug deep into her palms. She just knew that if she let go, she would lose her mother forever.

* * * *

Detective Dave Selten had decided to stop by Doreen's apartment on the chance he might see her, but she had not answered the doorbell and her Corvette was not in the parking lot. He had grabbed a couple of chili dogs from a hot dog vendor on the side of Route 1 and gone on to Roosevelt Park to eat them. He sat on the park bench by the lake's edge, throwing twigs into the water. A group of five ducks swam rapidly toward him, hoping that what he was throwing was edible. Another large brown duck just sat where he was and watched. Dave smiled.

"A loner, huh? Me, too." The brown duck paid no attention to him. A smaller, white and black duck swam around the brown duck. She seemed to be trying to get his attention, but it wasn't working. She flapped her wings, splashing water up in the air. The brown duck swam closer to her. She kept it up, so he swam closer still. Suddenly she flapped her wings, skittering across the surface of the lake, stopping on the other side. The brown duck just stayed where he was. It looked at Dave, its unblinking eyes unreadable.

"Yeah, man, I know the feeling," he said, throwing the rest of his food toward the duck. "Here, have some chili dog."

* * * *

Deputy Joe Sterling had chowed down at the Inn, feasting on southern barbecued ribs and fried chicken. The other two deputies had long since gone home to their families and he sat alone at a round concrete table on the wooden outside deck overlooking the waterway. There had been no need to rush home to an empty house, so he had decided to sit and watch the boats go by.

Darkness was setting in around him, but the deck lights cast an uneven glow on the dark water. Small red lights adorned the side of the bridge, warning boaters of its presence. Joe looked up at the small glass enclosure sitting on top of the bridge, and at the man sitting inside watching a small television set. He could never be a bridgetender, he decided. Too boring, sitting in there hour after hour, doing nothing but watching TV, reading books, and opening and closing the bridge for every large boat that wanted to pass through.

What could he get Debbie for her birthday, he asked himself. For that matter, would she even be home in time to celebrate it? It was only two days away. Saturday. November 11th. She had said she would be home on Saturday night, if all went well. What could be wrong, he wondered. A twenty inch gold chain, with a little gold butterfly on it. Deborah loved butterflies. Where to find it was the hard part. He decided to try the large malls in Daytona Beach. They had the biggest jewelry stores and therefore, the biggest selection of jewelry. That made sense, didn't it?

Joe listened to the sounds of the night: katydids and crickets chirping their songs, bullfrogs and gators croaking, the muffled sounds of cars and trucks whizzing north and south on Interstate 95 a few miles away. The sweet sound of organ music floated out to him from inside the Bridgetender Inn, occasionally broken by bursts of laughter from the few patrons inside the lounge. He loved the sounds of the night in this small fishing town, but tonight without Deborah they made him feel lonely and deserted.

Joe picked up his heavy glass by its thick handle and downed the rest of his beer. Slowly he stood up, kicking his leg to be sure his slacks fell back over his western boots, and with his hands in his pockets, started the walk home.

* * * *

Judy Price sat staring at her daughters, unable to believe they were grown women. She had finally come out of the fog and into the light of the setting sunset and found her daughters sitting on her bed watching her. At first she had not known who they were, so she had not spoken to either of them. She had looked from one to the other until finally one had called her "Mom". Tears had welled up in her eyes and she had cried till no more tears would come.

Judy had hugged her twins, her beautiful grown-up daughters, until she was too weak to go on. Doreen and Deborah had cried with her. Doreen had told her about her job as a nurse, about her apartment in the park, about her new Corvette. Deborah had told her about her husband, Joe, about their home in Florida, about her job as a lab technician, and about the baby. She did not dwell on the subject of her unborn child, but moved quickly to another subject. She did not want a repeat of the conversation on the telephone, especially in front of their mother.

"Time for your mother's medication," the nurse said, bouncing into the room.

"Not yet, Nurse," Judy Price begged weakly. "I still want to talk to my daughters. There's so much

I want to know. So much time has passed between us. A little longer, please."

"Tomorrow's another day. You can talk to them then. You need to rest and get your strength back slowly. You ladies understand, don't you?"

"Yes, of course," Deborah said, rising, "I need to check into my hotel anyway."

"Why don't you stay with me?" Doreen asked her, picking up her purse. "I have room. Besides, it will give us a chance to talk. Just like old times."

Deborah hesitated. "Are you sure you don't mind? I already have a reservation at the hotel down the street."

"Mind? I'd really appreciate it. I hate being alone at night lately. Please say yes, Debbie."

"Okay, sure. Mom," Deborah said walking back to the bed, "I'll see you bright and early in the morning. We'll fix your hair and spruce you up pretty again. Sleep tight."

"I have to work tomorrow, Mom, but I'll run up at lunchtime, if I can, and we'll have lunch together. The hospital won't mind if I take a long lunch," Doreen said, giving her mother a hug and kissing her forehead. "And welcome back, Miss Price."

"I love you both," Judy answered, tears again in her eyes. "And it's great to be back."

Chapter 23

"Make yourself at home," Doreen told her sister, setting down Deborah's lavender Samsonite weekender by the front door. "You can either sleep on the sofa bed in the living room, or with me in my king size bed. Take your choice."

"Doesn't matter to me. Either one."

Deborah walked around the living room, stopping to observe the different fish swimming back and forth in the large glass tank. There was a plastic green and gold mermaid sitting on the multicolored stones at the bottom of tank, her tail waving slowly up and down, and a plastic diver opening and closing a colorful trunk full of pretend treasures.

"Okay. Then you can sleep with me. I'll throw a couple of steaks in the broiler, you can put together a salad, and we'll have dinner in bed, watch some TV and talk till the sun comes up. How does that sound?"

"Sounds great! I'll put my luggage in the bedroom, call Joe so he knows everything's fine, and be right back."

* * * *

"Who are you?" Detective Dave Selten asked the papers spread out before him. "I know the answer's here! Damn it to hell!" He shuffled the papers around, peering first in one folder, then another. Something was nagging at him. The pipe. Something about the pipe. And the cigarette butts found in the ashtray at Parker's. He continued to stare at his notes, digging deep into his subconscious, hoping to bring out the answer. Virginia Slims. The metal pipe and Virginia Slim cigarettes.

Dave took a long swallow of his cold beer and glanced at the clock on the wall. 10:45 p.m. Automatically he got up and walked over to the worn couch, clicking on his favorite news channel, so he could catch the eleven o'clock news. Probably thousands of people had pieces of pipe somewhere around their car or house. A common thing to have around. And probably twice as many people smoked Virginia Slims cigarettes as those who had pipe. He gulped his beer, crushing the empty can in his hand.

Whoever his murderer was, she had to be one of the hospital personnel -- unless she was a private duty nurse caring for someone there, he reasoned. They would just have to fingerprint all the personnel. He'd set it up with the administrator, and have the fingerprint officers go from floor to floor, one nurse's station after another if he had to. He'd leave no one out: lab technicians, secretaries, nurses, doctors. Even the patients, if necessary! She was there somewhere and he'd flush her out, one way or another.

He decided to start the fingerprinting and intensive inquisition with the lab personnel. He closed his tired eyes, listening to the newscaster's voice drone on. Within fifteen minutes Detective

Dave Selten was in a deep sleep, the papers of notes slipping gently to the floor.

* * * *

"That was great," Deborah said, wiping her mouth with a napkin. Both Price sisters sat cross-legged on the large bed, a tray with empty plates and wine glasses in front of them. Deborah wore a long sleeve, blue flannel nightgown, tiny pastel colored daisies dotting the material. Doreen preferred beige satin lounge pajamas, and sliding to the side of the bed, slipped her feet into matching slippers.

"It was good, wasn't it?" Doreen replied, picking up her tray.

Deborah nodded, and following her sister's lead, picked up her tray. "How do you feel about Mom being more alert again?"

"What do you mean?"

"Oh, I don't know, Dory. Part of me is happy about it," Deborah said, following her twin down the hall toward the kitchen.

"But?"

"Well, I feel kind of strange with her. I mean, we really don't know her any more. She left when we were ten years old, we find her, or rather, you found her when we were eighteen or nineteen, and she's been catatonic all these years. I just feel strange. Don't you?"

Doreen placed the dishes in the dishwasher. "I guess I do a little. But not much. Remember, I see her every week, so I've kind of gotten used to her. I think it's exciting, myself."

Deborah walked to the living room window and stood looking out into the darkness. "Dory, why are there bars on your windows?"

"To keep John out while I'm asleep," Doreen answered flatly.

"John? John who?"

"I already told you. John McClusky. Don't you even listen to anything I tell you?"

"Who is this John McClusky? Your boyfriend?"

Doreen did not answer. "Dory, are you in trouble? Or in danger?" Deborah was becoming anxious about this whole subject.

"No, I'm not in trouble. I'm just having a bit of a problem with him. Nothing I can't handle." Doreen snapped off the kitchen light. "Let's see what's on TV and catch up on your Florida news."

"I'd rather hear more about this John McClusky. It must be important or you wouldn't have put bars on your windows," Deborah said, again following her sister down the hall toward the bedroom. "Come on, out with it."

"Look, Deb, I'd rather talk about something else, okay?" Doreen snapped at her.

"Okay, okay. Forget it." Deborah grew quiet.

Doreen clicked on the television and turned to look at her sister. Deborah was again sitting Indian-style on the bed, her finger tracing the pattern on the comforter, her eyes downcast. Her long dark brown hair was swept back behind one ear, while the rest cascaded down her right shoulder. Her swollen abdomen seemed to rest on her crossed legs.

"All right, but you have to promise me that you won't tell a soul. Promise?"

"Of course."

"I mean it, Debbie. It's very critical that you never tell a single person, not even Joe. Swear it!"

"I swear, I swear! Now will you please tell me?"

"Do you remember Ma telling us when we were little that the reason I have a scar was because

the doctor could only keep one twin from being
badly scarred?"

"Yes. So?"

"Well, he hasn't finished with me yet. I guess
he won't be happy till he does."

"Does what?"

"Kills me, of course."

"Who is 'He'?"

"John. Dr. John McClusky! Aren't I getting
through to you?" Doreen was getting aggravated.

"Dory, John McClusky is dead. Mom told us
that when we were kids, didn't she? Didn't she tell
us that he had died a few years after we were born?"

Doreen stopped to think this over. "I think he
just wanted everyone to think that, but I know for
a fact that no matter what is done to him, he always
comes back."

Now it was Deborah's turn to be confused.
"Comes back? What are you talking about? When
what is done to him?"

"Oh, shit! What's the sense of talking about it.
You obviously don't understand, or don't want to!
I knew you wouldn't believe me!" Doreen went into
the bathroom.

"Dory, I am trying to understand. I really am.
But I'm confused. Are you trying to tell me that
this, this doctor McClusky is trying to KILL you?"

"I know it's hard to believe, but I tell you it's
true!" Doreen said, coming out of the bathroom, a
paper cup of water in one hand and a pill in the
other. "He shows up when I least expect him to,
and tries to sweet talk me, but I know what he's
up to." She popped the pill into her mouth, and
followed it with the cup of cool water.

"Have you called the police and told them?"

"No! I told you I don't want anyone to know! I'll
handle him myself!" Doreen climbed into bed. She

began to flip the channels with the television's remote switch. "Let's talk about you. How's Joe?"

"He's great. Working hard. There's been several murders down there, and so he's working long hours. He's really a great guy. But, Dory, please, let's talk about this Dr. McClusky. I'm really scared for you."

"Scared for me? Why?"

"Why? Because you're my sister. Because I love you. Because I don't want anything to happen to you."

"Oh, yeah? Since when?" Doreen asked sarcastically.

"What?" Deborah looked like she had been slapped.

"Never mind, Debbie. I'm tired. Shut the television off when you're ready." Doreen rolled over on her side, turning her back on her sister.

Deborah sat there dismayed, but she said no more. She clicked the remote to "OFF", rolled over away from Doreen, and lay there staring at the wall, sorry that she had told Doreen that she would stay there. She decided that in the morning she would move to a hotel.

Chapter 24

"Mrs. Browne, we'd like you to come over to police headquarters on Monday morning to do a police sketch for us. It's the earliest we could get the artist to do it. We've already cleared it through your supervisor. Do you need a patrol car to come get you?" Detective Selten asked the cafeteria worker.

"No, Sir. I have a car," she answered, "but I already tole you that I only saw her for a second. I didn't even have to serve her. I don't know if I could do it."

"Do you see her anywhere?" Detective Selten said, momentarily ignoring her protests. "Maybe you'll remember if you spot her in here."

Alma Browne took another look around the cafeteria and shook her head. "Sorry, I don't see her anywhere." She sighed. "What time do you want me there on Monday?"

"Around 9:30 in the morning, okay? The sketch artist will be in then."

"I'll be there. Well, I guess I better go help with clean-up, so I can get on home. Can I leave you now?"

"Yes, Mrs. Browne. Thank you," Dave said.

"Nothing?" Sergeant Tacker asked him.

"No. Did the fingerprinters get here yet?" Dave

asked, getting himself a cup of coffee.

"About twenty minutes ago. They started on the bottom floor in the lab. They'll work through everyone on this shift, and then the late night shift. Tomorrow morning they'll do the day shift. Hospital administrator is getting them a total computer listing of all employees, their shifts and their positions here. Should have it in about another hour. Don't worry, Dave, we'll get her."

* * * *

Doreen had spent her lunch hour sitting with her mother and sister at the institution, and she had been forty-five minutes late getting back to work.

"I can't believe they're doing this to everyone," Nurse Linda De Garre said, preparing medications. "Imagine fingerprinting the lab people and soon it will be the whole hospital staff. How can they believe that one of us killed those three doctors?"

Three? What three, Doreen wondered. Oh God, they must have found McClusky. And now they were fingerprinting everyone? *Don't panic, don't panic*, she warned herself. They can't prove she killed McClusky. The only thing she touched was the powder, and he had eaten that. So why the fingerprinting? Probably looking for the killer of Walters and Parker. So let them fingerprint her, she thought. She knew she had nothing to do with their deaths. Only McClusky's, and they would have no way of proving that.

"I just can't help wondering what the hell is going on. I mean, three doctors within a month?" Nurse De Garre continued. "It's got to be the same killer. I mean, all of them were surgeons here at this hospital."

"I just can't believe someone would want to kill any of them. Especially Dr. Kaufman. Those beautiful green eyes, closed forever."

Dr. Kaufman? "Did you say Dr. Kaufman was one of them?" Doreen turned and asked her.

"Oh, yeah, didn't you hear? He was poisoned in the cafeteria a couple of days ago. I can't believe you haven't heard, Doreen."

"I've, uh, been very busy at home. I have out-of-state company staying with me," Doreen stammered. "You mean the three doctors are Walters, Parker and..."

"Kaufman," Nurse De Garre said, finishing Doreen's statement. "Isn't it awful?"

"Was there another doctor killed?" Doreen asked, trying to sound nonchalant.

"Not that I'm aware of. Why, should there be? Personally, I think three's too many already."

"I was just wondering. I, uh, missed all the hospital gossip over the past two or three days," Doreen said, trying to sound like one of the girls. "I just wanted to make sure I hadn't missed anything else. I just can't understand why this is happening."

"Some psychopathic nut is on the warpath with doctors. Who knows why. Anyway, they're fingerprinting the bottom floor now. They'll get to us eventually, I suppose," she replied, locking up the meds. "Well, I'm leaving. It's quitting time and I'm gone."

Doreen watched her get her purse, and along with another nurse, walk to the elevator. What did this all mean? Doreen's mind tried to sift through the facts, but the answer always came up the same -- McClusky was still alive. One more escape from the cocoon of death. Her mind searched, sifting through a maze of deceptive plans and possibilities, until it settled on the surgeons seminar which was to take place soon. She'd get him. This time he would not escape. This time he'd pay. She'd see to it.

"Doreen, don't you have anything better to do than hang around here?" one of her colleagues laughed, pushing the button for the elevator.

"I'm coming," Doreen answered. Yes, she had plenty to do, all right. *Besides*, she thought to herself, *tomorrow's my birthday*.

* * * *

Judy Price sat by her window looking over the gardens which surrounded the sanitarium. So many years had passed while she had mentally roamed around in the fog. Her daughters were now beautiful full-grown women, each with her own life and career. She was about to become a grandmother. It was all too much and she was having trouble comprehending the entire overall picture.

A butterfly fluttered by the window and Judy watched it till it was out of sight. She let her thoughts wander back to when her daughters were little girls. She could see them playing, fighting, going to school and coming home again.

Judy Price also began to remember other memories, memories which had plagued her even through the fog. She remembered the day she had come home to find her pet parakeet dead in the bottom of its cage, its little neck broken. Each twin had denied doing it, but Judy had known which one was guilty.

She remembered the other time she had come home late from work one night and had found her little kitten lying stiff and dead on the porch. It had been strangled with a shoelace. Again both twins had denied her accusations, but she had dragged the girls screaming and crying into their bedroom. There Judy had gone through their closet until she had found the small sneaker that had its shoelace missing.

Checking the inside of the shoe, she had learned the identity of its owner, and Doreen had had a spanking with the leather strap which had belonged to her grandfather in his barber shop. Assuming that she must have also killed the parakeet, Judy had spanked little Doreen harder and longer than she normally would have, all the while screaming at her about killing animals, especially pets. She had turned around to see Deborah sitting quietly in a small rocker, watching her sister take the punishment.

Judy could still feel the guilt she had felt back then at having struck one of her daughters. Doreen must have hated her for having done it. But then she had had to repeat the spanking when her neighbor had come knocking on the front door screaming at Judy that Doreen had tried to cut her daughter's throat with a knife. Doreen had cried, repeating over and over that she had not done it, but why would her neighbor have lied? So Doreen had again been spanked and told to stay in her room. Deborah had stood to one side, watching.

There had been many such incidents. Then had come the fire. Judy could remember taking the twins with her when she had gone to try to talk to her parents. She had left them in the car while she had begged her father to please let her talk to her mother. He had told her to just go away and leave them alone, that they had no daughter. Judy had pleaded with him, but her father had just closed and bolted the front door. She had stood on the porch crying. Finally she had walked down the front steps, and having smelled smoke, had searched the area surrounding the house.

As Judy had walked around to the back of the house she had found one of her daughters standing there staring at the flames that were quickly devouring the old frame home. Her daughter had had a small flame burning at her feet, which had turned out, upon closer inspection, to be a rolled up coloring book. Judy had grabbed her daughter and had dragged her kicking and screaming to the car. She had then turned and run back toward the house, but the flames had moved quickly with the help of the strong breeze and the home was in total flames. She had screamed, backing away from the heat that had seared her body.

Judy had looked up and caught a glimpse of her mother trying to smash the upstairs window. She had seen the anguish on her mother's face as she had frantically banged on the window glass with her hands. Judy had screamed over and over. It was to be the last conscious thing Judy Price would do for fourteen years.

Now as she sat by the window of the hospital, tears ran down her cheeks. Oh, how wrong she had been back then. Poor Doreen! How she must feel about her mother now, Judy thought. All those spankings! Spankings and punishments over and over. Her guilt became painful again. So painful that when the fog began to cloud her mind once more, she welcomed it.

* * * *

Deborah had checked into a hotel close to the hospital. She had not told Doreen. She had pretended to still be asleep while Doreen had gotten her uniform on to go to work. As soon as Doreen had left for the hospital that morning, quietly closing the door behind her, Deborah had gotten up, repacked her suitcase and left. She had left Dory a note of explanation, claiming that she had wanted to stay in a hotel to be near their mother. After she had checked into her hotel she had unpacked her suitcase, taken a hot steaming shower, and had dressed herself in one of her new maternity slack sets.

She had spent over fifteen minutes looking at herself in the bathroom mirror, trying to get used to her new motherly image, all the while gently rubbing her swollen abdomen. She had smiled at the woman in the mirror. Yes, it was true, she had decided. Expectant women definitely had a glow around them. A pink and blue glow.

Wait until her mother saw her, Deborah thought to herself as she walked proudly down the hospital corridor which led to her mother's room. The sickly clean smell of disinfectant mixed with the pungent odor of ill people filled her nostrils, but she took no notice of it. She opened the heavy wood door of her mother's small room and quietly peeked inside. Her mother lay on the bed staring at the ceiling, her face expressionless, her blue eyes shadowed and blank.

"TAAA-DAAA!" Deborah said, throwing her lightly tanned arms open wide and turning herself around several times so her mother could see her new look.

Judy Price kept her eyes on the ceiling.

"Mom?" There was no response. "Mom, what's wrong?" Again no response. Deborah walked to the side of the bed and stared down at the mother she hardly knew. Disappointed that her mother would not look at her new clothes, Deborah slapped Judy Price sharply across the face. "I hate you! Do you hear me? I hate you!" she screamed. "You'll never see me again! And you'll never see my baby! Not EVER!"

* * * *

Joe Sterling didn't mind doing chores around the house. In fact, he enjoyed it. Except laundry. He hated washing, drying, folding and hanging up clothes. It was a boring task but one that he couldn't avoid doing when Deborah wasn't around. He had contemplated taking the dirty laundry to the Laundromat in town where they would do it all for you at a reasonable price, but then had decided that he really had nothing better to do. Besides, he could watch television and do the laundry during the commercials.

Joe suddenly realized that the commercial was almost over and he had not yet worked on the laundry. He jumped up and went to the small laundry room just off the kitchen. When he lifted the door of the washer he was shocked to see the clothes still sitting in water. He turned the dial only to learn that the machine would do no more than hum.

"Damn transmission must have jammed," he said aloud, "or the stupid motor burned out." He swore under his breath and pulled the electrical cord out of the socket. "Always something!" he grumbled, pulling the washer away from the wall and turning it sideways so that he could take the back panel off to try to figure out the problem. He suddenly stopped, his anger forgotten. There on the floor behind the washer lay some of Deborah's clothes in a heap.

That's unlike her, Joe thought to himself. Deborah was a very tidy person, who insisted that everything had a place and that everything should be in its place when not in use. He bent down and picked up the beige slacks and the brown knit maternity blouse. Both were darkly stained. Joe studied the stains up close. It appeared to him to be blood. Now how the hell would her clothes get covered with blood? And why would she hide them behind the washing machine? It didn't make any sense.

Joe had a sinking feeling in his stomach. Had she aborted the baby? That was a stupid thought, he decided. They had waited so long for her to get pregnant. She had really wanted the baby, had been so happy when she had found out that she was finally pregnant. Was that why she had gone up North, he wondered. Had something happened to the pregnancy and she just didn't know how to tell him? Oh God! Maybe she wasn't even planning to come back!

Joe could feel panic mounting inside him. This was ridiculous, he decided. All he had to do was call and talk to her. They had always talked things out. There had never been any secrets between them. Not until now, anyway. He placed the clothes gently on the kitchen counter. He seemed unable to take his eyes off of them, and a foreboding ominous feeling hung over him like a large storm cloud that sent flashes of lightening everywhere to warn of heavy rains coming.

He sat down heavily at the table, resembling a man whose spirit had just been broken. He just didn't know what he should do. Maybe he should just forget it, put the clothes back where he had found them and pretend the washer and dryer had never been moved. Just make the cloud disappear.

But he knew he could not and would not forget it. Better to accept the approaching storm and maybe it would all turn out all right. Maybe he and Deborah would not get wet.

Joe got up and slowly reached for the phone. What would Deborah say when he told her that he had found the clothes she had hidden. Would she deny it? He put the receiver back down in its cradle. What if she didn't deny it. What if she told him how the blood ended up on her clothes and why those clothes were hidden behind the washer. Did he really want to know? He picked up the telephone receiver and dialed Doreen's number. He HAD to know.

"Hello," Doreen said after three rings.

"Doreen?"

"Yes. Who's this?"

"It's Joe. How are you doing?" Joe asked, his fingers caressing the material of the clothes.

"Fine, Joe. How about you?"

"Good. Look, is Deborah there? I just want to say hello."

"Oh, miss her, do you? Well, so do I. I have no idea where your wife, and my sister, may be."

"Oh? Is she out running around, shopping for more baby things?" He could just see her going from store to store, packages cradled under her arms, shopping bags hanging from her hands.

"Well, Joe, I don't know about that. I came home today and found a note from her telling me that she wanted to stay in a hotel closer to our mother's hospital. Other than that, I have no idea what hotel she went to or where she is. She really is in a weird mood," Doreen stated flatly.

"A weird mood? Like what?" Joe was getting alarmed.

"I don't know, really. Just kind of touchy.

Maybe it's due to her pregnancy. Maybe it's because our mother came out of her comatose state."

"But I should think that those two things would make her happy. Do me a favor, Dor, if you should talk to her, please tell her to call me, will you?"

"Sure, Joe. If I see or talk to her, I will. I'm going over to see my mother later. I'll try to locate her for you, okay?"

"Thanks. I would appreciate it. She hasn't been feeling well. Between her migraine headaches and her pregnancy she's been kind of weak and dizzy. I just want to know that she's okay."

"Sure, I'll do it. You take care of yourself and don't worry. I'm sure she's fine."

Joe thanked Doreen again and hung up. Everything seemed to be getting out of control. A couple of days ago, his world was great. Now he didn't know what was happening.

He picked up the clothes again and absently traced the stain on the slacks with his finger. He stared out the window, his mind trying to decipher the facts from the fears. There could be a logical explanation. Joe watched the Spanish Moss on the trees outside sway in the cool Florida breeze. A red male cardinal landed on a branch and fluttered back and forth. It was soon joined by a female brown one, who stayed for a few seconds before flying away. The male followed.

Joe turned away from the window and again picked up the telephone. "Pete? This is Joe. I need a favor."

"Sure, what?" Pete asked

"I have some clothes I want checked. They appear to have blood stains and I thought maybe you could tell me for sure."

"Hey, Joe, that's no problem at all. Just drop

them by my lab and I'll handle it for you."

"Well, I'd like this kept just between us. It's very important, Pete, or I wouldn't ask."

"Something personal, huh? No sweat, Joe. Consider it done and then forgotten. Okay?"

Joe thanked him and hung up. He got a brown Publix grocery bag from the kitchen drawer and put the clothes in it. With the washer long forgotten he left the house.

Chapter 25

Judy Price sat in front of her dresser mirror and stared at her reflection. When had she grown old? she wondered, holding lifeless strands of her hair away from her head. She wrapped them around her finger, held them that way for a few seconds and then released them. They fell straight again, limp and drab. The last time she remembered looking in a mirror she had been young and not too bad looking. In fact, she decided, she had been pretty.

She smiled at herself. One top incisor was missing and one front tooth on the bottom. How had that happened? She could not remember. Her eyes scanned her face, taking note of the dark circles under her eyes, the sunken cheeks and the cracked lips. Tears formed in the corners of her eyes until they slowly fell down her hollow cheeks.

Judy reached up and wiped the tears away with one thin hand. She noticed how thin and bony her hands and fingers were. She stood up and opened her bathrobe. Her flannel nightgown hung on her frame like a sheet on a pole. She pulled the nightgown tight around her body, holding the soft material behind her back. "My God," Judy said to herself, "there's no shape left. None at all."

"Don't worry! We'll fatten you up again," Doreen said, standing in the door, her arms loaded with packages.

Judy quickly let the material go and her nightgown fell back down. She stared at Doreen, the tears still glistening in her sad blue eyes.

"Come on, Mom, don't cry. It's my birthday, but the presents are for you." Doreen opened the door wider and a woman about Judy's age walked in carrying a medium size suitcase in one hand and a large Indian burlap pouch with embroidered western symbols of different colors in the other. Doreen held a large white box, a slightly smaller one, and a shoe box.

Judy's gaze went back to the woman. She had platinum blonde hair cut short in the back and the sides were feathered back over her ears. The top was curly and appeared to be wet, the tips of the curls framing her face were colored a light brown. The woman's face was perfectly made up in eye shades of blue with her cheeks and lips pink.

"Mom, this is Dana, my hairdresser. She's going to make you look wonderful." Doreen set the boxes on the bed. "When she's through, these new clothes will add to the final picture." She opened the large box and took out a pretty blue cotton shirt dress with a white collar and white cuffs on the sleeves. She laid it on the bed and opened the second box, which held a pale blue uplift bra, matching panties and half slip, and suntan colored panty-hose. From the shoe box, Doreen pulled out a pair of new white leather pumps.

"What do you think? Nurse Durfmier said I could take you to the cafeteria for lunch, so I thought you'd like to go dressed up. And look! I even remembered to bring earrings," Doreen said, holding a small white button earring in her hand.

The woman, Dana, started opening the suitcase, which carried curlers, brushes and combs, shampoo and conditioner and styling mousse. The red, yellow, blue and green decorated Indian pouch contained make-up of all kinds, nail polishes and creams. She looked up and smiled at Judy Price, who had remained where she was as if in a shocked trance. Judy gave her a weak smile in return.

"Okay, Mrs. Price," Dana said, "shall we get started?"

* * * *

Deborah laid on the full size bed in her hotel room decorated in shades of blues and greens, and stared at the TV screen. She had not bothered to go see her mother last night, nor today, either. Her suitcase was packed, ready to take her home. Home to Joe. Home to familiar surroundings. Home to friends, and warm sunny days which would take the New Jersey chill out of her bones. Home to where she would again be away from Doreen with her paranoia and away from her crazy selfish mother. To think that either of them would be excited about her baby, or the fact that she was even there at all, was a stupid assumption on her part, she decided. She might as well have stopped strangers on the street and saved herself the plane ticket.

She rolled over onto her right side, folding her knees slightly up and tucking her hands together under her pillow. She was bitter and angry and she knew it. She just didn't understand why. The rage that burned inside her was not new -- it had burned there always, smoldering since she was very young. Deborah sometimes wondered if she had been born with it, because she could not remember when it had started.

It wasn't that she didn't love Doreen, but why couldn't Doreen have been an older sister? Or a younger one? Why did she not only have to be the same age, but she had to have the same face, the same hair, the same body. The same body. No, not the same body. Doreen's body was ugly! She was a freak! Deborah smiled and turned to again lay on her back, her hands behind her head. The thought and the smile brought feelings of guilt to her consciousness and it laid heavy on her chest.

Deborah suddenly felt a kick in her upper abdomen. She lay perfectly still. It happened again. A kind of fluttery soft feeling rippled across her insides. She put a hand palm down on her stomach. Again the sensation occurred, a little stronger kick this time. *It's kicking harder*, she thought, *it's kicking harder and longer than usual.* She reached over, picked up the receiver and asked the operator for her home phone collect. After a few seconds, her home phone twelve hundred miles away began to ring. And ring. There was no answer.

Deborah hung up the telephone, disappointed that Joe had not been home to hear her wonderful news about how active their baby was now. She'd tell him when he picked her up at the airport tonight. "Must be out working," she said to her unborn baby, her hands lovingly caressing her enlarged abdomen. "Daddy's trying to catch a bad murderer. Don't worry, my little baby, your daddy is a wonderful deputy. He'll catch him."

Chapter 26

Alma Browne had spent the morning trying to describe the mysterious nurse she had seen in the food line the day Dr. Kaufman had been killed, but no matter what the artist had done on paper, the woman had shook her head. Finally they had given up. The portrait could be one of any number of people.

Detective Dave Selten sat frustrated at his desk, a lit cigarette burning between his fingers, the files of Drs. Walters, Parker and Kaufman lying open on his desk. There had to be a motive, a link to all three. Except for the fact that they were all men, all surgeons, and that they were associated with Metropolitan Hospital, there was no other obvious connection. He was sure that they were all killed by the same person, but who was she? And why?

"Here you go, Dave," Sgt. Tacker said, dropping a manila folder on Dave's desk.

"What's this?" Dave asked, opening the folder.

"The report on the fingerprints for the first and second shift personnel in Met's lab."

"And?"

"Nothing. Not even close. Not one person's fingerprints even came close."

Dave said nothing. His eyes read the report, his mind absorbing the facts, and his stomach churned some bile up into his throat. He took a roll of Tums out of the top drawer of his desk, popped two white tablets into his mouth and chewed slowly.

"Look, Dave," Tacker said quietly, "why don't you let it alone for a while. You're supposed to be off today. Go home, watch television, drink a few beers. Better yet, go get laid. You'll feel better if you get the tension out of your system."

Dave stared at him. Maybe he was right, he thought to himself. Sometimes you can't see the forest for the trees, as his father used to say. If he tried to forget it for a while, maybe he would see something he was missing. Besides, he had a date with Doreen tonight. He had almost forgotten.

"You're right, Tacker," he said, closing all the files and setting them to one side of his desk. "If you'll excuse me."

After Sgt. Tacker had left the room, Dave called Doreen and confirmed their date, telling her to get dressed for dancing and dinner and that he would pick her up between seven and seven thirty. He then called for an appointment to get his hair cut. Finally he cast a final look at the folders resting on the desk. Picking up his cigarettes, he walked out the door.

* * * *

"Yes, Operator, I'll accept it," Joe said into the telephone.

"Hi, Sweetheart! Miss me?" Deborah asked.

"Where the hell are you, Debbie?" Joe barked at her.

"I'm at the Atlanta airport," she replied

sheepishly, hurt in her voice. "I tried to call you last night and again this morning, but there was no answer."

"I'm sorry, I shouldn't have snapped at you, but I was worried sick. I called Doreen and she told me that she had no idea where you had gone. I waited to hear from you, to find out where you were. You scared the shit out of me, Deb."

"I'm sorry, Joe. I, uh, just couldn't stay with Doreen. She was acting weird."

"Funny. That's what she said about you. Are you sure you're all right?"

"I'm fine, really. I'm sorry. I didn't mean to scare you. But I have some good news!"

Joe wondered if he should bring up the bloody clothes or the baby. "What is it?" he asked her.

"The baby's moving a lot now. Really kicking hard!"

Joe wasn't sure he had heard it right. Did this mean everything was okay?

"Joe, did you hear me? I said the baby is really getting active. It really is. I mean, it wasn't much at first, but the kicks got harder and harder." Deborah hesitated. "Joe, are you still there?"

"Yes, honey, I'm still here." He couldn't believe it! The baby was fine. And alive! "Are you sure the baby's all right?"

"Oh, yes, Joe. YES!" She couldn't contain her excitement. The airport loud speaker announced that her flight was now boarding at Gate 33.

"Deb, why did you move out of Doreen's? What's the matter up th ... "

"Joe, I've got to run and board my plane. I'll be home in about an hour. Don't forget I'm coming into Daytona Airport. I'll explain everything when I get home. I love you."

"I love you, too. Have a good flight home," Joe

said, but Deborah had already hung up. He went to the coffee table, picked up the lab report and again read the words: HUMAN BLOOD :TYPE AB NEGATIVE. Not Deborah's blood type. Whose then? And why? Had she lent her clothes to someone else? Joe doubted it. Again, it was uncharacteristic for her. He picked up the telephone.

"Hello?" Dr. Donald Turner said, answering his telephone.

"Hi, Doc, it's me, Joe."

"Hey, Joe, how's it going?"

"Fine. Listen, can you tell me the different blood types of Martin and Baines. I don't have the files here at the house, but I'm trying to balance it out," Joe lied.

"Sure. Hold on," the coroner answered. After a few moments he said, "Joe? You still there?"

"Yes."

"Martin was O positive and Baines was AB negative."

AB negative? The fact was seeping into Joe's brain. But how could Debbie have had anything to do with an old migrant worker's death?

"Joe, anything else?" the M.E. asked, puzzled by the deputy's non-response.

"Oh, sorry. I was writing. Thanks, I appreciate you looking it up."

"No problem. See ya'." The M.E. hung up.

Joe held the receiver in his hand until the dial tone whined in his ear. AB NEGATIVE. Baines was stabbed over and over. He hid the report out in the garage in his tool box, and picking up his truck keys, he headed out the door to pick up his wife at the airport.

* * * *

Dave held Doreen close to him, swaying to the old tune "Tiny Bubbles", smelling the mixture of the sweet clean scent of her hair and the light scent of her rose bouquet cologne. She felt right in his thick muscular arms, her slender taut body pressed against his. He made a slow turn and she automatically followed his every movement. He moved his face slightly toward her, and taking a chance, lightly kissed her ear. He felt her body tense and then again relax when he made no further overtures.

"Dance Ballerina Dance" started, and Dave, reluctant to let her go, began to twirl her around the dance floor. Doreen did not miss a beat. He loved the old songs of the swing era of the forties and the rock tunes of the fifties, so he had taken her to a little club in Linden, New Jersey, where they featured this type of music, except on Sunday nights, which was strictly polka music night.

The Starlight Lounge was almost completely filled to capacity. The single men and women (and those that wished they were single) all stayed around the bar area, while the couples and the married people sat at the wooden tables surrounding the larger dance floor. To the back of the dance floor was the band platform, where a five piece band played for a half hour and then broke for a twenty minute rest by the bar.

Dave led Doreen back to their table and motioned for the waitress. Doreen pulled a cigarette from her purse and Dave picked up the matches in the ashtray and lit it for her. As soon as the waitress appeared at their table, Dave ordered another round of drinks.

Doreen watched the couple at the next table holding hands, whispering secret words to one another around small intermittent kisses. She glanced back at Dave who sat smiling at her, his soft brown eyes shining. She leaned forward slightly and warmly smiled back. There was a small fire growing inside her that Doreen could not identify. Sometimes it was just a fluttery feeling, sometimes a real hint of desire. She tried to ignore it, hoping whatever was causing it would just simply go away.

Dave reached across the table and covered her small delicate hand with his large one. The heat from his touch sent small electrical sparks through her, making the fire inside her flare up as if it was being fanned.

"Doreen, do you believe in love at first sight?" he asked her quietly. When she didn't respond he continued. "I never have. I mean, I've always felt that love was a feeling that grew as you got to really know someone." He paused, looking deep into her big blue eyes, trying to see what she might be feeling. There was not so much as a hint of reaction to what he was trying to say.

"I've kept myself busy with my work most of my life," he went on. "There never seemed to be time for feelings. Maybe because I never allowed myself to have any emotions. Until I met you. I don't understand what it is about you that keeps me feeling like a clumsy adolescent. I mean, I'm a full grown, middle-aged man, but you make me feel young. Even restless. There's an urgency building up inside of me that I can't fully explain." He hesitated, removing his hand from hers, and sat back in his chair, his colloquy stayed.

Doreen reflected for a moment, and then extended her right hand palm up to him. Dave took it and closed her slim hand, her fingers stroking his. Her eyes glistened, her smile warm and sensitive. Dave had never seen her look more beautiful or more feminine than she did at this moment.

"I feel good around you, too. Safe. That's it. I feel safe, as if no-one will hurt me ever again. David, you've put..." Doreen searched for the right words. "You've put a warm glow inside me, one which I can't describe."

The waitress brought their drinks to the table. She smiled at them knowingly. Dave took out his black tri-fold wallet and handed her a five dollar bill. She thanked him and moved back into the dimness of the lounge. The small candle on the table cast a deep amber glow on both their faces.

"Doreen, I think I..." Dave began, but the band had returned to the stage and were now playing "Heart and Soul". Dave took Doreen by the hand and led her to the dance floor.

As the night wore on, Doreen had found herself wishing more and more that this night would never end. She had not wanted to leave the safety of Dave's presence. And by midnight she knew she had gotten her wish. Although Dave's apartment was shabby in comparison to her own, his large king size bed was comfortable, his love-making sweet, considerate, and for the first time in her twenty-five years, climatic. As she slept peacefully in Dave's arms, her breathing soft and deep, he kissed her pretty face lightly.

"I love you, Doreen," he whispered to the sleeping woman. "And you'll always be safe. I promise."

* * * *

As Deborah slept serenely, her husband, Joe, sat in the pale green bedroom chair watching her. He had not brought up the bloodstained clothes or the fact that the blood on them matched one of the unsolved murders in Flagler County. She had told him on the way home from the airport all about Doreen's fear that a long deceased doctor was trying to kill her and that Doreen needed mental counseling.

Joe had held Deborah as she had tried to tell him about her mother's empathy regarding her pregnancy, had held her as she had cried it all out. He had wanted to take her out to dinner at La Crepe En Haut, an exclusive French restaurant in Ormond Beach, to celebrate her twenty-fifth birthday, but Deborah had not been in a celebrating mood. They had stopped at McDonalds on the way home, for burgers and fries instead.

Now as he sat there quietly watching his wife sleep, the inner turmoil continued. Should he ask her about the clothes and face the consequences the question may bring, or leave it alone and go on as though nothing was out of the ordinary? He decided that he did not want to know, and so, for the time being anyway, he would not mention it. Joe slowly stood up and walked over to his side of the bed. After he had settled himself comfortably between the crisp white percale sheets, he rolled onto his left side and gathered his wife into his arms. Deborah murmured faintly and snuggled in against him.

"Happy birthday, Sweetheart," he muttered softly, kissing her ear. "I love you."

Chapter 27

Thanksgiving came and went. In Florida Joe and Deborah Sterling had celebrated with a quiet turkey dinner for two followed by a lazy stroll on Flagler Beach, holding hands and walking ankle deep in the cooling Atlantic waters.

In New Jersey Doreen had spent the day with Dave and her mother, having their turkey feast at a small restaurant close to the sanitarium. It had been Judy Price's first day away from the hospital and she had been like a child seeing the outside world for the first time. Judy Price had liked David, hoping that Doreen would settle down with him in the near future.

Christmas was fast approaching, and throughout the United States, things were being decorated in red, white, green, silver and gold. People were in festive moods, shopping for presents, baking cookies, pies and fancy desserts, and entertaining family and friends, new and old.

The Price sisters were no different. Deborah and Joe Sterling were busy, not only decorating their home for the holidays, but redoing the second bedroom into a nursery for their soon to be born child.

Dave Selten had decided to move into Doreen's apartment, and the arrangement had proved to be a happy one for both.

There had been no further migraine headaches for either twin.

Chapter 28

Doreen stepped off the elevator on her floor at Metropolitan Hospital to find that the Edison Crime Lab crew had set-up a fingerprinting section, where every staff member was taking a turn being fingerprinted. She glanced around and spotted Dave standing to one side by the nurse's counter talking to one of the new student nurses. The pretty young brunette was smiling up at him while he talked. They both laughed at something he said. Doreen could feel the rage boiling up inside her. She turned and pressed the down button for the elevator. The dull pounding had started behind her eyes and was rapidly spreading to her temples.

"Dory? Where are you going, honey?" Dave asked, coming up behind her.

"What? What did you call me?"

"Honey. Hey, you're white as a sheet. What's wrong? Are you all right?"

"Yes. I mean, I have a migraine starting. I've got to go home. I've got to lie down." The elevator door opened. "I'll see you at home later."

"No, you won't. I'm coming with you. We'll leave your car here and come get it later, or tomorrow I'll bring you to work," Dave said, getting into the elevator with her, his hand on her arm for support.

"You don't need to do that. I'll be fine. Really."

"Now, don't argue with me, young lady. I still wear the trousers in this twosome," he said smiling. "I think."

As the doors closed Sergeant Tacker walked over to one of the nurses. "Doreen Price is next. Could you point her out to me?"

"Sorry. I haven't seen her yet today. She must be late. Unless she called off work today."

"When you see her, send her to us, okay? How about De Garre? Is she here?"

The nurse pointed to Linda De Garre going through the patient charts. Sgt. Tacker walked over to the strawberry-blond nurse behind the counter. "Mrs. Linda De Garre? Please step over there to the table for fingerprinting."

* * * *

Deborah stood staring at her reflection in the large oval floor mirror which hung suspended in a maple frame on a stand. She had found it at an Estate sale and had decided that she must have it. She had always loved standing before it and seeing her reflection smiling back at her. Today was different, though. Today in her beautiful mirror she saw a fat woman. A woman whose swollen abdomen was making her look grotesque. And ugly! Even her face, arms and legs looked fatter.

Deborah pulled her long brown hair up behind her head, some shorter strands falling around her face. She quickly let her hair fall again, realizing that with her hair up she again looked like her sister, Dory, with her short haircut. She looked at her abdomen again. *Oh God*, she thought, *I'm ugly. A freak! A freak like Dory!* Joe wouldn't want her anymore if she was a freak! He'd find someone else.

Someone young, someone pretty, someone slim.

She walked over to her nightstand and looked down at the picture of her and Joe which was taken two years before when they had gone to Busch Gardens in Tampa, Florida.

Her head started to ache, starting at the base of her skull and slowly working its pain to her forehead and temples. She put the picture face down on the maple nightstand, and opened the little drawer. She reached in and took out a pair of scissors. *A freak! Sisters to the end! Identical twin freaks*, she thought, walking back to the oval mirror.

The pain now stabbed her behind the eyes, causing blurred vision. She reached up and grabbed a lock of her beautiful long, shiny brown hair with one hand, and with the scissors, cut off a chunk of hair. Twin freaks should look like twin freaks, she decided, and continued until the gold carpeted floor around the base of the mirror was covered with shiny brown swatches of curls.

* * * *

Dave had gotten Doreen home and into bed, had made her some tea with honey and lemon, and had then sat on the bed rubbing her temples. She had been arrogant and hostile, but had refused to talk about whatever was bothering her. He had finally chocked it up to PMS and let her sleep while he went back to the hospital. He knew he loved her more than he would have thought possible, but the realization was more pleasurable than worrisome. It was time that he settled down, got married again and had a home. A real home.

There was no need for Doreen to work anymore, unless she preferred it that way. He could take care of her on his income. Maybe they could even have a child of their own. He wasn't so old really, he decided. Men older than him were fathering babies, so why shouldn't he? But would she say yes if he asked her to marry him, he wondered, stepping out of the elevator onto the fourth floor at Metropolitan Hospital.

"Hi, Dave. I wondered where you went off to," Sgt. Tacker said when Dave reached him.

"Had to leave for a bit. How's it going?"

"Fine. We finished the day shift, except for..." The sergeant riffled through the computer sheets on his clipboard. "Except for a Betty Miller and a Doreen Price. We'll do them tomorrow. The shifts just changed and we've started on the second shift for this floor. Sure is time consuming. You never realize how many people work in a hospital until you start something like this."

"Well, you don't have to worry about doing Doreen Price. I know her personally. In fact," Dave said, lowering his voice, "I'm about to ask her to marry me. If she'll marry an old flatfoot like me."

"Well, hey, that's great! She couldn't find a better guy and I mean that, Dave," Tacker said, shaking Dave's hand.

"Detective Selten? You'd better come over here for a minute," Officer Joan Warner said, coming up to the two men.

"What's the problem?" Dave asked, looking toward the fingerprinting area.

"There's an LPN refusing to be fingerprinted. Claims it's unconstitutional, against her legal rights, etc."

Dave walked over to the irate nurse. "What seems to be the problem?"

"Look here. Am I charged with anything that I need to be fingerprinted for?" she asked hotly.

"No, ma'am, you're not charged with anything, but I am sure that you must know that three doctors, all associated with this hospital, and this floor in particular, have been murdered. Everyone who works here at Metropolitan is being fingerprinted. By allowing us to fingerprint you, unless you had something to do with those victims, you will be cleared and can go on your way," Dave tried to reason with her. He looked at her long dark hair tied up in a bun on top of her head, and then down at her feet.

"Well, I'm not going to do it! I had nothing to do with those killings. And I want to talk this over with my attorney. I'll sue the police department, the city, the county and YOU!" She was beginning to get hysterical.

"Would you please come with us and we'll discuss this at the precinct?" Dave asked her, taking her by the arm.

The nurse pulled her arm away from him. "Not until I talk to my attorney!" she screamed at him, tears forming in the corners of her eyes.

"You can talk to your attorney from the station house. There's really no reason for you being this upset. Or do you have good reason to be alarmed?" he asked, again taking her by the arm, holding her a little tighter this time. Sgt. Tacker took hold of her other arm.

"You're going to be sorry about this, I promise you both!" she threatened, crying openly now. She pulled her arm free from Sgt. Tacker's grip and smashed her fist into Dave's chest. He grabbed her with both hands and pinned her arms until Tacker got his handcuffs on her.

"I haven't done anything! I swear! Please!" she begged them.

"Yes, you have," Sgt. Tacker coldly replied to

the weeping woman. "You just assaulted a police officer!"

* * * *

"Debbie, I'm home," Deputy Joe Sterling announced as he came through the garage door into the kitchen. He looked at the stove and was surprised to see that no dinner was cooking. He walked over and peered into the oven. Nothing. "Debbie?" He walked through the small dining room and down the hall to their bedroom.

Joe stood in the doorway and surveyed the room. Deborah lay sleeping across the unmade bed, the crumpled sheets almost on the floor. His eyes stared at her chopped up short hair, then moved their gaze to the locks of long brown hair lying scattered on the floor by the mirror, and finally came to rest on the scissors now lying among the cut hair, their jaws wide open.

Joe was puzzled as well as alarmed. "Debbie? Are you all right? What's wrong? Debbie?"

She opened her eyes slowly and blinked several times until her eyes focused. She looked up at Joe's worried face and smiled.

"Debbie, what the hell happened? What did you do to yourself?"

"What do you mean?" she asked, still groggy with sleep.

"What do I mean? Debbie, why did you chop up your hair?"

Now it was Deborah's turn to be puzzled. She reached up and ran her hand through her hair, feeling the shortness. She pushed herself to a sitting position, rubbed the sleep from her eyes, and yawned. Again she felt her hair. She looked at Joe questioningly. He pointed to the floor by the mirror. Her eyes followed his direction until she saw the hair and the scissors. Still perplexed, her hand continued to stroke her short hair.

"Well?" Joe asked again.

"I, uh, don't know," she stammered. "I had this dream that Doreen was cutting my hair to look like hers. Said we should look like the identical twins that we are. She, uh, said that I was fat and ugly. That I was a freak like her! I'm not, Joe, am I? I'm not a freak like Dory, am I? Am I?" She was crying now.

"Deborah, listen to me," Joe said softly, trying to calm her down.

"It's not true, is it, Joe? I'm not fat and ugly. You still love me, don't you, Joe? She said that I was fat and ugly and a freak and that you would find someone else and leave me! You won't, will you?" She was hysterical now, holding onto the front of Joe's uniform shirt.

"Debbie..."

"Doreen did it! She cut my hair short to look like her! She wants me to be ugly like her! She's always wanted me to be ugly -- to be a freak like her! Don't you see, Joe, she's always been jealous of me because I was normal. I was pretty. I am pretty, Joe, aren't I?" she sobbed, leaning against his chest, her tears staining his tan shirt.

"Debbie, Doreen is not here in Florida. She's up in New Jersey. She couldn't have cut your hair, Sweetheart."

"She did it. I'm telling you she did it! She doesn't want me to have you. Oh, Joe, please keep her away from me from us! She might want to hurt the baby, or you! Oh, please, Joe, promise me that you will keep her away!"

"I promise, Debbie, I promise. Here, you lie down here and I'll get you something to drink..."

"I don't want anything to drink! Please, don't leave me, Joe! Please! I'm afraid. Don't leave me!"

"I'm only going to get something from the kitchen. I'll be right back. I promise. I'm not going to leave you." He laid her back down on the bed, and covered her sobbing body with the top sheet. When he reached the bedroom door he looked back at her. Deborah lay on her side mumbling over and over that Doreen had done it.

Joe hurried into the kitchen, and picking up the telephone, called Dr. Brenner's office.

Chapter 29

Judy Price was getting stronger each day, mentally and physically. She spent her days reading everything she could get her hands on, especially newspapers and old magazines. She wanted to know not only what was going on today in the world outside the hospital, but also what had gone on while she was "sleeping" for all those years. The old magazines helped provide that missing information.

The attendants brought in all the magazines they could find, and Judy was very appreciative. She found herself amazed at the many changes that had occurred in the world, in the outer space race, in fashion, and particularly in the way women themselves had changed. According to the different articles, women were more career minded than before, more aggressive in social situations, more demanding of equal rights in general.

Judy had decided that as soon as she could she would go to college and get a degree of some kind. She didn't know what it was that she wanted to learn, but she would figure that out when the time came for her to go.

Judy walked over to the mirror and looked at her new reflection. Her hair was looking healthier, shinier and thicker. Her face had more color in it and she was eating more than she could remember ever eating, so she had gained almost ten pounds already. Her eyes no longer had that deep sunken look and her cheeks had filled out slightly, giving her a more rounded smooth complexion.

She spoke to Doreen almost every day now, either by telephone or in person. She was happy that Doreen was finally in love and that David loved her also. She had given her daughter her blessing when Doreen had told her that David was moving in. It truly seemed to be working out well for them.

Judy had tried to call her daughter, Deborah, on several occasions, but the first time she had called there had been no answer, the second time the line had been busy, and the third and last time she had called, Joe had told her that Deborah was ill and couldn't come to the phone but that he would have her call as soon as she was able. Deborah still had not called.

Next week was Christmas. Judy was going to New York City with Doreen and Dave to see the lit-up Christmas tree in Rockefeller Center, and she couldn't contain her excitement. She decided that she would try to reach Deborah again on Christmas Eve. The doctor said that if her progress continued, she would be able to leave the hospital before the first of the year. If so, she decided, she would take a trip to Florida to spend time with Deborah when she had her baby. Imagine! A baby! A grandbaby! Judy Price couldn't wait. It was going to be a wonderful new year for all of them!

Chapter 30

"Mrs. Wellington is discharged, Doreen," Dr. Willett said, sitting down at the nurse's counter to write prescriptions and orders. "Make sure that she takes these two scripts with her for her meds. I don't want her to have to call me Christmas Day because she forgot them. That woman can be so demanding."

Like you doctors aren't, Doreen thought. "Yes, Doctor," she said aloud.

"Hi, Detective Dave," the little dark haired student nurse chirped in a sing-song voice. Doreen turned sharply and stared at Dave and Bonnie Trimball.

"How are you doing, Bonnie?" Dave asked.

"Fine. Are you doing more fingerprinting or have you moved up to frisking everyone," Bonnie chirped again.

"No to both," Dave answered.

"Miss Trimball, have you cleaned up Mrs. Rodriguez yet?" Doreen snapped at the girl.

"I was just going, Doreen," the girl answered, her eyes still on Dave.

"Miss Trimball, I would appreciate your addressing me as Miss Price and not as one of your friends," Doreen corrected her. "And move your fanny and get your work done."

"Yes, ma'am, Miss Price. Bye, Dave," she said, hurrying down the hall to room 417, her young face flushed pink by Doreen's crisp words.

"Don't you think you were a little hard on her? She's just a kid," Dave said to Doreen. She glared back at him in response.

"Do you always get so chummy with KIDS? Or is she an exception?"

"Why, Miss Price, could it be that you're a little jealous of a student nurse?" Dave asked her with a wry smile.

"What are you doing here, Dave?"

"Come to take you to lunch in the hospital cafeteria. We're finishing up our fingerprinting on the top floor, so I thought that we could have lunch together. Kind of a celebration."

"Wouldn't you rather take Miss Bonnie Trimball? That way you could flirt with each other for a full hour," she retorted.

"Hey, come on, Dory. Give me a break, will you? I have no interest in that child nurse. Besides, I love you. And I have a surprise for you if you'll behave yourself and stop this nonsense."

"What is it?"

"Never mind. I'll tell you later in the cafeteria. Say in about five to ten minutes?"

"Try a half-hour and I'll meet you there. I have to wait until some of the other nurses come back from lunch. We're short-handed due to the holidays."

"Half an hour it is. Love you, Dory."

"I've asked you not to call me that. I hate that name."

"Sorry. Forgot. See you shortly," he said, running for the open elevator.

Dory! How dare he call her that? Doreen turned

to the bulletin board to tack up a memo to her
nurses regarding a training session on the AIDS
virus. He had never better call her that again or
she'd show him a Dory he'd never seen before. He
was just like every other man she had ever known
fickle. Imagine him living with her and then flirting with a damn snot-nosed little student bitch!
Men! Doctors! All the same, she decided, sticking
in the last thumbtack.

Doreen backed up to see how the memo looked
on the board.

"ATTENTION ALL SURGEONS!!!

You are cordially invited to attend the Bembbar
Seminar Dinner to be held at 7 p.m. at the Emerald Restaurant in Rahway on December 27th.

Topic of Discussion: Multi-By-Pass Surgery
Guest Speaker: Dr. Robert McAllister
RSVP by December 12th
ALL SURGEONS INVITED!!"

Of course! The seminar. She had almost
forgotten about it. Dr. Robert McAllister. The guest
speaker was him!! Dr. John McClusky! Coming out
into the open again. Well, she'd show him this time!
Him, Dave, ALL OF THEM!!

"Doreen, going to lunch?" one of the nurses
asked her.

Doreen looked at her and smiled. "Yes, I sure
am."

* * * *

Dave was waiting for her when she arrived at
the cafeteria. He kissed her lightly and they got
into the buffet line. As they moved down the aisle
of food, Doreen chose a peach yogurt, a cup of tea
with lemon and a small dish of brown rice.

"How can you live the way you eat? You need

meat, potatoes, protein foods. You eat like a canary," he said, motioning to Alma Browne for French fries, meatloaf and gravy.

"Do you want me to be fat?" Doreen asked him.

"No, I guess not. But it really doesn't matter. I'd love you either way."

"What's your surprise?" she asked him, picking up her tray.

"I made reservations at the Brass Bucket in Woodbridge for us for New Year's Eve. I wanted someplace special. Someplace romantic."

"That's nice. Okay."

"That's nice? Okay? Is that all you can say?" he retorted, setting his tray on a table for two. "I know it's not the Tavern-On-The-Green, but I thought it was pretty nice. What's the matter, Doreen? You've been awful edgy lately. Did I do something?"

Yes, you're alive, well and fickle, she answered to herself. "No. I'm just a little uptight. I don't know why. By the way, I'll be a little late coming home tonight."

"Oh? Working late?"

"No, just going shopping for a few things I need. I won't be too late. I'll bring a pizza home with me. Okay? Feel like having pizza?"

"Sure, with sausage, onions and pepperoni. And I'll stop and pick up a six-pack."

"Well, I've got to get back upstairs," she said, picking up her tray.

"Hold on, I'll walk you back up," Dave said, stuffing the last piece of meatloaf in his mouth as he stood up.

Doreen and Dave set their trays on the moving conveyor belt which took the dirty dishes to the kitchen. Alma Browne stood behind the food counter and watched them, thankful that the police had found that nurse and would leave her alone now. See, she told herself, it all worked out without her. Black folks should never get involved where white folks were concerned.

* * * *

Doreen stopped at Rickles Hardware store after work and bought three kerosene cans. Next she went to three different gas stations and had each one filled, which she hid in the back of her Corvette under a blanket. Lastly, she stopped at a pizza place next to the Pickle Barrel Deli on Route 27 to get the pizza. Finished with her errands, Doreen headed home.

Chapter 31

"Hello, Sweetheart," Joe said, coming into Deborah's hospital room. "Merry Christmas! And how are you feeling today?"

"Okay. Did the doctor say I could go home now?" she asked softly.

Joe held her hand. "He didn't say, Debbie, but I think he's going to keep you here until the baby's born. That's the safest way. It's only another week or two at the most. Besides, aren't you going to wish me a Merry Christmas?"

"I'm sorry, Joe. Merry Christmas, but..." Deborah's voice trailed off, the tears slowly falling down her cheeks.

"What, Sweetheart? What is it?"

"I don't have any presents for you," she sobbed, her small hands covering her face.

Joe took both of her hands in his. "Debbie, you give me a present every day that you're my wife, every day that you love me. And this here," he said, patting her enlarged abdomen, "is the best gift you could ever give me. I love you."

"Oh, Joe, I love you, too. I'm sorry about ..."

"Never mind that. Forget it. Like Dr. Brenner said, too much stress. Besides, I brought you presents that Santa left at the house." Joe reached down and picked up the packages on the floor and set them on the bed.

Deborah again began to cry.

"Oh, Debbie, please don't cry anymore."

"I...I can't help it. I don't understand what's wrong with me anymore."

Dr. Brenner had said it was depression due to the oncoming delivery of the baby, mixed with fear and stress and anxiety caused by her sister's and mother's problems. It had all piled up and exploded. The doctor felt that she needed quiet bed rest for the termination of her pregnancy. Also, she could be watched, so that she didn't hurt herself or the baby. They had not bothered to tell her this, only that it was depression caused by the pregnancy.

"It's all going to be fine, baby, I promise. Pretty soon you'll be busy changing diapers, feeding and washing the baby, going for walks on the beach with the baby strapped on your back. You'll be very busy and you won't have to worry about being depressed. You won't have time to be depressed."

"I guess you're right, Joe," she sniffled.

"By the way, have you decided what you want to name it?"

"Well, I guess Joseph Junior if it's a boy, after you. Judith if it's a girl. After my mother, you know."

Joe wondered if he should tell her about the telephone calls. He decided it was Christmas, so maybe she would be happy about it. "Your mother's called a couple of times asking for you. She wanted to wish you a Merry Christmas. She sent you a card, too. And the top gift there is from her also. You can open your presents when you're up to it, okay?"

"Time for her medication," said a tall thin nurse

with gray hair coming into the room with a small white paper cup.

"Debbie, I have to go now. I'll call you later and see you again tomorrow. I love you." Joe bent and kissed his wife sweetly. He patted her tummy. "Bye Joe Junior or Judy."

* * * *

Joe decided to spend the rest of Christmas Day cleaning Debbie's car for her. He washed and waxed the Camaro until his reflection smiled up at him. Next he scrubbed her vinyl seats and dashboard with leather and vinyl cleaner. Joe grabbed the industrial vacuum cleaner and plugged it into the garage socket. First he vacuumed the trunk, then the floor behind the front seats. He reached under the front seat and pulled out the street map and the police flashlight which he made Deborah keep in the car in case of emergency. As he started to put them on the front seat he noticed that both were stained with a dark substance. He examined the light up close and saw the indentation in the metal.

Oh God, no, he prayed silently. *Please don't let it be so. Not again.* First the clothes, now the light and the map it rested on. What was happening? His brain told him that this dark substance was blood his heart again prayed that it wasn't.

Joe sat there for about twenty minutes staring at the flashlight and the map. His mind tried to cope with the facts and the theory that was building in his thoughts. He jumped up and ran into the house, through the kitchen, through the dining room, down the hall to the bedroom. There on the bedroom floor sat Deborah's purse. He quickly grabbed it and turned it upside down, all its contents falling out onto the carpet.

Joe did not know what he was looking for, but he searched through his wife's wallet. He felt guilty. Deborah and Joe had never trespassed on each other's personal belongings or possessions. But he had to. He had to get to the bottom of all this. He felt like he was losing his mind.

He spotted the knife he had given her for protection lying on the carpet, and gently picked it up. Joe turned it over several times in his palm before he pulled the blade out. It, too, was streaked with a dark tar-like substance. Joe knew he would have to have all three things checked as he had done with the clothes; would it prove to be human blood again? The blood of Baines and Martin? It was all too much. Deputy Joe Sterling hung his head, and for the first time since he was a child, he cried.

Chapter 32

She was running, running hard, but it was in slow motion and she seemed to not be going anywhere. She could see her little girls far ahead of her, their little arms extended out to her.

"Mommy, help me. Please help me," they were both saying at the same time, although Debbie stood on the left and Dory on the right with about thirty feet between them. She didn't know which one to run to first.

"Me, Mommy, please help me," Dory softly called to her mother.

"No, me first, Mommy, please," begged Debbie.

There seemed to be smoke filling the all white room, then red flames licking at the walls.

There was no furniture in the large sterile room, only her and her two ten-year-old twin girls. She tried to run faster, but the fire was heading toward each girl. Which one should she save? She knew she could only save one, but which one?

"Please save me, Mommy," Debbie cried. "It hurts, Mommy, it hurts."

She looked at Dory. Dory had lowered her arms and was now smiling, her face turned towards the fire. "It's all right, Mommy. The fire feels warm. The light makes me feel pretty. Do you think I'm pretty, Mommy?"

She did not seem to get any closer to either girl. Oh, God, help me, she prayed aloud. Help me save my daughters. The flames were now devouring her little twins. Debbie was screaming. Judy Price began to scream.

She opened her eyes. Her body was drenched in sweat and her face was covered with tears. Her whole body shook. It was a dream! A God-damned dream!

Judy laid back down on her pillows, inhaling large amounts of air and then exhaling slowly, trying to regain her composure. She wiped her tears with the top sheet. She glanced over at the clock sitting on the nightstand. Nine-thirty. The bright morning sun poured in the window, lighting up her hospital room. She suddenly remembered to-day was December 27th! Judy became anxious and happy, her nightmare all but forgotten. Tomorrow she was going home to live with Doreen and David! Tomorrow she was finally leaving the hospital! Tomorrow everything would be wonderful! She'd be free!!

* * * *

Funny, Dave thought as he hung up the telephone receiver. *No answer*. Doreen had called off work today. She had told him that she didn't feel well. She should be home in bed, but there was no answer. Maybe she went to the doctor for a check-up, he decided, heading for the hospital cafeteria. They had finished the fingerprinting of all the hospital personnel, and had come up blank. No-one's fingerprints had matched. Even the nurse who had refused to be fingerprinted had been innocent.

Innocent of the murder charges anyway. It seemed that her real name had turned out to be Lucy Peters, whom the FBI had been trying to locate since she had kidnapped her own two small children from her husband in Washington, DC the previous summer.

A blank! Back to square one. *Do not pass go,* he thought, *do not collect two hundred dollars.* He picked up a brown plastic tray and set a pint of milk on it.

"Can I have the roast beef with French fries and lots of gravy on both?" he asked the black woman behind the counter.

"Yessir, Detective," Alma Browne said with a wide smile. "I sure was glad to see that you had found that nurse. I guess it wasn't her that had killed those doctors, huh?"

"What?" Dave asked her. "What nurse? What are you talking about?"

"That nurse that had been in line with that young doctor who died here in the cafeteria. The one you had wanted me to describe. Remember? The artist at the police station had tried to draw her picture? That nurse."

"What do you mean, I found her?" Dave was confused. What the hell was this woman talking about?

"Well, ah, I thought that you had found her. I mean, you were here with her the other day. Don't you remember? You and her ate lunch in here the other day, sat right over there," she said, pointing to the table where Dave and Doreen had sat two days earlier.

"Are you sure?"

"Of course, I saw you."

"No, are you sure that that was the nurse?"

"Oh, yessir. That was her," she said, handing

him his plate of food. Dave turned and quickly walked out of the cafeteria. "Now, what the hell did I say?" Alma Browne asked herself, still holding the plate.

Dave ran to the pay phone outside the cafeteria and called Sergeant Tacker at the police station.

"Tack? Get the fingerprint boys back up to the hospital. I want everything on the fourth floor nurse's station dusted. Next, run all the prints against the prints on file." He thought for a minute. "I'll be at home. Call me there."

* * * *

"Deputy Joe Sterling. Can I help you?" Joe asked, answering his office phone, the hot Florida sun streaming in the small office window.

"Joe? You better get over to the hospital. Deborah's started labor early," Dr. Brenner said, a smile in his voice.

"What? It's now?"

"It's now. You're going to be a daddy today! Congratulations!"

* * * *

Doreen's New Jersey apartment was quiet when Detective Dave Selten opened the door. He looked in the small kitchen. Everything was immaculate and in its place. He walked down the hall to the bedroom. It was the same story: the bed was made, the drapes were open, and everything was spotless. Dave had tried to get Doreen to remove the bars from the windows, but she had become very upset and had been very adamant that they remain where they were. He didn't understand her fear, especially with him there now.

Dave checked the ashtrays. All had been emptied, washed and replaced in their individual locations. He opened each of her dresser drawers and examined the contents. Next he checked the kitchen drawers and cabinets. How could she be involved with those killings? he wondered. She was a brunette but she had short hair. But then it could have been long and she had cut it.

Dave went back to the bedroom and into the bathroom. He took a comb from the drawer and ran it through her hairbrush, pulling off strands of her hair which he took back to the kitchen and put in a plastic sandwich baggy. Some of the strands were longer than Doreen's hair.

Going back to the bathroom, he resumed his search through her cosmetics, her toiletries and her bathroom medicine chest. He looked over each prescription bottle: Tylenol #3 tablets, Valium, Librium and Erythromycin. He took out his note tablet and wrote down the medication names, the dates, the doctor and the pharmacy. He found that the cabinet under the sink contained shampoo, conditioner, Witch Hazel, alcohol, feminine products, her hairdryer, assorted size curling irons. He was about to put it all back when he noticed a small brown bottle in the back corner. He reached in and took it out by the cap.

Could Doreen be into cocaine? It appeared to be the type of bottle coke users carried their drug in. Dave unscrewed the cap, trying not to touch the bottle. He sniffed the contents. It didn't smell like cocaine. He put his finger over the top of the small bottle and tipped it so that a few grains of the powder was on his finger. He tasted it and spit it out. There was no taste. He replaced the top and carrying it by the cap, again went to the kitchen for another sandwich bag.

As he walked back toward the bedroom he stopped and peered into the hall closet. Coats, sweaters and formal dresses hung in clear plastic garment bags. He unzipped each one and pushed the clothes around. When he had finished this task, he started going through the boxes on the top shelves. One box contained photograph albums. Dave sat down on the floor and began to look through each one.

Oh my God, he thought. *She's a twin! She has an identical sister*. He stared at both faces in each picture, when they were babies, when they were pre-teens, when they were grown. There were no pictures of either girl when they were teen-agers. Another fact that was strange: in each picture only one girl was smiling, the other was somber. And on the somber girl, someone, probably Doreen, had drawn a zigzag line down the right side of that girl in each photo.

He tried to remember. Every time he had made love to Doreen she had insisted that all the lights were off, but he had felt something on her side as his hands had explored her body. Was it a scar? Was that the reason for the lights always being off during sex, the reason she would change in the bathroom, the reason she had always refused to take showers with him? He had thought her overly modest, that she would get over it as time went by and she felt more comfortable with him. Where had she gotten the scar, if that's what it was? If she was a twin, where was her sister? Why hadn't she or her mother ever mentioned her?

Doreen's mother! Of course. He admonished himself for not thinking of it sooner. He would go to see Judy Price. He would learn from her all the answers to this mysterious girl whom he wanted to marry. Dave hurriedly shoved the boxes back up on the shelf, dropping a hat which sat perched up there. He reached down and scoffed it up and spotted the piece of pipe hidden in the corner behind one of the garment bags. He pushed the bag aside and took out the pipe. He stared at it for a few seconds, and after putting the hat back in its place on the shelf, took the pipe and the two sandwich bags with evidence and left for the coroner's office.

* * * *

"May I help you, Miss?" the saleswoman asked Doreen politely.

"Yes, I, uh, would like to try on the gown in the window. The one with the stars," Doreen answered, a far away glaze in her shiny ice-blue eyes.

"Stars?" the woman asked, puzzled.

"I mean, the one with the sequins. Also, the skull cap that matches it."

"Oh, that's a wonderful choice. It will be beautiful on you, what with you being so slender and all. What size do you wear?"

"Seven, I think."

The woman disappeared to another section of the store. Doreen looked around Damion's Designs Boutique to see who was there. It was not very busy, with only a couple of thirty-ish type women looking through the sale racks, and sales clerks standing around trying to look busy or, at the very least, interested.

Doreen had decided to splurge and buy the pretty gown and cap that she couldn't help but look at each time she had passed the shop's window. Besides, she had told herself, why shouldn't she wear the shiny gown with the stars to her final rendezvous with Dr. John McClusky at the restaurant seminar being held that night.

She wanted to be beautiful tonight, to catch not only his attention, but every other doctor's attention, too. She wanted them all to know that she, Doreen Price, the freak, could be as beautiful, if not more so, than anyone else. She wanted them all to know that the scar made no difference. She wasn't a freak! She was beautiful just as beautiful as Debbie! And more beautiful than that stupid student nurse! She'd show Dave! Maybe she'd invite Dave to the seminar tonight. This way he'd see how beautiful she could be. He'd see it all right! Him and all the other men!

Chapter 33

Judy Price had been surprised and pleased when Detective Dave Selten walked into her room. He had chatted with her for a few minutes, then had invited her out for a cup of coffee. She had happily accepted and he had taken her to a diner down the street from the hospital.

"I can't tell you how happy I am to finally be leaving this place, Dave," Judy said, blowing on her hot coffee.

"Mrs. Price, is Doreen a twin?" he blurted out suddenly.

"Of course. Didn't Doreen tell you that? She has an identical twin sister named Deborah." She sipped her coffee carefully, in case it was still hot.

Could her sister be the killer and not Doreen? "Does she work at the hospital, too?" he asked, trying to sound as if the question was idle curiosity.

"Yes, as a matter-of-fact she does. She's a lab technician."

Dave was getting excited. A lab tech. She would have had access to the poison. She probably knew the doctors. She probably had long dark hair. That would be why Alma Browne had mistaken Doreen for the murderer. But then why hadn't her fingerprints proven it? Or hadn't they fingerprinted her? But Tacker had told him that every employee had been fingerprinted -- except Doreen.

"I think I'm going to go visit her as soon as she has the baby. It will do me a world of good, give you and Doreen some privacy for a while, and also help Deborah with the baby," Judy was saying.

"She's pregnant?"

"Oh, my, yes. She's due any time now. Another two weeks, I think. You'll like her husband, Joe, when you meet him. I haven't met him yet, but Deborah just raves about him. You two have a lot in common. He's a deputy sheriff or something. Law enforcement of some kind."

"What's their last name?"

"Sterling. Deborah seemed to be truly happy when she was here. I hope she really is. I worry about her."

"Why?"

"Oh, I don't know really, Dave. I think back to when the girls were young, and then I worry." A frown settled across her forehead and she seemed to drift into another time. "It makes me feel guilty to think back," Judy continued. "So many times I punished Dory. Punished her for killing the cat, the bird; punished her for hurting other children; punished her for lying, for deliberately breaking things, for continually hitting her sister, Debbie."

"You shouldn't feel guilty about that, Mrs. Price. That's a parent's job. As long as a parent doesn't physically or mentally abuse a child. All children need to be disciplined when they do something wrong. That's how they learn." He motioned for the waitress to bring more coffee.

"But that's the problem, David. I had punished the wrong child! Doreen had never done any of those things. It was Deborah who had done them and then had blamed Doreen. I had chosen to believe Debbie. I think it was because I felt guilty about Dory that I chose to take everything out on her. Punish the child who was a continual and constant reminder that I had sinned, that God had punished me by giving me an imperfect child. My parents told me that the twins were my punishment and I guess I believed them, so I blamed Doreen for the reminder." She stared out the window, lost in the past.

"A reminder of what? What had you done that was so bad?"

"My twins are illegitimate," she answered softly. "I was supposed to marry my high school sweetheart, so I went ahead and had, had an affair with him. When I found out that I was pregnant, he got cold feet and left me. I had the twins. Abortion wasn't in then. It was an awful time. My parents disowned me, my friends shunned me..." Her voice trailed off. She stared down at her coffee cup.

"But why was Doreen the only reminder of this? Why not Deborah also?"

Judy looked confused for a moment. "I'm sorry, David. I forgot to tell you. The girls were Siamese twins. They were joined on one side. Deborah ended up with just a small unnoticeable scar. Doreen, on the other hand, was unfortunate enough to have a full discolored scar down one side.

"The other children made fun of her. Adults even treated Doreen differently when they found out. It was as if Dory had leprosy or something, as if her imperfect body was somehow contagious. Even when I found out that it was Debbie who had told everyone, had made sure that no-one got away without knowing that Dory was scarred, I ignored it as sibling rivalry. Debbie would say 'Dory,

show them your scar' and Dory would become
embarrassed, but she would show it anyway. I
should have realized. I should have stopped it, but
I didn't. And then my parents..." She stopped, tears
glistening in her big oval blue eyes. Dave waited
for her to continue.

"I finally had to face it. When my parents
burned to death, I had to face it. I had to face the
fact that Debbie needed help. Psychological help.
But it was too late. Too late to save my parents,
too late to save Dory, probably too late to help
Debbie. I gave in. I broke."

"How did your parents burn to death, Judy?"
Dave asked softly.

"My daughter set their house on fire. It went
up like paper. I couldn't help them. I just stood
there and screamed."

"Which daughter did it?"

"Doreen had always liked fire. She would play
with matches every chance she got. Said it felt
good, warm. So naturally I just assumed that it
was Dory I caught with the burning coloring book
that day at my parent's house. But it had been
Deborah," she answered, her voice just above a
whisper.

"Judy, where can I find Deborah and Joe? I'd
like to meet them."

"Huh? Oh, they live in Florida. Flagler Beach,
Florida."

Florida? If they lived in Florida, how could
Deborah have killed the doctors? "You mentioned
before that Deborah was just here. When was
that?"

"About a month ago. Maybe a month and a
half. She flew up from Florida."

"How long was she here?"

"Only a couple of days. I only saw her once,

when I first... when I became conscious of where I was. She never came back again, and Doreen told me that Deb had gone home. I don't know why, nor have I talked to her since. I think something's wrong, but I don't know what it is. I've called several times, but her husband told me that she was sick, so I guess that's the reason she left."

So much for the sister theory, Dave thought. "Have you heard from Doreen today?"

"No, why? Should I have?"

"No, not really. She said she wasn't feeling too good, so I thought maybe she had called you. I'm sure it's just a cold."

"Dave, could you take me back now? I'm a little tired from this backward journey in time. Do you mind?" she asked, gathering her purse.

Dave motioned the waitress for the check. "Who took care of the girls while you were in the hospital?"

Judy thought for a while. "I don't know, Dave. Maybe a foster home. I just don't know. I'll have to ask Dory when I talk to her later."

* * * *

"It hurts, Joe! It hurts!" Deborah cried, one hand rubbing her abdomen, the other holding onto her husband.

"It's okay, baby. It will be over soon. Take a deep breath. It's our baby, Debbie. It's ready. It's almost over," Joe said, trying to console her, a feeling of helplessness overpowering him.

Dr. Brenner came into the labor room. "How are we doing in here?" he asked cheerfully. "Ready to be parents?"

"Make it stop, Doctor. Please, make it stop! It hurts, it hurts!" Deborah pleaded.

Dr. Brenner gently spread Deborah's legs, and not seeing any difference, slid on a plastic glove and slipped two fingers slowly into her. There was no change. She wasn't dilating any further. She had opened only one centimeter and then her body had just stopped. He motioned for Joe to follow him outside.

"Joe, she's not dilating. I will need to take the baby by Cesarean birth," he said when they had left the room. "I'll set it up immediately and then I'll be back to tell Deborah."

* * * *

After Dave had dropped Judy Price off back at the hospital, he had gone straight to the coroner's lab for the results on the articles and hair he had found in Doreen's apartment. The medical examiner had been waiting for him.

"Where did you find the stuff?" Dr. Bill Daniels asked Dave before he had even closed the door behind him.

"Why, what did you find out?" Dave asked, dropping his large frame into the old leather chair in the M.E.'s office.

"The small bottle definitely contained traces of cyanide powder. The hair samples matched the hair found in Dr. Parker's apartment perfectly. The bottle and the pipe both contained the same fingerprints, which matched the fingerprints also found in his apartment. The pipe, which incidentally matched the skull depression on Walters, had blood smears on it, and those smears matched Walters's blood type identically. I even cross matched it. Looks like you found your murderer. Who is she?"

"Are you sure?" Dave asked, ignoring the

doctor's question.

"Hundred percent sure. I'm going to run the DNA to back it up, but I'm sure. Where did you get the stuff, Dave? Who is she?"

"You wouldn't believe me if I told you. See you later, Doc," Dave said as he slammed out of the office door.

* * * *

Doreen turned first to the left and then to the right. Her reflection in the full length mirror told her that she was beautiful. She had decided to take the sequined dress in royal blue instead of green, and she was more than thrilled with her decision. The blue from the gown enhanced the color of her eyes, making them appear to be a deeper shade of blue than normal. She had spent almost forty-five minutes applying her make-up, making sure that her appearance was perfect.

The light blue shadow accented her face, and the bluish-pink lipstick offset the effect just enough to give her a little pouty look. The blue-sequined skull cap with its small beads cascading lightly around her delicate face, covered her brown locks of hair totally, and it gave her a sophisticated stately look. The V-neckline in the bodice showed just enough cleavage to be tasteful, her ivory skin a sharp contrast to the deep blue of the gown which covered her slender body with a perfect hour-glass fit. Her new shoes were royal blue satin pumps, as was her clutch bag. She was radiant, and for the first time in her life, Doreen knew it.

She gave herself one final inspection in the mirror, picked up her clutch purse, and headed for the door. Suddenly she turned and went back to the kitchen, pulling a small steno tablet and pen from the kitchen drawer. Two minutes later she was seated behind the wheel of her white Corvette. The note for Dave sat propped up against the toaster.

* * * *

Deputy Joe Sterling paced the worn carpeted floor in the father's waiting room at Beachside Memorial Hospital. He absently chewed on his thumb cuticle as he walked.

"Officer Sterling? There's an urgent telephone call for you. They said it was the lab. You can take it here on that phone," the hospital floor secretary said, pointing to the beige phone sitting on the end table.

Joe picked up the receiver and after only five minutes of conversation he hung up, the reality of the information he was given registering slowly and loudly in his brain, the excitement of the baby draining from his body. His worst fears had come to life. The blood on the flashlight and the map matched those of victim Thomas Martin, and the blood on the knife matched victim Willie Baines. He could no longer ignore it. His beloved wife, Deborah, the mother of his almost born child, was a murderer. There could be no doubt now.

But why? And now what? Now that he knew the truth, what should he do about it? There were only two choices: ignore it and keep quiet, or bring justice her due.

His stomach felt sour and his head ached. He wanted to cry, to scream out, to break something, everything. His hurt and his anger were like bullet shots to his heart. He could quit the department, just take Debbie and the baby and move somewhere else. But suppose she continued to kill?

What then?

Keep running? Keep hiding? Could he, should he, put himself and the baby through that? Deputy Joe Sterling was a law enforcement officer, and had been for too long now. He would have to face Deborah on it. He would stand beside her and they would get through it together. He loved her deeply, but she would have to turn herself in, or he would have to do it for her. He sat down heavily on the couch, put his head in his hands and cried.

Chapter 34

The strong cold New Jersey winter wind sliced through Dave's cocoa brown leather jacket, chilling him through to his skin, burning his ears and nose to a bright pink. He fumbled with the apartment keys, his fingers too cold to follow the instructions which his brain directed to him.

Once in the apartment he hesitated and listened. There was no sound, but all the lights were on. He removed his jacket and laid it quietly on the arm of the sofa. Slowly he walked down the hall toward the bedroom, glancing sideways toward the kitchen as he passed to see if Doreen was in there. When he reached the bedroom door he paused.

Her gray woolen slacks, thrown recklessly, lay in a heap on the massive bed, her black turtleneck sweater in a heap on the floor. Large plastic shopping bags lay scattered over the bed and there was a large box on the bedroom chaise lounge. Damion's Designs Boutique was written in bold black ink across the lid. Dave looked in the box and picked up the yellow sales slip. Why had Doreen bought an expensive evening gown? Where was she going? And with who?

Dave checked the bathroom to be sure that

she wasn't in there, but all he found was a total disarray of cosmetics. It was all too unlike her, he thought. Doreen was a meticulous person about herself, her possessions and her home. She had to have been in a tremendous hurry for her to leave this mess. He walked over to her closet and rummaged through the clothes looking for the $500 blue sequined gown which had just been purchased according to the sales slip. Nothing there. Next he checked the hall closet, where she kept her better clothes. Not in there, either.

She must be wearing it. But to where, he wondered. A date? Was she seeing someone else? How much did he really know about her? Only what he had seen, only what he had learned from her mother, only what the M.E. had found. She had lied to him, lied about having so many brothers and sisters, lied about her father being a truck driver, lied about her mother and her background. She had hidden the fact that she was a twin, had hidden the fact that she was scarred. What else had she hidden from him, and lied to him about? Maybe the fact that she loved him. Was that also a lie?

Dave sat on the bed and put his face down into his large meaty hands. *Dave, you jerk*, he admonished himself silently. *You big dumb flat-foot! In love with a mysterious girl you really know nothing about. Nothing except the fact that she's murdered at least three doctors*, he reminded himself.

He'd call Doreen's sister and talk to her. Maybe he'd learn more. He slowly stood up and lumbered toward the kitchen, his shoulders slumped like a man who had been beaten down by eighty years of life. Dave was sure that Deborah's telephone number would be in the telephone index which

Doreen kept in the kitchen by the telephone.

He looked first under S for Sterling. Finding no number listed there, he began to flip back through the pages to D for Deborah. He suddenly realized that there were NO telephone numbers listed under ANY of the alpha index cards. Didn't she call anyone, ever? When he reached the Ds, there it was...the only phone number in the book: Debbie, 1-904-555-7919.

Dave quickly dialed the number. After six rings he hung up the receiver. He ran his hand through his thick brown hair. Now what? Sit and wait for her to come home, he decided. What else could he do? Put out an APB? He turned toward the refrigerator to get a cold beer and spotted the propped up note:

"Detective Selten:

If you can tear yourself away from your student nurses long enough, you'll find me at the Surgeon's Bembbar Seminar at the Emerald Restaurant in Rahway. Whether you decide to come or not, please be kind enough to remove your belongings and yourself from my apartment and leave your key.

Doreen."

Remove my belongings and myself? Over a student nurse? Dave could feel the anger welling up inside him. Well, that was fine with him, too! He would go to a motel ...surgeon's seminar? Why would she be at a surgeon's seminar? Oh, Christ! A SURGEON'S SEMINAR!

Dave grabbed the telephone book and looked up the address of the Emerald Restaurant. Next he telephoned Sgt. Tacker and explained what he had learned and where he was going. He then instructed Tacker to put out an APB on Doreen Price and her Corvette, and for him to notify the

Rahway Police Department. Grabbing his leather jacket, Detective Dave Selten ran for his car.

* * * *

Doreen had taken great pains not to get any of the gasoline on her beautiful star-filled gown as she poured the acid sweet smelling liquid around the base of the large wooden restaurant. She had wondered if that would do the trick, and then before discarding the cans, had spotted an open screened window. She had peered inside. It was the storage room, filled with large cans of vegetables, soups, potatoes and more. The room also stored shelves filled with white paper bags, napkins, paper tablecloths, food wrap paper, toilet paper, adding machine tape and other assorted paper products.

Doreen had then pressed on the base of the screen and it had popped right out. Next she had poured the remaining contents of the cans into the room from the window, mesmerized by the design which the gasoline made as it spread across the storeroom floor. Finally she had let the last of the gas wash down from the window sill, down the outside wall of the restaurant, to join the rest of the liquid at the bottom base.

Satisfied with her work, she had entered the restaurant through the front door and had gone upstairs to the ladies lounge to wait until all of her guests had arrived for her party.

* * * *

Dr. Brenner glanced at Deborah's sleeping face and smiled beneath his surgical mask. He reached into her open abdomen and gently removed the tiny baby.

"Oh, my goodness, Doctor, look," one of the nurses exclaimed, staring at the open gap.

"Well, I'll be damned," Dr. Brenner exclaimed, "another one hiding in there!" He chuckled. "Deborah will be excited. She's a twin, too."

"Excited?" the nurse said. "Shocked would be more like it if it was me!"

Dr. Brenner cut the cord on the first baby. "One baby boy," he said, reaching for the other tiny baby still lying quietly inside the womb. "Come here, little one. Your turn."

"Something's wrong, Doctor," the anesthesiologist said softly. "She's hypotensive. Blood pressure's dropping like a rock."

"What? Why?"

"I don't know! I don't know!"

"What is it down to?" Dr. Brenner quickly took the second baby out of Deborah's abdomen and smacked the soles of its tiny feet. The baby let out a wail.

"Seventy over forty and still dropping. Heart rate is at 130 and climbing!"

"Quick! Set up volume of saline by IV, and give her Lidocaine and Veratnil."

"Heart rate is up to 160!" the anesthesiologist called out. "Respiration is 4!" He stood up and opened Deborah's eyes with his fingers. "Pupils are small and non-reactive."

"Hurry with that med!" Dr. Brenner yelled to the nurse preparing the injections.

"She's gone into cardiac arrhythmia," the anesthesiologist yelled. "We're losing her!"

* * * *

Doreen sat in the upstairs lounge window, staring down at the Cadillacs, Lincolns, Mercedes, BMWs and Rolls Royces filling the restaurant parking lot. She smiled. Everyone was coming to her party! It would be the social event of the year! She stood up and walked slowly toward one of the large mirrors which totally decorated all the walls of the lounge. She stared hard at her reflection, blinded by the light radiating from the stars on her dress and her cap. Radiant, she decided, absolutely radiant!

Her small hands continually rolled the papers she had taken when she had entered the restaurant. She had read them, discovering that they contained the evening's agenda as well as the menu for her guests. Oh, yes, she would feed them all very well, she thought. Her mind kept focusing on her sister, Deborah, and she was having some trouble breathing. Something must be wrong with her sister. *Shit, not now, Debbie,* she said to herself. *You are not going to ruin my party! Whatever it is can just wait!*

She decided that she would wait another five or ten minutes to be sure that Dr. John McClusky was downstairs with the others before she made her slow and breathtaking descent down the carpeted winding stairs to the dining room. Her hands continued to roll the agenda into a cylinder, the inside of the paper tube stuffed with toilet paper.

* * * *

"Come on, come on!" Dave yelled at the cars in front of him. He had cut across Edison, through Iselin, racing down Route 27 heading for Rahway. As usual, the New Jersey traffic was jammed. Dave pressed down on his horn, loud and long. The woman driving the car in front of him put her hand out the window and stuck up her middle finger, all the while staring at him in her rear-view mirror.

"Bitch!" he mumbled, pulling his car to the right and trying to get around her. His path was blocked by a large dump truck loaded with gravel. "Move, damn you!" he yelled in desperation, his words hanging in the air.

* * * *

Doreen waited impatiently for the two women to finish primping themselves before the mirrors.

"I love your outfit," the older woman said to Doreen.

"Thank you," Doreen replied sweetly. "I'm glad you could come to my party. I think you'll enjoy it very much."

The two women exchanged glances. "Your party?" she asked Doreen.

"Yes, of course. It's my debut party. Everyone who's anyone is here. You two go on down and enjoy yourselves. I'll be down shortly."

The two women again exchanged looks, and after opening the lounge door, turned to look at Doreen again. She sat smiling at them. As soon as the door closed, Doreen unlocked the window and slid the bottom up. The frigid winter wind hit her like a cold slap across the face, but she continued to smile. She took her cigarette lighter from her clutch bag and lit the rolled up agenda. The paper caught the flame immediately.

Doreen held the burning torch out the window and let go. She stuck her head out and watched the red and yellow color float to the bottom. Suddenly there was a pop. The fire had caught the edge of the gasoline and spread around the building at such a rapid speed that it reminded Doreen of a fireworks display which she had seen one fourth of July when she was nine years old.

She again walked over to the mirror and surveyed her reflection. "Time for your grand entrance, my lady. Johnny, ready or not, here I come."

Chapter 35

"Joe?"

Deputy Joe Sterling raised his head. Dr. Brenner stood in front of him, still clothed in his green surgical scrubs, his mask now hanging around his thick neck.

"Are you all right?" the doctor asked him. "You look awful."

"Boy or girl?" Joe asked quietly.

"Boys." The doctor waited until the word sank in.

"Boys? Plural?" Joe asked, somewhat puzzled, not sure he had heard the doctor correctly.

"Plural. Twins. Fine healthy twin sons, Joe. Each weighs a little over five pounds, but we'll fatten them up before they go home. I've had them put in life support cribs to be sure they get a good chance for survival. If we keep them in a highly sanitized environment and watch them, they'll be fine." He hesitated.

Joe studied the older man's face. Why was there no happiness on his face? Where was the glimmer that was usually in the doctor's eyes? "What is it? What's wrong?"

The doctor sat down next to Joe. "Sometimes things happen, Joe. Things that we cannot foresee, things that we can do nothing about. Sort of God's will."

"What is it? Deborah? Is it Deborah?" His every word was laced with mounting fear, his eyes open wide with a cloud of dread covering the irises.

"Joe, she had an allergic reaction to the anesthesia. Something which we could not know in advance. We did everything we could…"

"DEBORAH!" Joe screamed out loud, jumping to his feet.

"Joe, please," Dr. Brenner said, his hand on Joe's arm.

"My Debbie? Dead? Is that it? My Debbie…my wife…dead?" A nurse appeared at the door with a hypodermic. Dr. Brenner nodded his head.

"Joe, I have something to calm you down," he said, taking the syringe from the nurse.

"I don't want it! Oh, Jesus H. Christ!! Why? Why?!"

* * * *

The fire spread rapidly through the old restaurant, devouring everything in its path. People were screaming and running everywhere. Suddenly there was an explosion in the kitchen. A chef ran out of the swinging doors screaming, his white pants and smock ablaze. A plump woman of fifty fell at the bottom of the stairs, but before her husband could help her, she was trampled by other fleeing patrons.

Sirens wailed in the distance. The maitre d' and the owner, both dressed in black tuxedos, were trying to calm everyone down, begging them to stay calm and quickly exit through the front and side doors of the restaurant. A young waitress was trapped on the staircase as the fire spread across the carpeted steps. She turned and ran back upstairs to jump from one of the second floor windows.

"Come on! Hurry!" she yelled to Doreen as she ran up the stairs.

Doreen stood on the third step from the top, her hand resting on the mahogany banister.

"Come on, Lady! We've got to get out of here!" the girl yelled again, grabbing Doreen by the arm. Doreen pulled free.

"Don't! You'll mess up my stars! This is my party and I want every star in place," Doreen retorted, her glassy blue eyes watching the fun and excitement below her.

"Are you crazy or what? Come on!"

When Doreen did not answer, the girl hurried up the stairs to the ladies lounge. Doreen watched the bright light of flames, felt the warmth it cast upon her. The light. The light was good. It was warm and safe. The light would make her perfect, make her pure. It was exactly like it was supposed to be. Exactly like she had dreamt it would be. The spotlights were on her now. Her stars glimmered -- glimmered on her head, glimmered all over her perfect body. She took another step down closer to the fire.

Nobody can ignore me now, she thought. *No one will call me a freak again. This is my day, not Deborah's. I'm the center of attention now and she's not here to ruin it for me.* Doreen lifted her face and let out a small laugh.

"DOREEN!" Dave yelled up to her.

Doreen looked down at him. He looked so handsome standing behind her light. Finally they were face to face, her and John McClusky.

"Well, what do you think now, John?" she called down to Dave. "Am I beautiful enough for you now?"

"Doreen, stay there," Dave shouted, looking around for something to cover himself with.

"I've missed you, John, darling," she said, going down to the next step. The wood made a cracking sound.

"Doreen, don't move! Please, honey, don't come down. Go up, Dory, go upstairs," Dave pleaded with her. He tried to go up the stairs, but the heat of the fire made him back up.

"Don't call me that!" Doreen screamed at him. "I hate the name Dory! My name is Doreen. Doreen Price. D is for Dory, Dirty, dirty, Dory..." She descended another step.

"Go upstairs to the window. Go UP, Doreen, not down!" Dave was choking now, his vision blurring from the tears as the fire burned his eyes.

"You scarred me, Doc, but I forgive you. Can you hear me, John? I forgive you now because I'm perfect. S is for scar, Johnny, but I don't have one anymore. You can come to me now. I won't hurt you anymore. I forgive you."

"D...D...DOREEN, PLEASE," Dave called as loud as he could.

"Why won't you come to me? Don't you trust me anymore? That's it, isn't it, John? You don't trust me not to hurt you. Isn't that right? Then I'll have to come to you," she said, stepping down another step. The wood under the carpet cracked loudly as it split, giving way under her weight and sending her straight down to the marble floor below. Doreen's head hit the cool marble floor first, creating a large cracking sound and sending a red hot electrical shock through her body.

"Get out, mister!" the fireman yelled, shoving Dave out the door.

"DOREEEEN!!"

"Get out! It's too late!"

Doreen laid in a widening pool of her own blood, her beautiful brown hair now matted with the sticky substance, her twisted and broken body sprawled in a graceful pose on the ballroom floor. Doreen watched the brilliant lights from the fire surround her, felt the heat soothing her body, making her whole again.

"See, Momma," she whispered, blood trickling out of the corner of her mouth, "I'm beautiful, too. Now Debbie and I are really identical. Aren't we, Momma..." She smiled at her mother's face in the flames. Slowly her mother's face began to fade. "Don't go, Momma, please don't leave me again. I'll be good this time. I promise, Momma, please...don't go..."

Her mother's face was replaced by the beautiful mirror image of herself, and Debbie stood above her in the flames. "Go away, Debbie!! This is MY party! MINE! Do you hear me?"

Debbie reached her delicate hand out to Doreen, palm up, her long thin, graceful fingers together. "I know, Dory, but it's time for you to come with me into the light. There we'll be fine. Whole again. Just you and me together again. Forever, Dory. No one will hurt you again, I promise. Please take my hand, Dory. We need to go now."

Doreen hesitated. "Please, Dory, please."

Doreen slowly raised her arm to clasp Debbie's hand. Doreen smiled at her twin sister, a sweet and loving look on her beautiful face, and took her hand firmly. As Debbie smiled down at her, Doreen sighed and slowly closed her beautiful ice-blue eyes, her pain ended forever.

Epilogue

Dave Selten sat in his small office on Beach Street in Daytona Beach, Florida, staring out the front window at the passing shoppers. He tapped his pen softly on his desk blotter. It had been six months since he had made his decision to take early retirement from the Edison Police Department and move to Florida to open his own detective agency. He had, so far, not regretted his decision. Dave glanced over at his secretary, who sat at her desk filing her long nails.

Oh, yes, he decided. This is where he wanted to be. Away from the cold, away from the reminders of Doreen, and away from the total insanity of up North. Here it was a new, fresh and peaceful environment, and Dave loved it. He would be happier here. It was definitely, as far as he was concerned, a more serene existence.

* * * *

The warm spring waters of the Atlantic crawled slowly up the sandy shores, kissing the grains of sand until it went back out, only to repeat the process again moments later.

Deputy Sheriff Joseph Sterling walked leisurely and quietly next to his mother-in-law, Judy Price, the still cool Florida breezes caressing their hair and faces. Each carried a small baby boy on their shoulders. A small wire-haired dog passing by the quartet suddenly let out a yelp and turned its head to look at them. It started a low growl in its throat as it eyed the twin boys, its tail tucked between its legs, its ears back and teeth bared. The twin babies just smiled back.

About The Author

Marjaree Mayne was born and raised in New Jersey. As a working single parent of four sons, Ms. Mayne attended college later in life, majoring in Psychology and Deviant Behavior.She has always had a stong interest in twins, and in the psychological profiles of mass murders.

Ms. Mayne now lives in Ormond Beach, Florida with her Pomeranian, Fluffy. When she is not writing novels, she is a successful REALTOR.